The Malta Job

Notes on a Wee Island

Alwyn James

Ringwood Publishing
Glasgow

First published in Great Britain in 2014 by
Ringwood Publishing
7 Kirklee Quadrant, Glasgow G12 0TS
www.ringwoodpublishing.com
e-mail   mail@ringwoodpublishing.com

ISBN 978-1-901514-17-9

British Library Cataloguing-in Publication Data
A catalogue record for this book is available from the British
Library

Typeset in Times New Roman 11

Printed and bound in the UK
by Lonsdale Direct Solutions

Acknowledgements

The manuscript of *The Malta Job* owes its existence to my wife Jean. As I exhausted the meagre library shelves of the hotel on our second long stay on the island, she insisted that holiday writing would be far more satisfying than holiday reading. I took her advice - and it was.

If Jean was 'the onlie begetter' of the manuscript, the book exists thanks to the 'midwives' at Ringwood. Isobel Freeman and Sandy Jamieson read *The Malta Job* and liked it. I am indebted to them. Finally, editor Lorna Stallard gave the newborn a reassuring pat on the bum and sent it off into the wide world.

The two real heroes of the book are Malta itself and Scottish banking.

I owe my love of the first to the islands themselves and to the many Maltese we met there, often by chance encounters on our walks, sometimes followed by invitations to visit their homes.

My admiration for Scottish banking is the result of many years spent working with the people of the Royal Bank of Scotland, as, among other things, editor, chief press officer, speech writer, gossip columnist and television presenter . A customer of Bank of Scotland for forty years and a grateful recipient of Clydesdale Bank sponsorship of my book *Other Men's Heroes*, I have those banks to thank too.

Dedication

To Jean, of course

About the Author
Alwyn James

While creating a successful career in Scotland in editing and later in corporate communications, both external and internal, Welshman Alwyn James had several non-fiction works published. Two of these, *Scottish Roots* and *Other Men's Heroes*, became well-respected leaders in their field.

The Malta Job is his first work of fiction but he is already well-advanced with a follow-up, *In a Dead Man's Chest*, which Ringwood hope to publish in 2015.

He has almost finished a fascinating mixture of history and travelogue, *Other Folk's Scotland*, which Ringwood will be publishing in early 2015.

He is also working on *Cursèd Leaf,* a history of Scottish Banknotes.

The Moment
Friday 3 December

The engine of the white Renault Mégane with its distinctive black windows shrieked into life. Instinctively, I looked around the bleak Maltese slopes to see if the noise had attracted any attention. Of course, it hadn't. There was no one there to hear it. Well, no one who mattered.

The car accelerated down the steep track. I willed it to ignore the sharp right-hand bend at the bottom of the hill. It did, of course it did, bumping over the worn and insignificant kerb and then lurching sideways as it hit the more challenging line of stones marking the cliff-edge.

And then I heard the screams coming from inside the Renault, the screams that should never have been. Katy's fingernails bit deeply into the back of my hand.

Something had gone wrong, dreadfully, horribly wrong. As the car corkscrewed into the blustery air above the bay, we both turned to Tony for some explanation.

He was smiling.

Chapter 1

The Mission

It was almost exactly a month before that heart-stopping moment that I had arrived on the island. I should have been shivering in a moist Edinburgh flat, trying to carbon-date the remains of a tin of baked beans. Instead, I had found myself munching juicy prawns and quails' eggs in a Maltese hotel and wondering whether to go for the pork escalope or swordfish for the main course.

Even now I find it difficult to allocate credit for the transformation of fortune fairly between Geordie Ballantine and Don Blaikie. Geordie's contribution was huge, but unwitting. He had just managed to type the heading '*MacAbre*' and the line 'Never in the long, dark annals of Scottish crime have there been.' before a finger on the wrong key of his weary Remington became his last act on earth. Alcohol and nicotine shared responsibility for both full stops.

It was a bad start to Geordie's second book, a sure-fire best-seller after his first very profitable venture into authorship as opposed to journalism.

The eccentric Geordie, a seemingly eternal player on the Scottish newspaper scene, had been the chief crime chronicler on Glasgow's leading Sunday paper. His unmistakable figure, reminiscent of Ron Moodie's Fagin in *Oliver!*, and his bulbous, questioning profile was an essential part of any police briefing. Indeed, at one time, he alone among us could actually postpone the start of such briefings merely by arriving late.

These late entrances had become more and more common however and his career appeared to be winding down, with his own paper resorting to sending younger scribblers along to cover for him.

Then, in sight of his sixtieth birthday, he came up with the counterblast no one had been expecting. He wrote *MacMurder*, a pacey round-up of Scotland's most infamous homicides, got Malkie McCormick to produce some of his best and most gory cartoons and persuaded Blaikie Books to publish it. The book rapidly became a cult buy among tourists and locals alike and gave Geordie a new career on TV chat shows in Scotland and further afield. These appearances provided Geordie with some extra drinking money – and the TV makeup artists with a challenge they never really got to grips with.

The success of *MacMurder* took everyone by surprise and there were shouts of 'Encore' from all corners. People were just crying out for the First among Sequels.

And that brings me to Don Blaikie who bears more direct blame than Geordie for what turned out to be my far-from-restful hibernation. Don was a chatty, sixty-something Pickwickian gentleman-publisher, quite unaccustomed to best sellers or even, his unkindest critics among the new wave of Scottish publishers might suggest, to sellers.

He was now determined that the most successful publication ever to be launched by Blaikie Books should get a speedy follow-up, applying the same formula of Geordie's earthy prose and McCormick's breathless illustrations to some of the more grisly happenings in Scottish history. The title said it all – *MacAbre*. It was certainly applicable to the demise of its author after typing only those fateful thirteen words.

There had been a good turnout at Geordie's cremation, despite some bitterly cold rain sweeping the gentle slopes to the south of Edinburgh around Mortonhall Crematorium.

The ceremony had been memorable, with Don Blaikie delivering a eulogy crammed with references few if any of us grasped. He even managed to find a biblical text to underline Geordie's powers of journalistic persistence. In the tale of the trusty friends who clamber on to the roof to get their ailing mate to Christ, Don rejected the Good News style of 'because of the crowd' and went for Jamie Saxt's 'could not get nigh to him for the press.' The image of Geordie, even in his youth, resorting to the rooftop to get an interview brought smiles to all of us who knew him.

The climax to the service came when Geordie's widow Effie, her outfit inspired by that of Morticia Addams, dramatically placed a copy of *MacMurder* on the coffin as it disappeared from view to the strains of the Dead March from *Saul*. It must have been the first time that that particular piece of music ever got a round of applause and whistles.

With my motorbike grounded at the garage until I could afford to pay for a couple of essential repairs, I'd taken a lift out with some of my old mates from the radio station. As I was contemplating a sprint through the icy shower from the chapel to their distant car, an ageing Singer saloon lurched over to me, almost colliding with the hearse arriving for the next cremation. The driver's window cranked down erratically. Don Blaikie's head emerged, reminding me of Johnny Cope, the ancient tortoise who, when not asleep and immobile, patrolled the family backyard in Glenbraith. The publisher called to me in the distinctive armour-piercing accent of Edinburgh's best fee-paying schools.

'Come along, Smiffy. There's something I need to talk to you about.'

I apologised to the driver of the hearse and the rest of the funeral party, as Don seemed oblivious to their presence let alone their anger, and got into the Singer.

I admit I had been looking forward to the post-cremation crack at McGuffie's or at the overflow at Jinglin' Geordie's, but Don had inherited, from his mother's side I had been told, formidable if gentle powers of persuasion.

We spluttered into Edinburgh in a vehicle that must have turned heads in the immediate post-War years with its pace-setting curves, but now did so for entirely different reasons.

Don was not one to let the heather grow under his brogue-shod feet and, within half an hour of waving goodbye to the late, lamented Geordie, we were discussing Don's project and my problems in the haphazard drawing-room office of his Georgian New Town flat. It somehow felt perfectly normal to be nibbling, in the middle of the morning, a slice of Dundee cake and slurping Madeira of all things poured from what looked like a Victorian medical receptacle of some sort into claret-sized glasses.

Don sat at a huge mahogany desk, flanked by dark oil paintings of earlier Blaikies, as sombre in aspect as Don was amiable. That was surely a question of artistic fashion, as those gents were no doubt just as jovial as Don. Chuckles and twinkles were thin on the ground in Victorian portraits.

Around us were stacked untidy clumps of books, the flotsam and jetsam of Blaikie Books' less popular productions, *Place Names of Badenoch*, *An A to Z of Fife's Wild Flowers*, *Borders Yesterdays*.

The publisher spoke of Geordie's untimely demise – 'just as he would have wanted it' – and of my unique suitability 'to take up his mantle' or 'quiver' as he inexplicably corrected himself.

He had already paid Geordie a sizeable advance, but was so convinced of *MacAbre*'s money-spinning potential that he was prepared to offer me £500 on the nail, £500 on delivery and a 50/50 split of the royalties with the grieving Effie. And all I had to do was convert a bulging sack of scribbled notes into a neat manuscript.

As the grapevine had had plenty to say about Geordie's earnings from *MacMurder*, the offer was tempting, not to say mouth-watering. I had just been made redundant as our local radio station went in for the rationalising or downsizing I had so often reported at other companies. I had done the same old story time and time again, asking men what it felt like to be out of work at the age of 50. And now I was asking myself the very same questions – and me only half their age. Still, it was last in, first out and I had only been with the station for eighteen months or so.

The rent agreement on my Bellevue Crescent basement was running out and the renewal would certainly show a hefty hike as the new Scottish Parliament was shunting up prices at all levels. Don, an old friend, was aware of my plight.

I had first met him five or so years earlier. As a green cub reporter with *Capital News*, one of the city's evening papers, and with little under my belt other than my degree in Communication Studies at Edinburgh's Napier University, I had found myself next to him at a press conference. When I mentioned, entirely in passing, my passion for the cinema, he persuaded me to pen a contribution for his compendium to mark the centenary of Robert Louis Stevenson's death.

I churned out the RLS and the Cinema piece, covering not just the many film versions of *Treasure Island, Kidnapped* and of course *Jekyll and Hyde,* but also taking in *The Wrong Box, The Body Snatcher, Ebb Tide* and *The Suicide Club.* Don even took advantage of a young man's desire to see his name in print to get me to supply all that without payment. He owed me one – and, to his credit, he remembered and this was his repayment.

I was attracted by the challenge and the money, but unsure. A lad of no fixed abode, cut off from my office word-processor, my time should surely be spent looking for a real job. I shared these thoughts with Don.

Don pondered for a while, swilling his Madeira around the generous glass with a vigour that threatened to turn it airborne but never did. I could see he was thinking – his eyes were closed and his head nodded in time to the Madeira's merry-go-round.

'What do you know of Malta?' he asked eventually, in what I took to be just another of his characteristically rapid changes of subject.

'*The Malta Story*, 1953, John Mills, Alec Guinness,

Anthony Quayle. I've bought the Cinema Club video,' I suggested helpfully. 'Or perhaps *The Maltese Falcon*, already made once in 1931, but then, superbly, in 1941, Humphrey ...'

'Good film, but a load of codswallop, Smiffy,' he interrupted. 'The Knights of Saint John never gave the Emperor Charles V a valuable sculpture or anything like it. It was a real falcon, every year. I read it on the door of a gift shop in Mdina, but that's not what I meant. Get a long-stay holiday there, take the office lap-top, get stuck into Geordie's notes and you'll live like a lord in the sun for less than rent and gas bills here.'

I was still reluctant to take the plunge and came up with another worry. I pointed out to Don that Geordie's style was inimitable. No less an authority than the reviewer for *The Herald* had said so – and had said it in print. To be honest, Geordie's tabloid writing had always been colourful, even when reined in by the newspaper subs. Under Don's passive editing of *MacMurder*, it had become positively psychedelic.

'You're a journalist, for God sake. It's Geordie Ballantine I'm asking you to churn out, not Sir Walter Scott.'

I could feel my objections evaporating in the face of Don's enthusiasm, the Madeira and the attraction of being able to postpone most of the hard decisions I would have to take if I stayed in Edinburgh, such as where to live and how to earn some money. Don was offering me a lifeline.

To be frank, I began to see the book as a useful run-in to my real career as a writer, which was in dire need of a kick-start. I should have been named Hugo Catchpole, Dwayne Lightning or something equally swashbuckling. I'm sure it would have given me a better start in life. Instead, fate and an unimaginative pair of parents had shackled me with 'John Smith'.

Somehow, while I had never really resented their physical legacies – a gangly six-foot-something frame, freckles, carroty hair defying all fashions, past, present or future, spindly, disjointed limbs and left-handedness – I did feel they had let me down at the font. 'John Smith!' I know that the tragic Labour leader had made it to the top, but politics was not the same.

Life as a media man was going to be hard. Very hard. Would they have picked Magnus Magnusson to run *Mastermind* if he had been called 'John Smith'? Just look at the production and script credits on any television show and you'll see what I mean. It's a help, no it's essential, to be called Barnaby or Dominic or Cressida or Natasha.

If you're into showbiz, you can change your name, but not if you're on a newspaper. I toyed with introducing a spurious middle name – J Baskerville Smith, with overtones of classic typeface and ruthless hound and, after Sean's *The Name of the Rose* effective detective. I never had the courage to go through with it. Besides, W. Gordon Smith, a late and well-loved Scottish pro, had beaten me to that idea, although I think his 'Gordon' was authentic.

I guess the answer is to let your parents provide a name for your first fifteen years at which stage it expires, leaving you to choose your own. As a teenager, I could then have gone for something dramatically Scottish – Ben Lomond, Glen Coe, Scott Monument, Campsie Fells, all sound better than John Smith. Then maybe when you reach the age of sixty, your kids can get their own back and give you your third and final set to remove the embarrassment of adolescence excesses. After all, you can't go on a Saga holiday with a name like 'Dwayne Lightning', can you?

I cautiously suggested he upped the advance to £750.

'I can do better than that, dear boy, much better.'

Don rather sheepishly picked up a miniature leather-headed gavel and tapped on a brass gong on the table. Before my eyes, a section of the bookcase behind him swung back and a little grey lady scurried in.

'Miss Murgatroyd, your cake is as delicious as always. I don't believe you know Mr John Smith.'

'Yes, I do. I didn't meet him, but I do remember him coming here with those bits about the films. He was two days late with his manuscript if I remember rightly. And there were lots of split infinitives.'

'What a memory,' Don enthused, 'awesome, awesome. Johnny is back again, here to save us.'

She stared at me with a mixture of disbelief and gratitude. Maybe I didn't fit into her idea of a white knight. She looked at Don for enlightenment.

'Johnny is going to finish Geordie's opus for us. But he needs to get away for a while. I believe the young people call it "space". Ring Hector and see if he can fix a stay in Malta, about a month or so. As soon as possible. Back well before Christmas. And put it on my bill.'

He looked at me for agreement. I nodded more from bewilderment than from enthusiasm.

Miss Murgatroyd disappeared as dramatically as she had entered. Don poured out another Madeira, explaining that Hector was an old school chum who ran the family travel agents.

When the efficient Miss Murgatroyd returned with the news that she had got me a last-minute seat on a Glasgow flight on 2 November and a five-week, half-board Airtours holiday, we still had enough Madeira left to toast the success of 'The Malta Job' as Don described it.

'You'll love it,' Don enthused. 'It's a great wee island, not as big as Skye, but packed with history and all that stuff.'

Miss Murgatroyd, a stickler for detail, I suspected, interrupted. 'It's only about the size of Mull, Mr Hector said.'

The publisher smiled appreciatively, as if his faithful dog had performed a favourite trick.

10

'I would,' Don explained, looking at the neatly penned notes handed to him before the wraith in grey lace melted back into the books, 'be staying at the Seacrest, a splendid hotel overlooking Mellieħa Bay in the north of the island, less frantic than those areas in the south of the island.'

Looking through the tall windows to Queen Street Gardens, I could see that the cold rain had turned to sleet and there were even a few fat snowflakes clinging briefly to the panes. I was warming to the Madeira (the drink) and to the idea of Malta (the island).

My redundancy payout would look after the beer. And I would be back on 7 December, well in time to travel north to Glenbraith and make the most of a family Christmas and, of course, the Millennium Hogmanay. All in all, it had been a good morning's work.

Part Two

Chapter 2
The Adventure

First impressions of what was to be my home for the next few weeks were most encouraging. I had arrived at Luqa Airport late at night on Tuesday, 2 November, reached the Seacrest just on midnight and gone at once to my room. A quick look around had identified the bed, the wardrobe and the loo. I had fallen onto the mattress and gone straight to sleep without taking in any other details of my surroundings. That had meant that the first real introduction to my new life came with the morning sunlight when I pulled back the curtains to reveal my office, the balcony.

It won hands down when set alongside the cubbyhole under the stairs at Bellevue Crescent. High on the top, fourth floor, over the arabesque curve of the swimming pool, it was at the back of the hotel and had no sea view, but made up for that by facing the sun from two o'clock onwards and offering an interesting and ever changing vista.

Around the pool were white plastic sun-beds, some covered with padded yellow mattresses and, as a fair barometer of the day ahead, some with bodies male and female in varying degrees of bronzing. At the far end of the pool, a few dozen bamboo sunshades and half as many palm trees marked the end of the pleasure pod and the beginning of the real world of work.

Small, hopelessly small, fields, some showing signs of careful tending and already receiving the attention of labouring men, others thick with neglect, were marked off with wooden picket fences, prickly pear hedges, beautiful dry stane dykes of precise blocks of the yellow Maltese limestone.

Eight spindly windmills reminded me of those crayon drawing of flowers I had produced as a toddler and which still, patiently framed by mother, adorned the walls of our Highland cottage. Silhouetted against the sky, two or three of them were birling to drag up the water from below the rocky surface. Water-tanks in stone or concrete held the water from the wells or the coveted rain.

As the left-hand wall of my balcony hid the precipitous perch of Mellieħa village and the other wing of the hotel covered the rising landscape to the Marfa Ridge, my horizon was low and my sky was big. Throughout the day I set about discovering the other delights of the hotel, the restaurant where we breakfasted and dined, the lounge and bar and, to bridge any lunchtime pangs, the noisy and bustling pizzeria. Notice boards promised weekly cabaret and nightly music groups, so that I would not have to spend the whole day with *MacAbre*. Incidentally, that title might also be a good name for a Scottish band. I made a mental note to suggest it to a drummer friend when I got back home. He had already turned down my idea of 'The Gneiss', a very hard Scottish rock found in the islands.

Across the road was the broad and sandy crescent of Mellieħa Bay, an ideal spot for bracing rambles, short and not too demanding, to clear my head. More challenging walks threatened in the near distance and the village itself, with its shops and bars, was roosting on a rocky outcrop high above the sea.

This was indeed a place where I could really get down to work!

The plan started well enough. Sitting in my 'office,' relishing the rare appearances of a fitful sun and well wrapped against the wind – Don's hints of tropical conditions were somewhat off the mark in the first few days – I ploughed enthusiastically into Geordie's notes, oblivious of the banter wafting up from the sun-beds below.

The expensive laptop was a great boon to me and I knew that it was no loss to Don. The high powered salesman who had persuaded him to buy the technology had not been able to persuade him to try using it. At first, the keyboard and screen,

14

mean when set alongside the large desktops of the radio station, irritated me, but soon my fingertips were tripping along as speedily as they had ever done.

Slowly, I got to grips with Geordie's atrocious handwriting. More surprisingly – and more disturbingly – I began to find his writing style coming more and more easily to me. I would never live this down with the Press Gang back home. Geordie had always been a by-word for over-the-top tabloid. Still, five per cent of sales would anaesthetise me to the jibes.

He had understandably used most of the plums in *MacMurder*, but by no means all of them. He'd sought out every bludgeoning, poisoning, knifing or strangling from Darnley to Bible John via Madeleine Smith, but had, as always with any publication, missed out things which were remembered as soon as the printing was completed and when it was too late to do anything about it.

He had certainly left himself – and that meant me – plenty of material for *MacAbre*. The many titbits garnered included the Burke and Hare body-snatching and Half-hangit Maggie, but his meticulous if occasionally indecipherable notes left out completely my favourite tale – of Sawney Bean and his stomach-churning Galloway Cannibals. I could write that one blindfolded. All in all, I had no complaints. *MacAbre* could indeed turn out to be my lucky lottery ticket to fame and fortune.

By the end of the third day, I was confident that I would make Don Blaikie's deadline with days, maybe even weeks to spare. I might even manage to get a proper holiday out of it all. I had reckoned without the distractions.

The first of these were my fellow holidaymakers. There were plenty of easy opportunities for chitchat between mouthfuls at breakfast and dinner, in line at the buffet and in the deep armchairs of the bar. These were beguiling enough on their own account, without having to be set alongside the chore of tackling Geordie's handwriting. Within days, I was on bosom-pal terms with Sam and Sadie, a fun-loving couple from Shrewsbury; with a gentle Newcastle accountant named Sid and his wife Bonnie and with Norman, not to mention a host of others eager to make the most of their walkin'n'talkin' holidays.

Sam and Sadie were irresistible. Sam, lithe and chirpy and carrying his six decades lightly, had been a cricket umpire at the highest level and even done a few overseas tours. His tales of behind-the-scenes goings-on kept the bar laughing, even people, such as the local Maltese and myself, who never understood what cricket was about anyway. Sadie, tall, upright and flaxen haired, was an ex-hospital matron and could match any of his stories, focusing mainly on the waywardness of human plumbing. They both had that indefinable ability to accumulate like-minded companions. Time spent with them passed much more speedily and enjoyably than with the increasingly burdensome legacy of Geordie Ballantine.

Sid and Bonnie, met in the lift on my first morning, were less boisterous, but still good, cultured company, unstinting talkers, attentive listeners. Sid, only recently retired, was stooped and heron-like, with all the variety of interests that accountants seem to acquire as compensation for the routine of their profession. He was among other things a dedicated beekeeper and managed to get even me interested in that esoteric hobby.

Apparently there was a project to bring back the traditional Maltese bee to the island – it was after all honey that had given the island its old name of Melita. Sid returned one afternoon from a visit to his fellow-keepers involved in the crusade, laden down with jars of honey and bottles of mead. I took a jar of the first and helped him dispose of the second. I tried to prise from him the secret of how a bee-keeper from the north-east of England could possibly recognise his opposite number on Malta – and vice versa. Were there secret handshakes or special code words? Apart from muttering that they had met in a bar, he didn't seem to know.

His wife Bonnie was a buxom delight, with a mission to look after and bring or drag into the circle any lonely, single or shy holidaymakers who happened to catch her eye. I had noticed her working on some of the other guests with that warm Geordie ease and admired her well-disguised skill, before I realised that she had me firmly in her sights and I was just another of her poor souls to be saved from their own company.

Norman was another matter. He was a retired Rotherham fireman and a seasoned long-stay holidaymaker. His wife had died earlier in the year and this was his first holiday on his own. Short, rotund and topped off with a dandelion mop of white hair, he knew everything about everyone – and his grasp of the facts was spiced with a highly developed sense of rumour. Everyone soon got to know – and fear – his trade mark opening line, 'I couldn't help noticing …'

In my case, what he couldn't help noticing was my working at the laptop on my balcony. With his sharp eyesight and binoculars, he might even have been able to see what I was writing. His balcony was, after all, a mere 100 feet away on the other wing. Within minutes, he had wheedled, for starters, details of the book, of my redundancy, of my Highland home and the fact I was unattached. To be fair, he gave plenty in return – the pithy vital details of every Brit in the hotel. Sam and Sadie, for example, had already told me it was second marriage for each of them, but Norman added the colourful aside that Sadie had advertised for a man in the local paper. I soon came to the conclusion that no matter how effective he had been in damping down the fires of Rotherham, he should have been a journalist.

Another example of his skills. On one of the warmer days, we were lying around the pool – I was just giving my laptop time to cool down, honestly – when an embarrassed SOS sounded from a third-floor balcony. It came from a Birmingham couple we knew very little about, as they had until that moment kept well out of the Norman's clutches.

They had managed to lock themselves out on the sun-washed balcony, unable to get back into their room. We were prepared to jeer at them and, in jest, to threaten to let them stew – or at least burn – for quarter of an hour or so. But before anyone could move, Norman had rushed off on his figurative white charger and rescued them.

Later that evening at the bar, I discovered that he had tracked down the hotel housekeeper, accompanied her to the couple's room, over-ruled her objections that she should do the job herself and then had gone in to release the catch of the door to the balcony. In his slow, measured progress through the room, he managed to spot a couple of empty duty-free gin bottles, litre ones at that, on her side of the bed, a toupee stand on his and Christmas card envelopes that bore two different surnames. An awesome talent lost to our profession!

There were many others that I talked to from time to time. The Brits were generally a lot older than me, but when I chanced my arm with some of the younger female Continentals – the hotel was popular with Germans and Scandinavians – I found either a ten-foot brick-wall or a nine-foot blond boy-friend.

The lively owner of the hotel provided a further challenge to the dead Geordie's literary legacy. Mr Joseph – everyone called him that, not to distinguish him from the saint of the same name but to mark him out from Mr Rocco and Mr Godwin, his two brothers who were also involved in the Seacrest – was a pleasant and cultured man.

He had been around the globe, including a spell in Scotland's flagship Gleneagles hotel, before setting up back in his native Mellieħa. He would come up with proud and colourful answers or suggestions to anyone showing an interest in his beloved island – or, better still, in his own village.

The first few days saw me being enticed further and further away from *MacAbre*. I had never been to Malta before and it is an island easy to love, especially if you have any sense of history. In a tiny, confined space, not much bigger than

Edinburgh, you can get not just to wild, remote and tinglingly desolate places but also to the most evocative of historical settings. The span goes from eerie prehistoric temples to the dramas of the Second World War where the fight for Malta was arguably the key to final victory.

And there was no shortage of material in the thirty centuries in between, from the shipwreck of Saint Paul and the early Christian catacombs, to the charismatic Knights Hospitaller of Saint John and the invasions of Ottoman Turks, Italians, Napoleonic French and, of course, the British.

I became hopelessly infatuated with this untidy little rock, European history's microdot. The result? Instead of spending every moment at Geordie's sack of notes, I pitched into reading everything about Malta that I could lay my hands on – Ernle Bradford's *The Siege of Malta*, Nicholas Monsarrat's glorious *The Kappilan of Malta*, Joanne Trollope's *The Brass Dolphin* and even a book on the one and only – and now deceased – Malta Railway.

To be honest, from time to time, especially when I saw what luxury Don Blaikie's unusual extra to the advance for *MacAbre* had brought me, twinges of guilt would get to me and I would take out Geordie's ramblings and buckle down to my task. The words still came to me, but much more slowly now. There were times when I was convinced that even a damp basement in Auld Reekie would have been a more productive workplace.

And things didn't get any easier. In fact before long, *MacAbre* was to become a rarely visited No-Go zone for my thoughts, relegated to the bottom of a long list of priorities. My passion for Malta, aided and abetted by what seemed suspiciously like lightning strikes of divine intervention, eventually turned a writing commitment into something very different indeed.

I suppose it was Sid and Bonnie who set the ball rolling. 'Don't be a spoilsport. Come along with us on one of the trips,'

Bonnie urged. 'It'll give you a break from all that work and, who knows, you may meet a nice young girl.' My mother always believed that shortbread and a cup of tea sorted out all human problems, from shingles to homosexuality – she had only recently come across this new 'problem' with a teenage neighbour in the village. Bonnie clearly attributed the same magical properties to marriage.

I gave in without too much of a struggle, little realising that sight-seeing was going to involve me in even more distractions – and a couple of encounters from which I would never recover. The first of these came on that innocent sounding coach-trip that I took with Sid and Bonnie.

Chapter 3

Wednesday 10 November

There's always someone who arrives late on these coach trips. In this case it was me, a few pieces of tissue still sticking to the razor-damage on my chin that had held me back. I apologised to everyone as I rushed aboard. There was a seat near the front, but it was next to a strident London feminist who had loudly disseminated her views around the Seacrest's public rooms. I pretended not to notice it and made my way to the only other seat left – at the very back of the coach, of course. Nodding and shrugging my apologies à la Monsieur Hulot, I suddenly found myself looking at two faces I recognised, despite their dark glasses.

The last time I had seen Dougie Douglas and Gus Graham, perhaps a couple of years earlier, they were celebrating outside the High Court in Edinburgh after a jury had come up with a verdict of Not Proven in what had seemed like an open-and-shut case of extortion. I had been covering the case as a back-up junior reporter and recalled that a couple of the key witnesses had suffered from what looked suspiciously like terror-induced amnesia.

I hurried past, certain that they had not even looked at me. Besides, they would not have paid any attention to me at the court on the few occasions I was there. The Stars would not recognise the Stagehand. They must have arrived with the previous day's Glasgow flight. I'd been at the Seacrest a week and I would certainly have noticed them about the hotel or even on the pick-up coach if they had been on my flight.

Dougie and Gus! What on earth were they doing in Malta? Well, even villains need a break, I suppose. I looked back. No one else with them. Perhaps the two men were escaping from some heat back home – it's good for a young journalist to have a news sense. I made a mental note to ring Phil Dunne, Phil, the gentle oberstürmbahnführer of the *Capital News* reporters.

With his contacts in the Edinburgh Underworld, he would know if anything was in the wind.

The presence of the two men put a dampener on the trip. Yes, they looked as you would expect tourists to look, Dougie, smiling, slim and bearing his fifty years or so well in a brown linen safari suit, the enormous, glum, close-cropped Gus contributing less elegantly to the image of the British tourist in a green shell suit bristling with insignia to trumpet his support for Hibernian Football Club. But each time I caught sight of them, they looked as if they had wandered on to the set of the wrong film.

It was, coincidentally, Geordie Ballantine who, years earlier had explained to me the origins of Dougie's upturned eternal smile and Gus' drooping permanent scowl. Both could be traced to facial scars around the lips resulting from one of the most infamous gang fights to take place in 70s Edinburgh. The two men had won the leadership of the ultraviolent Leith Lynx Pack after an encounter with the Gilmerton Mob that may have left Dougie and Gus with those barely noticeable facial scars, but had bequeathed more restrictive handicaps to the losers.

At home in Edinburgh's underworld, they were surely out of place among my fellow rubber-necking tourists. At Mosta, our guide told us of the miracle of the 2000lb German bomb that had crashed through the massive dome of the Church of Santa Marija in 1942 and failed to explode, injuring none of the 600 worshippers. I found it no less incredible to see two of Edinburgh's most notorious criminals admiring the beautiful calm interior of the church and pointing out to each other the designs on the stained glass windows.

When we looked at the patient silversmiths creating their spider-web filigree at Ta' Qali craft village, I could not believe that two men with a life-long reputation for grievous bodily harm could possibly be sharing our fascination with the delicate and ethereal craft.

22

I had from the beginning ruled out religious conversion as an explanation of their presence on the trip. Maybe I was being uncharitable.

At last, the pair found something more suited to their reputations. At the end of the tour, in contrast to the creative artistry we could wonder at in Mosta and the Craft Village, we all stumbled in a crocodile along the rough hewn passageways of Mdina's medieval dungeons, peering through the gloom at the sadistic ingenuities of man when it comes to death and torture. Bloodthirsty Turks, sadistic Inquisitors, maniacal executioners were all spotlighted in gory detail in the crowded Chamber of Horrors.

But while the rest of us were reduced to nervous asides or mute horror, Dougie and Gus seemed amused by every exhibit, laughing loudly from time to time. And I swear I saw Gus actually making notes on the back of his guide-book at a display of racks, thumb screws and other compression or extension devices whose mechanics I never really fathomed, but whose capacity to inflict excruciating pain was all too apparent. I now definitely ruled out the religious conversion.

I was glad to get back to my room in the late afternoon, especially as I had found myself sharing the lift with my two sinister fellow citizens. I avoided speaking, anxious not to give away my origins. I even went so far as greeting the lady who joined us in the lift with a hearty, guttural 'Guten Abend!', trying to remember how Erich Von Stroheim would have said it. It was only later that I discovered she was French.

I sat on the balcony, taking in the last of the sun, warmer than it had been all day. Why were Dougie and Gus in Malta? They could be on holiday, of course, but I remembered that they were family men. Phil had pointed their wives out to me in court. That reminded me again. I must phone Phil!

I didn't get around to ringing him for some days – and then only because of another, rather pointed reminder. There were, I plead, other distractions, besides my inbuilt procrastination and the obvious inertia induced by a cosy hotel bar at 9 pm when the cheap telephone rate came into play, but when the nearest card-phone was two hundred windswept yards up the hill.

Chapter 4
Sunday 14 November

Although I didn't know it at the time, it was a Sunday morning 45 bus that was to take me to a second fateful encounter. It was no more extraordinary a bus than any other on Malta. Air conditioning was provided by a non-existent door, windows that refused to close and even a flip-up, fly-spattered windscreen. A bus designed for sultry summers, but it was windy winter. I had discovered that the best bet was the seat up front at right angles to the driver. Yes, I know! It had the nerve-twanging disadvantage of letting you see the road ahead, but at least you were in front of all the main sources of cold breezes.

The windscreen was surrounded by the usual array of religious images. Premier Division saints in the Christian drama appeared with a number of expressions from pity to pain, eternal bliss to human compassion, with a particularly animated contribution from Saint Christopher, who metronomed on a cheap, glittery chain with every bump and shuggle. Secular competition was provided by the photo of a glossy trotting horse, a faded print of faded footballers and a card offering the services of Tattoo Tony.

I soon shared the seat with Henry, a fascinating old codger from Kent. He did not select the seat for the same reasons as I had. He just fell helplessly into it as the bus started up. Henry had last been on the island in 1943. Compared with his journey then, this bus was bliss. His merchant ship had been torpedoed off Sicily and he had been stretchered to Valletta. The hospitals there were overcrowded and yet another hotel in Sliema was commandeered for the traditional healing activities of the Knights Hospitaller. Henry was back to see if the dance floor that had once been his ward was back to its original use.

At Mosta, I reluctantly left him and his tales for my morning challenge – my first-ever Mass. Not even the presence of

25

Dougie and Gus had stopped me being bowled over on my first visit and I decided that, if I was ever to sit in on a Catholic Mass, it ought to be a good one. What better than the Mosta Dome?

My Presbyterian upbringing had left me ill fitted to cope with the liturgy of an alien worship and I found a seat at the back so that I knew when to stand, kneel or sit. Eleven o'clock Mass was in Malti, so once again I had failed to find a use for all that Latin I'd sweated over at Inverness Royal Academy.

It didn't matter. The setting was stupendous, a dome, it was said, to snap at the heels of Saint Peter's, Saint Paul's and Hagia Sophia, yet in a community dwarfed by Rome, London and Istanbul. The gap had been bridged by local carvers and sculptors, painters and weavers, goldsmiths and silversmiths who had, without pay or stint, poured their reverence and duty to their neighbours into the fabric of the church. You could almost feel the honest sweat, the aching muscles, the straining sinews. The singing was divine, the acoustics were chilling, and the sermon, incomprehensible to me but well received by my neighbours, was delivered by a priest in a sinuous, hypnotic style more reminiscent of Peter Lorre than John Knox.

My strategic spot at the back had meant that not only had I followed my fellow-worshippers correctly if tardily, but also that I was among the first to make it back to the daylight, blinking uncontrollably as the sun bounced off the buttery Maltese stone of the church and the capricious streets of Mosta that clustered around it.

There was, I discovered, a wedding to follow. As the fortified faithful poured out, the fashionable posed, ready to move in. It was patently a very grand affair. The guests were decked out in the sort of finery that would have got them all past Cecil Beaton into the Royal Enclosure in *My Fair Lady*. Top hats and grey suits, classy frocks and the most flamboyant of Malta's millinery cried out that this was a society event. The immense church emptied, the ladies and gentlemen paused in their posing and moved up the warmed, broad steps and into the dark coolness, still chattering.

A young man, dressed smartly enough in blazer and grey flannels, but clearly not one of the guests, hauled a cumbersome wooden case up the steps to the porch of the church. I was intrigued. It was the wrong shape for a camera and, even if it was some strange unknown piece of photographic equipment, he had missed the arrivals. He, slick with practice, opened the box, assembled a large set of tubular bells and stood, a soft, padded drumstick in each hand, ready for … well, ready for … something.

At that point, another young man appeared, carrying a similar large wooden case. He looked distinctly put out by the presence of the first man and with some annoyance brandished a sheet of paper at him. They both peered at the sheet. The first man pointed triumphantly at some detail. The second man panicked, picked up his hefty case and hobbled off at some speed.

I walked over to the musician, a question on my lips, a camera in my hand – and collided with a young woman with, I am sure, the same mission. I had not seen her as she had been standing behind another of the six massive pillars forming the portico of the church. I turned to apologise, but I was the one to be bowled over.

Snow White stood in front of me and I was smitten. She was trying hard not to look like Snow White – no hair band, no puffy sleeves, no feminine dress but instead a purple, yes purple, T-shirt and nondescript black jeans.

I was not fooled. There was no doubt. It was her. The rounded figure – you can't have a *thin* cherub – the eponymous snow-white skin, the rosebud Disney lips, the thick curly black hair, with, did I imagine it or did the reflections from the Mosta stone reveal tiny sparks of bronze, auburn even. She was tall and willowy. Funny word that, willow trees are squat, droopy and wishy-washy, but perhaps 'willowy' refers to the individual branches. Level with my chin instead of down at my third shirt button as with most of the girls I met, I gazed into something Snow White didn't have – green eyes.

I don't know why I've always gone for that particular look. It must have been my mother's fault for taking me to see the Disney film when I was at an impressionable age. Certainly I have never quivered at the thought of the buxom blondes who populated the daydreams of my contemporaries. When the Glenbraith tycoon Rabbie Glass, who had become very wealthy indeed knocking down old buildings, returned from London with a Barbara Windsor lookalike as his bride, I was not among the stricken teenagers who whistled every time she tottered past.

A quick glance around failed to reveal any lurking lover and a more studied investigation located a ringless finger.

My Identikit of Love spoke. 'Sorry … my fault. I wasn't looking where I was going.' The voice was as soft and low as I had expected and more musical than any tubular bells. It exuded North America.

I tried an old ploy that had worked on the pavements of Princes Street and the pubs of Rose Street. 'Are you Canadian?' The Canadians are always flattered that you recognise them and the Americans invariably give you a cue for an equally good follow-up.

'No, I'm American. Why did you think I was Canadian?'

'Oh, I just felt you were – don't be offended – more sophisticated than the usual US tourist.'

She shook her head, but I could see she was pleased. 'I'm actually from Boston, as in "Tea Party".'

'You mean as in "Strangler".' It seemed a far better link to me.

She ignored the remark. 'Well,' she said, 'I wonder what's going on. I was going to ask the man with that contraption what's happening.'

The question was answered before we had a chance to ask it. As we approached him, the young man held up his hand to prevent any intrusion. We did as we were bidden. A large white limousine had pulled up at the foot of the flight of steps and bride and father were heading straight for us. We stepped back and, on cue, the young man did his duty, playing an echoing metallic tune, a vaguely familiar religious air but definitely not 'Here Comes The Bride'.

The local onlookers, and there were many, clapped and one, a large, emotional lady dabbing her eyes, explained to me that this was the traditional way to let the congregation know that the bride was on her way.

'But what about that other man?' I asked. 'He had a set of bells as well.'

'Oh, yes, but that was Conrad,' the emotional lady shrugged with an air of resignation. 'He'd come to the wrong church. He's always doing things like that.' Her friends nodded and tutted in agreement.

'Gosh, does that mean there's a bride somewhere who's not going to have the bell treatment?' The lovely American looked quite concerned for the other bride.

'No, the other church is just around the corner. And it's Vanessa Sammut's youngest. Every one of her sisters was late. She'll be no different.' The chorus nodded again.

The bride seemed to be taking ages to put her dress in order, helped by a few of the onlookers and hindered by a trembling father. The young American bubbled with pleasure and couldn't take her eyes off the bride. I was no less happy and couldn't take my eyes off *her*.

I searched my memory banks. No, the cinema had never produced a more romantic boy-meets-girl scenario than this.

Eventually, the bride and her father, with thanks to the helpers and self-conscious nods to us, walked into the holy shadows in time to the tubular bells. We all applauded enthusiastically. The women around us melted away, perhaps to their Sunday lunch duties, perhaps to catch the tardy Sammut girl around the corner. The two of us were alone.

'That was wonderful, really wonderful.' She turned to me and smiled. Then her lips puckered with frustration and her dimples deepened. 'And what do you know? After all that, I didn't get a picture of the bride,' she sighed, tapping the hood at the end of a zoom lens that looked capable of launching an Exocet missile.

'*I* did,' I consoled, tapping my little idiot-proof camera, '*and* a good one of that man on the bells. I'll get extra prints for you if you like. It would be a pity to miss all of this out of your album,' I said, silently offering thanks to whichever saint looks after infatuated young men. 'Where are you staying?'

'The Seacrest, Mellieħa Bay.'

My hotel! And I had never even noticed her there. I heaped more thanks upon Saint Whatsisname.

'So am I, but I've never seen you around.'

'Oh, I've noticed you, all right. I arrived a week ago and I've seen you using a laptop on your balcony, haven't I?'

I think I blushed.

'I'm an early bird,' she explained, 'first down at breakfast, first down in the evening, then up and out. How come we haven't met before?'

I cursed my idleness. 'I'm usually up with the lark myself,' I improvised, looking for a defence for being down when breakfast opened the next day, but never until then having been earlier than five minutes before the kitchens closed. 'But I've been working into the early hours to finish a job – I'll be back to my usual 7.30 start any day now. I'll look out for you.'

To my surprise, she hurried away from me, down the

shallow, stone steps towards the bus stop at the bottom.

'I'm getting this bus up to Mdina. I was just waiting for it when I saw the wedding party,' she called back. No invitation to join her!

I ran down the steps after her.

As usual, the delay of tourists trying to find the right change held up the bus long enough for me to make it. By the time I caught up however, there were four or five school kids between us.

When I got to the door the driver, swarthy and unwelcoming, held out a restraining hand.

'Full!'

I could not believe it. Crowded buses were a way of life on the island. I pleaded, but the scowl remained. Just as the driver made to return to his driving duties, he stopped and did a double take. He actually smiled at me. At least, I thought that was what was happening until I realised he was looking over my left shoulder.

'Rowena. Where have you been hiding? It's been ages. Come aboard.' He turned into the bus. 'Push up down there. Can't you see there are people trying to get on?'

The obedient passengers concertinaed, leaving room for Rowena and of course for me! To her confusion, I thanked the voluptuous Rowena profusely. I was saved.

A goodly proportion of the crush, noisy school kids and laden shoppers, poured out on the fringes of Mosta, allowing me to move further into the bus. My American had even managed to find a seat. I said 'Hi!' between the backpacks of a couple of Danish tourists. Instead of looking delighted or even pleased, she just seemed surprised.

Twenty minutes after leaving the Dome at Mosta, we were in Mdina. Even then, there was little chance of much communication, as we had arrived along with a couple of packed tourist coaches. The Silent City did not live up to its name. But for twenty minutes or so we tramped the lanes looking up at those strange covered balconies which are so Maltese. French *balcons* are open to the air and the neighbours, very public extensions of the home. Malta's are secretive and mysterious, covered and sheltered from prying eyes, like elevated bird-watching hides. I spotted a teashop and at last we were alone together.

'John.' At last I could tell her my name.

'Katy.'

The setting could not have been more idyllic. There we were in the ancient inland capital of Malta, lofty Mdina, Città Notabile, sitting at a small table, looking out over the ramparts to the fertile winter fields and beyond to the north-eastern sea, dark blue to the sharp horizon. Surrounded by centuries. Dripping with tradition. Soaked in history.

And Katy ordered a burger and Coke!

Reacting against such insensitivity, I went for a large glass of an unnamed local red wine from an unlabelled bottle and a helping of hobz biz-zejt. My thick slice of grainy Maltese bread, impregnated with tomatoes, capers and garlic and soused in olive oil, put the burger just where it belonged – in its johnny-come-lately place.

In return for a full confession concerning *MacAbre*, I discovered that she was Katy Mifsud from Boston, of Maltese extraction yet on her first visit to Malta.

'Why are you here in the middle of winter?' She was not a bit like the other hibernating tourists. 'It seems a strange time to come.'

She paused before answering. 'You know something? In twenty-five years I'd never been to Malta once. I thought it was about time I did and I've got a break before starting a new job after Christmas. So here I am.' She shrugged.

So she was twenty-five. Almost my age. Interesting, and it made me miss the fact that she hadn't answered my question very convincingly. I pushed for more information about her, but not about her reasons for being here.

Graduating in some strange American combination of psychology, anthropology and a few other subjects I pretended to comprehend, she was now some sort of glorified social worker with academic overtones. Frankly, I didn't really care about the details. She was the girl for me.

If her appearance lassoed me, her voice tied all the knots. If she had known what had happened, she would have described me as 'hog-tied'.

One day, I think I'll get a PhD based on my observation that men fall for accents that don't sound like their own. I'd always gone for the southern Irish lilt and could detect one at thirty feet in the noisiest Edinburgh pub. For my thesis, I'll get a thousand students – they're cheaper than anyone else – to listen to tapes of girls saying the same thing in all sorts of different accents. They'll tick the boxes (academics love ticks in boxes) to record sexiness. I'll back it up with an analysis of every broadcast of *Blind Date* and then declare that this preference for unfamiliar accents is a genetic safeguard to expand the gene pool and discourage in-breeding. And then it's *Dr* John Smith and a calendar full of TV chat-show slots. I vowed to put a note in my diary to remind me to get it all sorted out when I got home.

But back to the mellifluous Katy. She wasn't put off by my attempts to mimic every suave operator of the silver screen from Valentino to DiCaprio – and on the bus trip back even said exactly what I was willing her to say.

'Hey, that was nice. Why don't we meet up for dinner in the hotel tomorrow evening?'

I was cock-a-hoop. 'Yes, yes, that sounds great. About seven thirty?'

'That's fine by me.'

But why didn't she say 'tonight' and what was wrong with breakfast? Was there a rival in the hotel? I mentally ran through the few Brits of our generation and rejected them. The most likely was a fine physical specimen from Bristol, but he spent most of his time running around the countryside and always looked on the point of exhaustion. I tried to recall any unattached foreigners. There were far too many of them for my liking. I would keep a wary eye out.

Chapter 5

Monday 15 November

There was no sign of Katy on the evening of our encounter and to my disgust my ingrained habit of oversleeping meant that the resolution to be up at the crack of breakfast went unheeded. Instead I was down late enough to do no more than exchange a 'Hi!' with Katy on her way out. Never mind, there was dinner to look forward to.

After breakfast, I took a long slow stroll along the beach and had a beer at the alfresco bar on the other side of the bay. Half way back to the Seacrest, some time around midday, a squall hit the bay unexpectedly and sent me scurrying for the warmth and comfort of the lounge bar. There were quite a few guests with the same idea and the bar slowly filled up. I was toying with the idea of getting back to *MacAbre* when I saw Dougie and Gus come in. It was my first chance to observe them since the coach trip meeting.

There was nothing at all suspicious about their behaviour. They noticed a couple leaving a prized table near the big window and quickly took possession. Gus produced a pack of cards and the two settled down to a game of rummy.

There was only one incident of note and that came when the inquisitive Norman tried to take a seat alongside them. I could not hear what he was saying but whatever it was did not meet with Gus' approval. Norman got up quickly and moved on to another potential target.

Norman was not going to prove a useful source of information on these two guests. But there was nothing sinister in that. I would have been astonished to see the pair open up to a stranger, no matter what the circumstances. Still it did say something for the deterrent value of the giant Gus that he could brush aside the persistent Norman so easily.

*

That first dinner with Katy was enchanting and not even the sight, over her curving shoulder, of Sadie and the exuberant Bonnie winking dramatically and giving me the thumbs-up sign could spoil it. I was in confident mood, as there had been no signs of another man when I saw her coming out of breakfast that morning.

After handing over my photos of the Mosta bride and the tubular bellman, I got down to more personal topics. Our talk came readily and was as smooth as pebbles. She relished my tales of a boyhood in the Highlands, a world away from her own childhood in a bustling American city.

She would not be convinced that I regularly spent my schooldays feeding buns to the Loch Ness Monster, but maybe I cried 'Wolf' too obviously, as she just wouldn't believe either that we all spoke Gaelic at home or that my father earned a living catching wild salmon and smoking them for an eager band of customers far and near.

The busty Bonnie passed our table, despite the fact it was hardly in a direct line between hers and the display of mouth-watering puddings. 'Introduce me to your lady friend, Johnny.'

'She's no lady – she's an American. Bonnie, meet Katy and vice versa.'

I turned confidingly to Katy. 'Bonnie's run away from a respectable family in England with a man old enough to be her father. He may look like an accountant, but he's into glamour lingerie and naughty videos. Worth a fortune, they tell me.'

I pointed over to the buffet area. 'That's him over there, the tall thin guy with a scoop of ice-cream on what looks suspiciously like two slices of gateau.'

Bonnie giggled and slapped me playfully on the shoulder. 'Don't believe a word he says, Katy.'

'I don't, Bunny, believe me, I don't. That's one thing I've learnt about him already.'

She was getting to know me well and quickly. She just had to be interested.

'It's not Bunny. It's Bonnie, as in Banks. Will we see you in the bar afterwards?' Bonnie grinned knowingly. 'Or are you young people planning an early night?'

'We'll see you in the bar,' I promised emphatically. 'You'd better rush off, Bonnie. I think Sid is looking at a third scoop of ice cream.'

She slapped my shoulder again and wobbled off.

I devoted my whole attention to Katy.

'Your turn now. Sell me 'the States'. And don't forget, my knowledge of the USA comes entirely from Hollywood, so you have a lot of undergrowth to hack through. I see the whole country as populated by Spencer Tracy and Edward G Robinson lookalikes. They are pursued by Bette Davis, Lauren Bacall and Ingrid Bergman, through a landscape alternating between Brooklyn and Monument Valley. In the background, I can hear the theme music from The Magnificent Seven, Gone with the Wind and Breakfast at Tiffany's and the noise of police sirens and squealing tyres.'

After all that, I took a deep breath, before adding. 'Oh, and at this time of the year, the streets are filled with ruddy faced Father Christmas figures shouting "Yo-ho-ho" and ringing a bell as they walk past grinning sets of teeth, carrying shopping in large brown-paper bags.'

She smiled indulgently and sighed. 'You mean to say you haven't even watched Cheers or Friends to bring you up to speed on Boston?'

'I once saw ten minutes of a Cheers episode,' I offered, proudly.

'What about Ally McBeal?'

'Is she the emaciated one or the tubby Dawn French lookalike?'

'O boy, this is going to take some time, but what the heck, we've plenty of that.' She looked pleased to take on the evangelical bit.

'It's really the only place I know. I wasn't born there. My family moved there when I was only two, but it has been the whole of my life since then.

'All my friends live there, all the family I know. And it's a wonderful city. You've no idea, the galleries, the Common, the islands in the Bay, the museums, the coffee shops …'

'The drug stores,' I prompted in my best American accent.

'You're teasing! And that's an awful accent.' She wiggled a finger at me. 'Believe me, it's a place where I've cried of course, but for the most part I think of Boston as somewhere to smile, to talk and meet with friends either for a date or just coming across them in the street. And it's such an incredible mix of old and new, traditional British, today American.'

Katy was enjoying herself.

'You see guys jogging, flying kites, throwing Frisbees, playing chess, juggling even. There's one busker balances a shopping trolley on his nose.' She giggled. 'And all this can be in streets that even you would call Olde Worlde.'

She remembered something that appealed to her. 'Listen, this sums it all up. One afternoon, we were, well about six or seven of us from College, doing our cultural duty and looking at an exhibition of Impressionist paintings, you know the thing, all bright colours and excitement, all very … European.

'Then … someone … said, pointing to one of those out-door scenes in a Paris café, you know with lots of happy people having a darned good time, "That's Boston, man. All those guys chilling out in a staid, old fashioned gilt frame".' She relived the occasion. 'For me that just summed up Boston.'

She was really getting into her stride. 'I know that I get a privileged ticket to the city. Dad is wealthy – his software business meant that whatever we wanted, he could afford it. I had my own friends, but Joe and Paul, my brothers, weren't much older than I was and they supplied an army of their guys to make up a huge social circle. Whenever I stepped out into the street, I'd be pretty sure to run into someone I knew.'

She was happy with her memories. 'Teenagers complain of loneliness; I liked being alone. It was a change, it was welcome. Boston was just as great a place to wander around on your own as in a gang.

'And at this time of the year, Boston is at its wonderful best, crisp snow, crowded streets, smiling, laughing shoppers, Thanksgiving – I'll really miss that – and Christmas – I'll be home by then, of course …'

'When are you going back then?' I'd been so intent of catching up on my lost week that I hadn't until then thought that her stay might not be a long one. After all, not everyone can take off for a month or so. I waited anxiously for her answer.

'Oh, not until December.' It seemed a blissful world away when she put it like that.

Katy discontinued my personal guided tour of Boston when she noticed that we were the only people left in the dining room. We didn't have the brass neck to go up to the counter for our final course, but slunk out with a hurried 'Thank You' to the patient staff. I did however manage to palm a piece of pepper cheese en route to the door.

We joined Sid and Bonnie and sundry other guests in an ever-expanding circle around two tables in the bar, but as it was one of the evenings when the band was churning out something more akin in volume to fairground rather than background music, conversation was limited to shouts and sign language.

At eleven, the group broke up and we made for our rooms. Katy and I shared a lift with Sid and Bonnie and an engrossed pair of honeymooners from Australia, back to visit the Land of their Grandfathers.

Katy followed the couple out of the lift on the third floor and, inspired perhaps by their lovey-doveying, gave me, to my surprise, a sweet little kiss on the cheek, no more contact than two snooker balls, but enough to be going on with.

I cherished the moment and happily endured the nodding grins of Sid and Bonnie as we continued to the top floor.

Chapter 6

Wednesday 17 November

'You've not been to Valletta yet?'

'No, it seems to be something of a block with me, I guess.'

I could not believe it. Katy and I were having breakfast together, two days after that first dinner. The day in between had been lost, as Katy was already sitting with someone else each time I arrived. At breakfast she was with the London feminist and listening to her sermon on the evils of men, as indeed were most of the guests. I hoped she wasn't going to be too influenced. At dinner, even more worryingly, she was sitting with a pushy, handsome German lad with excellent English. I got close to him at the coffee machine and gave thanks to Saint Whatsisname when I discovered he was booked on a return flight to the Fatherland two hours after the meal. And I had no idea where she disappeared to in between.

It hadn't been to Valletta and I had to put that right.

'You must see Valletta. Immediately. Come on, skip the honey and toast and we'll get the quarter past ten to Sliema.' I took her hand, led her out of the breakfast room and made for the lift.

'I thought you said "Valletta". Why are we off to Sliema?'

'Patience, hen. I'll see you at the front door in ten minutes.' I rushed her out at the third floor.

We were both back at reception almost simultaneously, Katy surprising me with a quick change from denim to brown slacks, a woolly bobble hat and a T-shirt that looked as if it was made of antique parchment. I think the parchment bit was intentional, not a washing machine error, as the T-shirt carried selected quotations from the Gettysburg Address. I hoped that people didn't notice my habit of reading words on Katy's chest. She didn't seem to.

We only just caught the Sliema bus, sprinting across the road from the hotel and running in front of the yellow vehicle before it could get up speed. The absence of a door made it easier to get aboard and I placated the driver by producing the right change, a rare consideration from tourists.

I explained to Katy my discovery of the sheltered front seat next to the driver.

'But that's for disabled people and pregnant mothers.' She pointed at the incomprehensible sign in Malti. I was impressed with her ability to read the language until I noticed there was a smaller notice alongside in English. I followed her sheepishly to a draughty seat at the very back of the bus.

By eleven o'clock we were standing on the sea front at Sliema looking over to Manoel Island and beyond to the stern profile of Valletta.

'Wow! It's so dramatic. But how are we supposed to get there?' Katy looked up and down the quayside.

'I can't offer a gondola, or even the local luzzu, but here's the next best thing.' I gestured to the little ferryboat that was approaching. We paid our 35 cents apiece and set off for Valletta. The sea was calm, the swell gentle, the sky clear. We scorned the covered cabin and spent the journey standing as close to the prow as we could get, the sun in our eyes, the breeze in our faces. It was not quite Jack and Rose in *Titanic*, except in spirit.

Fifteen speedy minutes later, we were under the walls of Valletta.

'We'll start our tour of the city by walking around it. On the outside. There's no better way of getting the feel of the place – and I'll bet you don't know many capital cities you can trot around in an hour ...'

We set off under a cloud-free sky, sometimes walking on a track, sometimes scrambling over the rocks, and all the time under the brooding ramparts of the amazing city.

By the time we reached the end of the hump-backed peninsula, the open sea was beginning to show white-tipped waves and to add some life to the surroundings. We sat on the rocks and scoured the horizon for ships. A few cargo vessels and a tanker passed by and we watched a cruise liner make her way out from the Grand Harbour and into the Mediterranean, off perhaps to Naples and Sorrento, Venice or Dubrovnik, Athens or the Holy Land.

I got to my feet and took Katy's hand, pulling her up. 'No time for all this. As you Yanks say, how we gonna see Valletta if y'all keep stopping to look at things!'

She did not let go of my hand and, for the first time, we took advantage of a gap in the walls to enter the city proper, emerging on to the road at Valletta's apex.

'That's the War Museum,' I pointed with my free hand at a door that led back into the city wall. 'We'll keep that for another day. It'll need an hour or so. There's something you should see first.'

There were very few walkers abroad at that end of the city. Suddenly, the loudest noise I had ever heard frightened the two of us enough to make us recoil from the pavement into a fortunately empty road. The huge liberty bell or independence bell, I forget the exact name, boomed out its daily noonday message and set in motion jangling vibrations that homed in through my jawbone to my two most recent fillings – it was Edinburgh's one-o'clock gun and the final scene from Hitchcock's *Vertigo* rolled into one – and then some.

Holding our ears, we took refuge in the great building opposite, the very one I was aiming for as our next stop. We were making for the Malta Experience, the audio-visual show to bring Katy up to speed on her own history, but there was a surprise for her before we'd even reached the ticket desk.

'Now, Ms Mifsud, sceptical rubber-neck from the Land of the Superlative, how does this grab you?'

The way to the ticket desk led past the Infirmerìa, the hospital ward of the Knights of Malta. Lofty? Yes. Broad? Yes. But long? Yes, yes!

In its day, the ward was the longest room in the world, 150 yards – an Olympic sprint and a half. Katy was taken aback.

'Eat your heart out, ER. They'll never believe this back home,' she said, clicking away with that 1000-dollar camera of hers.

'There was nothing like it in those days – anywhere.' I'd read my guidebook. 'This is where the knights tended the sick, feeding them on plates and dishes of solid silver, with knives and spoons to match, because they thought it was the cleanest metal of all. And at a time when no European had even seen or heard of Boston or Massachusetts.'

I caught her arm. 'Well, now, let's get down to the show and start your education proper.'

I enjoyed seeing the show again, but even more I shared in Katy's enjoyment of it.

We meandered back the full length of Valletta, taking a long time, marvelling at the great langues or hostel colleges of the Knights Hospitaller and exploring the shops and alleyways and churches. We left the great cathedral for another time and ate pasta under the statue of Queen and Empress Victoria, retaining her dignity in the face of bird droppings, missing fingers and a location renamed the Square of the Republic.

It was a great day, exhausting but satisfying. And Katy was very appreciative. I could tell that from the 'Thank You' and the extra special kiss I got as we eventually left the city and made our way wearily to the confusion of the bus station outside the city gate. Despite the efforts of the walk and the dustiness of the city, Katy exuded a freshness that reminded me of home in the Highlands. I was beginning to sense that the visit to Valletta had helped move our relationship forward to a two-way affair.

44

The only disappointment was that, in the middle of Malta's rush hour, we couldn't get seats together until St Paul's Bay.

*

That evening, Norman sidled over to me at the buffet counter just as I was manoeuvring a spoonful of sauerkraut on to my plate. I had not seen him for some time and looked forward to catching up on some of the gossip. A new intake of Brits had arrived the day before and, if past performance was anything to go by, Norman would have opened a few of his special files by now.

'Norman, great to see you. Where have you been this last week? I've missed you like I miss the daily paper at home. Any scandal yet from this week's lot?'

'No, not really,' he grimaced. 'One of them's just retired as a prison governor, but apart from him, they're a sullen bunch, not like last week's.'

I returned my attention to the salads on offer, but Norman tapped me on the shoulder. He looked more pleased than usual with some other bit of his ferreting and he delivered his coup de grâce with immaculate timing.

'Oh, there's something else, Johnny. I couldn't help noticing that you're getting very friendly with Katy. Did you know that she is getting married next year?'

The German bomb plunging through the Mosta Dome did not make a more direct hit. And inside me, this bomb did not fail to explode.

'Of course I do, Norman,' I replied with as much aplomb as I could muster under the circumstances. 'Didn't I tell you I did a year in the States? Katy's… um … man and I are old friends. We shared rooms at …'

God, would he have been at Boston or where?

'… at … University, rowed in the same eight together. Great guy. I expect to be Best Man at the wedding, but keep that to yourself.'

Norman was taken aback, apologised profusely and crab-like made his way over to Sam and Sadie's table, prawns on his plate and gossip on his lips.

I returned robotically to my table. I was sitting with Sid and Bonnie that evening and didn't have to look at Katy across the meal. She was some tables away with the strident feminist.

I was, for once, grateful that she was not sitting opposite me.

It was cabaret night and after dinner we all trooped down to watch the dancers from Aceline. Again I was able to churn over Norman's news without directly confronting Katy.

Chapter 7

Thursday 18 November

Next morning, Norman's death had an impact on all of us, but especially on Emily Carstairs. His fall from the fourth-floor balcony destroyed the symmetry of a particularly fine palm tree, sent a hundred sparrows fleeing raucously and made a direct hit on the foot of Emily's sun-bed. She was catapulted into the swimming pool and those of us who had been foolish enough to put a toe or finger in the icy water earlier in the holiday feared as much for Emily's life as for Norman's. I joined the rescue party, avoiding contact with the frigid water and playing the key role of landing the shivering mass. It was impossible to dismiss memories of Gregory Peck in the final reel of *Moby Dick*.

A quick glance at Norman showed that we should turn our attention instead to the goose-pimpled, teeth-chattering Emily. In the interests of decency, the men involved in the rescue stood back and two of the ladies, the matronly Sadie and a rather fetching young German also claiming to be a 'krankenschwester', took on the task of drying her out and restoring some warmth to her body, changing blue to pink as if she was a mound of soggy litmus paper.

Norman was certainly in no need of such tender loving care. Most of his body was sprawled in the nonchalant, relaxed position of a sleeping holidaymaker. His head, however, was at a gruesome angle, as if added as some hurried divine afterthought, a Friday afternoon product from the Eternal Assembly Line. His eyes, spookily, peered out as inquisitively in death as they had in life, even if they were staring rather pointlessly at the back of his own shoulder.

Brought up on cinema deaths, I was surprised to find that subsequent events unfolded with humdrum sluggishness. 'Eventually' was the order of the day. Someone eventually phoned the police and the police eventually turned up. To my extreme disappointment, they did not arrive heralded by flashing blue lights and screaming sirens and, even more of an anti-climax, did not mark the position of Norman's body with a broad white line. In fact, they ignored it completely and took statements from everyone around.

The police must have contacted the ambulance men for they too eventually materialised. They put Norman on a stretcher, covered him with what I suspected was a hotel tablecloth and carried him away. Everyone in the hotel lined up to pay their respects at what had all the signs of a cut-price funeral. I was pleased to see that not even the Germans desecrated the occasion with a camcorder. Bonnie started to sing the 23rd Psalm, but no one joined in so she stopped.

Emily had recovered sufficiently to be among the mourners – and to collar a couple of newspaper reporters. I felt proud of my profession, as they had been the first on the scene, arriving with commendable speed and clearly having access to a vehicle and a grapevine more efficient than those of the emergency services. She had a tale to tell and she told it with all the restraint of Joan Crawford on pep pills. It was as much as I could do to resist applauding.

As the ambulance drove away, I felt a cold, trembling hand slip into mine. It was Katy's. And it was not the occasion to raise the subject of her wedding.

*

By midday, in what proved once more to be a vain attempt to jolt *MacAbre* into life, I was sitting in the shade on my veranda, laptop at the ready on my little table and yet another pile of Geordie's notes, annotated and amended, in front on me. It seemed as good a way as any to push Norman and Katy from my thoughts.

You know how difficult it is to avoid looking at something once you've told yourself not to. That's just how I felt trying to ignore the sad end-balcony, which had once been the domain of Norman and his binoculars. It was on the wing of the hotel that was getting the last of the morning sun and I kept glancing over.

I finally decided that, in the interests of the public impatiently awaiting *MacAbre*, I should remove myself from the distraction and take the laptop indoors. As I took a last look at the tragic balcony, I saw a movement behind the window of the room alongside and recognised the battered prize-fighter profile immediately. It was Gus Graham.

Dougie and Gus had the room next to the late Norman! The *only* room next to him! Occupied by two villains with a track record in crime which, as with the iceberg that hit the *Titanic*, showed only part of their evil doing.

Was there a connection or was I drawing silly, melodramatic conclusions from a simple coincidence?

I didn't have long to debate the question. Gus came on to the balcony, looked out, turned and called inside. He pointed, guffawing, across the fields to where a farmer was laboriously dragging a huge harrow across a cramped and stony plot.

Dougie joined him and studied the man intently – through the late Norman's distinctive bright blue field glasses! My God, I felt like Jimmy Stewart in *Rear Window*.

MacAbre was returned to the back boiler.

Had I been raking through Geordie's files for so long that I saw mayhem everywhere? I needed to talk to someone to persuade myself I wasn't just being paranoid. Katy was an obvious candidate, the only candidate. I went in search of her and found her, by chance, making for the warmth of the indoor pool, a rolled towel under her arm revealing her plans.

'Leave that for the moment. I need to talk to you. Come on, I'll buy you a coffee or a Coke.' I immediately kicked myself. I had never seen Katy out of jeans. I should have offered to walk up and down the pool as she swam. But it was too late for that.

Most people were out for the day or sunbathing or down at the pizzeria, so we had the coffee lounge to ourselves and found a pair of armchairs over at the large window looking on to Mellieħa Bay. I realised that they were the same chairs that Dougie and Gus had been sitting in when Norman had tried to strike up a conversation with them.

I had not mentioned my Edinburgh acquaintances to Katy before, so it needed a bit of background to bring her up to speed. At first, she saw nothing strange in a couple of hoods – her words, not mine – taking a holiday, but the fact that they had not only the room next to Norman but also his binoculars really woke her up.

'Are we supposed to believe those cops missed something?' she rationalised. 'They said he must have gotten dizzy and toppled over the balcony. You know what he was like, Johnny. He was always leaning over to see what was happening below. That's much more likely than these two guys murdering him. It's too risky. Anyone could have seen them throw him over. Besides, he could easily survive a fall like that.'

'Well, I admit he wasn't stabbed or shot or poisoned, but if someone had already broken his neck, it would have been an easy matter to toss him over the balcony and make that look like the cause of death.'

'You know what? He could have discovered something about those men next door. Overheard their plans or whatever.' She was beginning to share my doubts about the official explanation. 'I was behind them at the counter one morning, last week it was, and they were having a very strange conversation. The big one …'

'Gus.'

'… wanted to know why they couldn't go home for a week and come back later. I thought that was a very strange thing to suggest. But the smaller guy said that they might as well stay and enjoy themselves. He then added something like "If we have to book a flight back home, we've failed". I think he emphasised the word "flight".'

The remarks puzzled me, but I was becoming more and more convinced that they were somehow responsible for Norman's plunge. I could see a newspaper crusade looming.

'I don't know what all that meant, but if they had anything at all to do with Norman's death, they'll pay for it. They may yet find they were unlucky to have Norman next door instead of that dozy couple from Worcester.'

'I'd say it was Norman who was unlucky to have *them* next door.'

My next step was clear. It was time to make that call to Phil Dunne, the one I'd thought of making when I had first met Dougie and Gus and had all but forgotten about. I'd phone him that night. There must be something very big in the offing to push them to murder. The Casualty staff at Edinburgh's Royal Infirmary had plenty of evidence that they had come very close to it in the past, but I was sure there were never any suggestion that they had actually done anyone in.

The Dougie and Gus business intrigued both of us, but it was impossible to spend long talking about it. The facts were so few, the combinations hardly more numerous, the speculation pointless. It was annoying.

We needed a new topic of conversation. And there was only one topic on my mind. My last conversation with Norman. I paused to think of a suitable cue.

'Why are you here in Malta at this odd time of the year? And on your own?' I tried to sound nonchalantly interested instead of painfully jealous. 'I know you told me you were here to see the old homeland, but, I don't know, I feel there's something more.'

'Is this a journalist thing or a Scottish thing, all this curiosity?' She seemed irritated rather than angry.

51

'Neither, it's just that you know what I'm doing here and the retired couples are on the island with the simple aim of dodging the British winter. But until I grabbed your arm, you were hardly buzzing around the landscape. And you didn't seem to be tracking down and looking up your lost relatives.'

'There aren't any left,' she replied, sadly.

'But you must have a reason,' I persisted. 'Not even a little rich girl – one with Maltese grandparents, granted – drops everything and rushes off to Malta for a few weeks without a reason, missing Thanksgiving you said, remember.'

'It's all far too complicated, believe me,' she parried defensively.

'I thrive on complexity. Try me.'

She played with the collar of her T-shirt – this time the design showed the Boston Tea Party in full colour. 'I've had a long standing relationship with someone.'

She's been sleeping with him for years.

'I knew him at University and now we've decided to get married!'

She's pregnant. I stole a glance at her lap. It was impossible to confirm a bulge or the lack of one.

'But I'm not sure …' She paused. 'I'm not sure that I want to get married.'

She's not pregnant.

'What's the problem?' I probed. 'You must have discovered everything there is to know about each other by now.' The lucky bugger.

'I'm confused about … things. His family is an ancient one.'

'All families are ancient. You mean he's loaded because of something his great-great grandfather did?'

'His family,' she carried on as if I had not spoken, 'is so much, well, part of America and they all seem to radiate it. If there was a Family America contest, believe me, they would win it. I'm sure they don't mean to, but they make me feel, I don't know, something between inadequate and insecure. I can't get out of my thought processes that his family is so different from mine.'

'Oh, good for them,' I clapped.

'You've no idea, Johnny. In the States these things matter.'

She looked more determined than I had seen her before, her chin tilted forward earnestly. 'The first lot – the English, the Scots, the Germans – are in with the bricks. And even the next lot – the Irish, the Italians, the Jews – are now part of the fabric, but I'm down below them. If I had some other Maltese name, say Debono, there are lots of them around, I might at least have sounded Italian. But Mifsud,' she shrugged, 'that says it all.'

'Aw c'mon, don't come that one with me, Katy. *We*'re the country of the not-so-Merry Wives of Windsor, where Di and Fergie couldn't fit in. You're the US of A, Land of the Free, where the only monarch is King Dollar and where all men and women are equal. Isn't that good enough for … By the way, what's his name?'

'Seb, Sebastian Palmer.'

'Sebastian!' I couldn't believe I'd met someone who knew someone called Sebastian. I know I have a thing about distinctive names, but I draw a line at Sebastian.

She continued. 'He's happy with everything – he just sees that he's marrying *me*, an American. Malta doesn't come into it. He thinks I'm just being a witless woman. It's good enough for him, but I don't know if it's good enough for me.'

I could see that Katy wanted to explain.

'My grandfather came over from Malta to get out of the

bombsites left by the war. He had worked in the dockyards here and he was the only one of five brothers to survive.'

I could have kicked myself for getting her to sit through some pretty harrowing war footage at the audio-visual show the previous day, but Katy carried on without any signs of distress.

'The other four were killed at the beginning of 1941 and just three months after that, his wife, my grandmother, died, giving birth to my father. "There was so little to eat," Grandfather Mifsud always said. As soon as the war was over, he came to the States, bringing my father with him. He had an uncle there, I believe.'

'And what about your mother? Was she Maltese too?' In America, the newcomers always tended to stick together at least for a generation or two. And to find their partners in the same community.

'Oh, no, mother was Irish. That's where the Katy, Kathleen, came from.'

And the green eyes. And the flashes of auburn. And probably the Catholicism which would have drawn the Irish and the Maltese to the same church.

'But I can't equate all that Malta stuff with Seb's over-with-the-Mayflower lot. I wanted to get away and sort myself out.'

'Don't you Americans all have shrinks to do that?' I had my tongue planted firmly in both cheeks.

'I can't explain it, but that doesn't mean it's not real. It's something deep down where my logic can't reach. It's too primitive to fight. I know it's goofy, but I'm afraid of the feeling. You know that thing about "growing old together"? Well, I'm afraid something like this might, well, over the years, eat at what we have now.' She sighed deeply and looked perturbed.

'I've told Seb. He doesn't really understand, but he knows

54

that it matters to me. It was Seb who suggested that I should get a bit of time and space for myself. He's very sensitive, you know.'

Sensitive? The guy's mad, I thought, I wouldn't let a girl like Katy out of my sight and he's sending her half a world away for a couple of months. Where she could meet irresistible guys like me.

Katy continued. 'He was the one who came up with the brilliant idea of Malta. I'd never been here, I think I told you that. Grandfather never wanted us to come back. Although, strangely, Dad liked Seb's idea and even insisted on paying for everything.'

'But coming here alone? That's a bit drastic,' I said, 'I know that's just what *I*'ve done but that was deliberate, to get away from people and to get some work finished.'

'Oh boy, it was so scary when I set off.' Her eyes showed some of her fear and all of her pluck. 'But once I arrived here, it all seemed right.'

She sighed. 'Megan, Megan Adair, my very best friend, she's going to be the maid of honour at the wedding, she was coming with me. But, would you believe it, the week before we were to leave, her father, an architect, walked out on the family to live with someone he works with.'

I made sympathetic noises. 'The lure of a curvy young secretary, I suppose.'

'No, it was his boss.' She noticed my reaction. 'And don't make sexist assumptions, Johnny – it was a woman and not a man.' She was right. That was exactly what I had been thinking.

'Well, Megan couldn't leave her mother and two young brothers. Everyone said I should call the trip off too, but that only made me more determined to come and sort things out.'

I noticed, once again, a little stubborn set to that inviting mouth.

'And I told them all that I wanted to be alone.'

That was a line I recalled from somewhere.

'Do you know, I left my cellphone behind and didn't even tell anyone which hotel I was going to or how to contact me? Well, I told Megan, of course. In case of an emergency.'

Katy looked at me and came to a decision. She put a finger under the neck of her T-shirt and fished out, at the end of a gold chain, a stupendous emerald engagement ring. I bet Seb got his PA or butler to go and find it for him, I thought, uncharitably.

'And I brought this with me to keep me in touch with them all.'

'Shouldn't you be wearing that on your finger?' I asked. It would have saved me the embarrassment of wearing my heart on my sleeve, even if it wouldn't have stopped me falling for her.

She seemed not to have heard the question. 'We are planning to get married next year – and I know exactly how it will be. There's no way his family is going for a wedding in a Catholic Church. I don't feel strongly about it, so I can see the whole day stretching out before me now. It'll be pure Hollywood. A big white wedding out at Brookline, at the Church of the Redeemer, they call it the Church of the Social Register, with all the trimmings and nothing left out …'

'I didn't know Lee Cooper did white satin jeans,' I teased, trying to bring a smile to her face. I failed.

'… and hundreds of people … mingling … on the lawn at Seb's parents' mansion on Chestnut Hill, sipping champagne to the sound of a string quartet, professionals of course not cut-price music students, playing "Greensleeves".'

I grunted, loudly enough for Katy to hear.

'But, don't get me wrong, Johnny, everything is going to

be OK. It's worth it all for Seb. He is perfect. Understanding, witty, very intelligent. And it's not just me. Everyone loves him, even my brother Paul who can be very … difficult … goes sailing with him. My girl friends are all so jealous. Megan keeps telling me just how lucky I am. He does everything so well – the things that really matter and the small things. He always dresses, well, so … appropriately. And he smells … so manly … so meadowy.'

Meadowy? What's with the boy that he needs to smell like a meadow? The last meadow I walked through had the sort of smell no one would want to exude.

Her eyes were focused three thousand miles away. This Seb must have some faults, but it was obvious from her face that she had not come across them, or if she had she hadn't noticed, or if she had noticed, she had dismissed them.

I thought of her comment about Boston being like a cheerful modern painting in an old fuddy-duddy frame and reminded her of it. 'Was it Seb who thought that one up?'

'Why, yes, that's right. How did you know?'

I shrugged. 'You mentioned his many talents and I thought at the time that it was a very … poetic … observation.' It's one I would have been proud of. The man had a perceptive eye and a way with words. And he also had Katy. Who could blame me for being jealous? And feeling more than a tad helpless? What had happened to Saint Whatsisname?

'If *he* had red hair,' she said looking at me with a strangely motherly expression, 'he would never make the mistake of wearing that maroon thing.'

Not for the first time, she'd lost me somewhere along the alleyway with her Irish train of thought, but I proudly smoothed down my Heart of Midlothian sweatshirt.

'With your colouring, you should wear green or blue.'

It was pointless trying to explain to her the social

significance of those colours in Scotland, so I just shrugged externally and seethed internally.

Surprisingly, given the revelations, that meal was something of a turning point. From that moment onwards, Katy and I were constantly together at meals and for much of the time between.

*

After dinner, I waited for nine o'clock, the start of the cheap rate. 'Would you like to chum me?' I asked Katy.

She frowned and hesitated. 'Can you tell me what it means before I answer that?'

'It's just what it sounds like. In Scotland, a friend would chum you to the bus-stop or chum you to an interview or …'

Katy interrupted, quickly getting the gist. 'Or chum you to an icy cold phone box, open to the winds and half a mile away.'

'It's never half a mile!' I protested, but then noticed she was grinning.

'Of course I will. And I think it's a cool word. I'll use it in Boston and it'll sweep through New England.'

We walked up the hill to the cardphone box, much cheaper than the hotel, I had been told. The economies were no secret and, as it was only just edging into cheap rate time, a queue of fellow tourists outside the box drove us across the narrow lane to the comfort of Marco's Bar. Even when the queue eventually disappeared, it took five attempts to find Phil's phone free. And the box was so cold that we had to pop back and forth to the bar between attempts, just to warm my dialling finger. But we eventually got him.

'I heard you'd emigrated,' Phil grumbled, sounding distinctly bunged up as well as fed up.

'Your news-gathering is up to its usual standards,' I sighed and explained that I was finishing off Geordie's magnum opus.

'Yes, I knew that. I've got a bet on with Jackson that you'll never finish it.'

'Well, I hope it's for no more than a quid or two, because you're certainly going to lose it. Listen, Phil, I'm not on expenses and the units on my card are waltzing away. You'll never guess who are in the hotel with me – Dougie Douglas and Gus Graham.'

'Well, lock your door, Johnny – they've never been lovers of reporters! This is one instance where I would not suggest you pester them for an exclusive, face-to-face interview.'

I thought of mentioning Norman, but decided against it.

'Phil, can you get in touch with a few of those seedy mates you cultivate and find out if there's anything in the air? I haven't anything hard to go on, but, well, something's happened which is very suspicious.'

There was a bout of sneezing at Phil's end as my units reached single figures.

When the sneezing stopped, Phil said, pathetically, 'I doubt if I'll be here. I should be in bed, not trying to lash these buggers in the news-room into life – or running messages for you.'

'Give me your mobile number then and I'll get you no matter where you are,' I pleaded. 'I'll ring you tomorrow – eight o'clock your time – it's cheaper for me.'

He reeled off a number. I managed to jot it down before a long tone told me that my card had breathed its last.

Chapter 8
Friday 19 November

The next morning I was down to breakfast a little later than my usual time, meaning the new time since I met Katy, but didn't have to search for her. She was waiting for me at the door, hopping with impatience. I assumed that my boyish, mesmeric charm was beginning to pay off and she could not possibly miss a moment of being with me. It was in fact something entirely different.

'Guess what? They've hired a car,' Katy said. 'I saw it delivered to them only twenty minutes ago, a fancy affair, white with black windows.' She pointed out of the window to a Renault Mégane. Gus was squeezing into the driver's seat. I assumed that Dougie would already be seated, patiently observing his chauffeur's struggles.

'The windows could be just habit – they both wear sunglasses even in Edinburgh. But equally it could be they don't want anyone to spot them.'

'We could follow them. Let's hire a car.'

'Well, I ride a motor-bike at home,' I confessed.

'I could drive,' she suggested.

'Have you ever driven on the left-hand side of the road before?'

'You mean all these people are *trying* to be on that side?'

'Of course they are,' I huffed. 'That's the way we British …' I broke off as I noticed that she was laughing at me again.

'No, I think we should get a bike, more manoeuvrable, less noticeable. And the helmets will give us some anonymity.' I also quite liked the thought of Katy riding around Malta, holding tightly on to me, like some cuddly koala.

'Not to mention protective armour, if what you tell me about your fellow Scots is true,' Katy added.

Fortified with a breakfast of scrambled egg and sausages – Malta retains many commendable vestiges of British rule, from that left-side driving and red pillar boxes with monarchs' initials, to hop beer and proper sausages – we prepared to tackle the climb to Mellieħa village, only marginally less demanding than the north face of the Eiger. There, once we'd recovered our breath, we were able to shop around for transport. Scooters were easy but finding something with a bit more power took some searching. We couldn't find a match for my own Suzuki, but finally landed up with an ageing Kawasaki motorbike of modest performance. I think it was actually the hire-shop manager's own bike. And thanks to Katy's insistence and her wealthy father, we had it for the rest of our stay.

There was no sign of Dougie and Gus when we got back to the Seacrest, so, with nobody to follow, Katy and I rode off to Paradise Bay a couple of miles away on the northernmost tip of Malta to watch the Gozo ferry come in and to get to grips with the motorbike's idiosyncrasies.

We sat on the pier at Cirkewwa, legs dangling over the edge, and looked across to Gozo and Comino, the small islands, which with Malta itself, make up the Maltese Republic. The sun was strong, but so was the wind. Katy laughed at the things it was doing to my hair. It was not my favourite target for wit.

'I hate this red hair,' I complained. 'How can a man possibly be attractive with red hair and freckles? Women, I grant you – Ginger Rogers, Maureen O'Hara, Maureen O'Sullivan, Vanessa Redgrave – but a man?'

'It's sweet, I like it,' Katy objected, 'and I'm sure I'm not the only one. You keep going on about films. Well, before I came over we watched a film, which had Henry VIII in it. He was only on for about quarter of an hour …'

'Robert Shaw. *A Man for all Seasons*, should have got the

Best Supporting Actor Oscar. But at least it went to Walter Matthau,' I said automatically.

'… but he was so … sexy. He had red hair and he had the women standing in a line.'

'He *was* King,' I added dismissively, 'and that, correct me if I am wrong, can be an attractive qualification for most women! Your Mrs Wallis Simpson seemed to think so, at least.'

'Touché,' Katy acknowledged, 'but I'm sure I'll think of others.' She frowned in thought, those darting eyebrows doing amazing things to my inside.

She had not thought of any more sexy male redheads by the time we'd had enough of the bracing ozone and were back on the bike for the five-minute ride to the Seacrest.

*

Phil was easier that evening. One call to his mobile and he was on the line, sneezing between words. 'Phil – *sneeze* – Dunne – *sneeze* – here.' I could hear the theme music of *High Road* in the background. He was certainly not at *Capital News* or Jinglin' Geordie's.

'I'm glad you're at home in front of the fire with your slippers on and catching up with the bits you've videoed,' I observed. 'I was afraid you'd be out on the bevvy.'

'I'd be out on the effin' bevvy, if it wasn't for this effin' flu, believe – *sneeze* – me! Talking to smelly villains down draughty closes, while you are sunning yourself alongside some pool, didn't help.'

'Not me, Phil, it's freezing here,' I lied, hoping that would make him feel better.

'Not unless Malta's moved – *sneeze* – I've been watching the bloody weather maps, you jammy bugger!'

'Any news from the City of Crime?'

'Well, as you know, I never use one word when I can think

of three, but in this case, the answer is "No".'

I was in a strange way disappointed.

'There is something odd, though. They can't be on holiday: Maisie and Senga – *sneeze* – would never let that pair away on the razzle. Besides the Grahams are expecting their first grandchild any day now – or maybe that's the Bairds, there's no sign of Joe Baird with them is there? – they usually hunt in threes – and the Douglases have only just got back from Tenerife. I've even had a tip-off they're both planning to retire permanently to the sun.' That gave him an idea. 'Perhaps they're sussing out a villa in Malta.'

There had certainly been no signs of house-hunting. But I said I'd keep an eye out for anything out of the usual with the Dynamic Duo.

'Don't rush away, young lad,' Phil wheezed, controlling another bout of sneezing. 'You won't believe this. I'm following up a story with a Malta angle and you could earn yourself a few dozen Glenmorangies.'

'Bottles?' I suggested, hopefully.

'Nips, you greedy bugger! No, seriously, it's a genuine job and there'll be a quite a few quid in it for you. You don't expect me to have a stringer on Malta surely? Let me have the fax number at the hotel and I'll get someone back at the office to fax you the details. The job will be a piece of cake – or gateau I suppose in your pampered parlance these days. It was a good story but it's fizzled out and could do with a human interest boost from the Malta side.'

I hadn't put the Seacrest fax number in my little black book, but told Phil that Don Blaikie would have it, even if he had not felt it necessary to use it. 'But say you want to send me a Christmas card or something. Don't tell him it's work. He thinks I belong to him full time, working on *MacAbre* from dawn to dusk – and probably in between as well.'

'You can do this pretty sharpish though?'

'Have I ever let you down?'

Another round of sneezing brought the call to a close.

Chapter 9
Sunday 21 November

Sunday morning. And my pigeonhole looked lived in at last. Until then, apart from my room key, it had contained nothing, not even a pigeon. But now there was not just one but four items for me. I took the three coloured envelopes and two stapled sheets of paper over to the far side of the lounge and sat in a deep, comfortable armchair to read them at my leisure.

It didn't take too much effort to guess what were in the envelopes. They were birthday cards. As it was my 27th, I did not expect to find my age emblazoned on any of them – it's not exactly a round figure. But I had reckoned without my kid sister, the mathematical Popsy. Irrepressibly into desk-top graphics, she had produced a one-off, reminding me that I was 3 cubed years old – and pointing out that the next time I would be cubed, I would be 64. I noticed the envelope was franked 'Inverness' – she must have been home for a weekend.

The other cards were from my parents and, sent on from home, an old flame – or rather an old ash – Tandy Gray.

I read dutifully through the lengthy verse from home, as I knew just how long my mother had spent at the local post office, sifting through the limited choice and eventually culling a verse to express her love.

Tandy and I had been close, very close, during our years at Napier, but she had gone off to work on a newspaper in South Wales a year or so back. The relationship had just not been strong enough to bridge the 400-mile moat called England and our letters and telephone calls had grown shorter and less frequent. On the card, filling up every bit of blank space with her neat, small, meticulous writing, she brought me up-to-date with her own work and wished me luck with my job search. Her old newsy style was still there, but did I detect a little homesickness?

I would not have believed that anyone could have got birthday cards delivered to Malta, a notably unpredictable postal destination, on an exact date – especially when that date fell on a Sunday. Popsy had solved the challenge by posting early – and printing her envelope and my mother's with a garish warning: 'To the management of the Seacrest Hotel – under pain of death, do NOT deliver this before the twenty-first of November.' The receptionist had been clever enough to apply this order to Tandy's card as well.

The fourth communication was much more interesting, even if it lacked the psychedelic colours, rhyme and radiant art of Popsy's offering.

As threatened, Phil had got Jackson to fax me a photocopy of a story from *Capital News* dated 5 November, just after I'd left, reporting the disappearance of Dante Micallef, a Maltese businessman visiting Edinburgh.

From the heading and opening sentence it was clear that Jim Pepper, the chief sub, had a hand in the page. The story was straightforward enough.

MISSING MISSION MALTEASER STUMPS EDINBURGH CITY COPS

A twelve-man mission from Malta returned home from Edinburgh yesterday as an eleven-man mission. Dante Micallef, who disappeared after visiting the former Royal Yacht Britannia two days ago, had not rejoined the party in time to fly back to Valletta with his colleagues.

Mission Chief Paul Grech told *Capital News*: 'Dante was with us when we left Britannia, but when we got back to the mini-bus there was no sign of him. Some of us went back to the ship, but could not find him. Eventually we had to leave as we were due for lunch at the Scottish Office.'

'We are bewildered. Dante was a cheerful, popular member of a group, a happily married man expecting his first child in the New Year. We can think of no possible reason for his disappearance.' Mr Grech expressed his confidence that his colleague would turn up in the next few days.

Detective Inspector James Tucker of Lothians and Borders Police confirmed that they are still searching for Mr Micallef. 'It's early yet, but the fact that he has failed to join his colleagues in time for the scheduled return is worrying.'

Mr Micallef, a manager with a large vegetable export business based in Naxxar, is on his first visit to Scotland and is believed to have no relatives or friends here.

I knew Jim well and understood his language. It was clear that the local police had no idea whatsoever what had happened to Dante Micallef.

Jackson had added the phone number of the missing man's family in Malta, together with a few details not given in the cutting. Phil was 'very keen', the words were heavily underlined, to get a personal piece on the Micallefs – from John Smith, Our Man in Malta! This would tie in with an appeal for information from the good citizens of Edinburgh. None had so far been forthcoming according to the local police.

I read the piece, once, twice, three times. It was tempting to try and tie it in with my two villains, but that made no sense at all. Not even all the wall-to-wall media trumpeting of a united Europe could get Dougie and Gus to go Continental or Mediterranean with their criminal empire.

What could they possibly want with a Maltese potato merchant? Kidnap? Bizarre. A drugs link? Unlikely. Coincidence? That had to be the answer.

I was not at all unhappy when Katy brought my musings to a dramatic end. She rushed over, flopped into the settee beside me and whispered, 'Those two men have just handed their key in. I was in the lift with them and they were very excited about something. Of course, they stopped talking when I got in. But now they're going out. We just have to follow them.'

Our helmets were upstairs, so I told Katy to make sure she saw which way they were going while I dashed up to my room. Somebody's Law said that the lift would take ages to arrive. It did.

By the time I was back, the impatient Katy was astride the motorbike and pointing up the hill to the side of Mellieħa. I started the machine and we set off in pursuit. Fortunately, the car was finding the hill just as much of a challenge as my Kawasaki was and we came in sight of it in time to see where it was heading. Nowhere unusual, just the main road south.

Katy huddled up close to me and I thought at first that she was attempting to nibble at my right ear through my helmet. No such luck. She was in fact trying to talk to me through the sound of the wind and the struggling engine.

'You left your mail behind on the table. I gave it to Marisa at reception and asked her to put it back in your pigeonhole.'

I thanked her.

'I looked at your cards. You didn't tell me it was your birthday.'

'Well, of course I didn't. It's not the sort of thing you go shouting around the place.'

'What's the big deal? You don't look twenty-seven.'

I didn't reply. What could I say? Did she think I looked eighteen? I'd once tried to grow a beard when one girl friend told me that I looked young. It was a disaster, reminding my mother, she said, of my childhood days at the seaside when I always landed up with candyfloss stuck to my chin. But perhaps Katy thought I looked old! Thirty-five even. I always thought thirty-five would be a sort of landmark – halfway to three score years and ten.

I realised that my passenger was trying to say something else.

'Who is Tandy?'

'A friend from university. A very good friend. We lived together for a while. She went away. She was ambitious.'

'It's a funny name.'

'It's short for Tannadice.'

'Is that a Scottish name?'

'Sort of. It's a place in Dundee.'

I could never explain to her that Tandy owed her eccentric name to a rather downtrodden father who was ordered by his mother-in-law to go down to the Registrar and name his first-born daughter Euphemia after her, in the approved Scottish manner. He, fed up with her bullying, committed his only open act of rebellion and named his daughter after his beloved Dundee United's ground. He had left home before Tandy's third birthday, her name his only lasting legacy.

Katy chattered on. I kept my replies short to get through the din of the slipstream, but the effort was too great. We fell silent.

The miracle of Malta's indestructible buses is even more difficult to understand when you see the roads they have to contend with. We slalomed past potholes in a way that made Katy squeeze me almost painfully, but found it surprisingly easy to keep the car in sight – through Xemxija and Saint Paul's Bay, inland to Mosta and on to Marsa where the great floodlight towers of the sports stadium gave me a clue.

'They're going to a football match,' I shouted back, authoritatively, as I'd noticed from the Saturday paper that there was a team called Hibs in the local league. They were not. We carried on well beyond the stadium and soon we all pulled into a crowded car park. I realised from the posters and occasional diminutive jockey that we were going racing.

The motorbike took us nearer to the entrance than Dougie's car could manage. We therefore had the luxury of trailing them from the front. No problem. I'd seen it done in the films. We paid out one-and-a-half Maltese lire apiece at the turnstile and inside found several thousand Maltese, men, women and children, and a pale, sandy track, a mile or so around.

Now Maltese racing is not Epsom and it ain't Aintree. It involves horses trotting around a sandy track pulling a jockey on a light two-wheeled cart consisting of little more than a seat and two wheels. Katy told me trotting was big Stateside and that the cart was called a sulky. The jockeys were, like their British counterparts, dressed in that combination of primary colours and simple geometric shapes which in previous centuries had been the preserve of clowns and court jesters but which have now been largely taken over by jockeys, footballers and Formula 1 drivers.

Some teams were already out trotting. Two large covered stands took up most of the straight nearest the entrance. Katy and I sat in the centre of the left-hand stand, which looked to be the most popular.

It was ages before Dougie and Gus sauntered in, each with a race card. They sat in the front row, giving us a clear view of them. The buzz in the crowd told us that the race was about to start.

A large white Range Rover moved majestically along the track in front of us and pulled up to our right. Wide white wings unfolded at the back, spreading across the whole width of the vehicle and beyond. It was a signal for the horses and traps to line up behind it. The vehicle moved off, the horses following. When the Range Rover reached the far side of the track, it suddenly speeded up, accelerating away from the runners and folding back its wings. The race was on.

Twelve teams trotted around in unison, the horses' legs pumping up and down rhythmically, their tails blowing back into the jockeys' faces in what I would have thought would have been at best a distraction and at worst an ordeal. There was little separating the runners and they were soon around

70

on our side. The crowd in the stands showed surprisingly little excitement, but a lap later a real buzz started – it was obviously the final run-in. For the last 200 yards, there was a frantic lashing of whips on the track and wild shouting from the stands. Then it was all over.

Dougie and Gus got to their feet, tore up their betting slips (so that's what had kept them), threw them to the ground and sat back on their bench. They were, I noticed, the only ones to litter the floor in the traditional gesture of the disgruntled British racegoer. The Maltese, rarely litter conscious, were uncharacteristically tidy in this instance.

In the flat area of ten yards or so between the stands and the rails, lots of things were happening. Kids were noisily indulging in playground games I recognised. An old man crossed from left to right, carrying a singing bird in a cage.

Fashionable young men and women wandered as if on a catwalk. A thin urchin passed from right to left, also carrying a singing bird in cage.

Dougie and Gus studied their race cards and had a few words with a Maltese family behind them. Gus lurched to his feet and walked off.

'I'll follow him,' Katy said and did just that. I watched Dougie. A young man passed by from left to right, carrying a singing bird in a cage.

Gus and Katy returned, separately.

'What did he do?' I asked Katy.

'He went up to a counter and bought a ticket.'

'No,' I explained patiently. 'He went up to a counter and placed a bet.' A pretty, self-conscious girl walked shyly past, carrying a singing bird in a cage. Was this some bizarre relay race? I restrained my natural curiosity and made no attempt to try and find out. We had other fish to fry than singing birds, if that's not a mixed metaphor.

During all this time, two large tractors dragging wide agricultural rakes behind them were smoothing out the sand track. Their work completed, the second race was in progress. Exactly the same as the first. But this time I noticed something I had missed earlier, an extra cause for excitement which the British courses don't have – a scoreboard showing which horses were disqualified for breaking into a gallop. That, I learnt, made for considerable excitement, as all the jockeys, even those at the back of the field, not knowing how many of the horses in front of them had been disqualified, lashed their trotters to greater and greater efforts at the end in the hopes of making the first four – and a place in next Sunday's meeting. I wonder how that chap Dick Francis would have described all this palaver.

The race over, I found myself fascinated by all sorts of movement above me. Two exotically shaped kites floated up from a nearby park, to the right a helicopter from Gozo appeared to hop over the eye-catching bulbous rotunda of Qormi's church, to the left a jet returning holiday-makers to their colder climes emerged from the gleaming golden cruet set formation – two towers and a larger dome – typical of Maltese churches. The church looked too far away to be Marsa's. Perhaps it was Paola's.

In the air, it was all happening. On the ground, nothing. Dougie and Gus just sat there.

Then, as the third race started, they did something unusual. They both got up and walked away from the stand, along the rails to where there was a small gate.

A man was already standing there. He was wearing an expensive looking light raincoat and a smart tweed hat, an outfit more suited to a British racecourse than to Marsa's track. He appeared tense and keyed up, shuffling from one foot to the other, not watching the horses but seeming to be more interested in the crowd. He took quick, nervous steps towards Dougie and Gus as they approached him. There were all the signs that he had been waiting for them.

Katy and I made our way to the edge of the crowd nearest to the rendezvous. We could not go any closer without being very conspicuous indeed.

We were too far away to hear anything or even to see the man's face clearly. Gus was on guard, facing away from Dougie and the man, looking out for any intrusion to what was obviously an important conversation. There had been no shaking of hands nor any sign of greeting.

I gave an instinctive start when Dougie put his hand in his inside pocket. To my relief, he produced not a gun but a mobile phone. He punched in a number, listened for a while and then handed the phone to the man.

We couldn't see the man's face, but after thirty seconds or so, Douglas snatched the phone back. From the body language of the man and the finger-wagging ferocity of Dougie, this was not a friendly conversation.

The encounter went on for a little longer than the race itself, something like five or ten minutes and came to an abrupt end when Dougie turned on his heel, collected Gus and made his way back towards the stand. The man they had been speaking to stayed where he was. It was impossible to see any detail of his face in the shadow cast by the brim of his hat, but he was utterly dejected if the line of his shoulders was anything to go by.

Katy and I pushed back into the safety of the thick crowd. We let the two villains barge past us and allowed a few minutes to pass before following them. They paid no more attention to the circling trotters and made straight for the car park. It was obvious that their business was over.

We followed their car for a little while, but soon realised they were going back to the Seacrest. We dropped back. No need to risk being noticed when we knew where they were going.

As we slowed down to a leisurely sightseeing speed, the noise dropped too and we were able to have a conversation again. I turned my head to the clinging Katy.

'What does Seb actually do?' I asked, silently adding, 'other than smelling like a meadow.'

'After Harvard, he joined his father and uncle in their legal firm,' she told me through the wind.

'So they've made him a part of the partnership, Cable, Cable and Cable,' I called back.

'No, Palmer, Palmer and Palmer.'

'I was quoting from *South Pacific*,' I explained. Cable, the good-looking rich boy, John Kerr, got the beautiful girl in that too. They don't come much more exotic than 'Happy Talkie Talkie' France Nuyen. But then I remembered that he died in the end. I cheered up.

'What colour hair does Seb have?' I lobbed the question over my shoulder into the slipstream.

'Oh, very blond, very Anglo-Saxon. A bit like Sting.'

I made no comment, which she took for ignorance.

'Or rather like the young Olivier in *Hamlet*. You remember him?'

Of course I remembered the handsome bastard, but I pretended not to hear her reply. At least, not the bit about Olivier. I speeded up to kill the conversation and turned my thoughts to dinner. Sunday cold buffet was the best of the week.

Chapter 10
Monday 22 November

Maybe the lack of coherent conversation on the trips to and from Marsa set Katy against the idea of the bike. At that Sunday dinner she had suggested we should leave it behind and do some serious walking.

'From A to B – that's all they're any good for. But you can't go for a regular walk. You always have to come back to where you left the bike. That sucks.'

So she had her own way and we were in for an early start taking the bus to Bur Murrad. Map in hand and calling on all my skills honed in the Glenbraith Boys' Brigade, I managed to get lost. Temporarily, of course. Just as I was calculating exactly where we were, Katy decided that we should ask the way.

'Għargħur?' The kind woman, sitting on the windowsill of her little white cottage as she fed a pride of snarling feral cats, looked disbelieving. She stared upwards, shading her eyes against the sun, and pointed to the crest of a great ridge. 'It's up there.'

We followed her finger. Yes, it did look a bit of challenge. I had obviously got the compass bit of the map right, but had not noticed the contours. Mr Joseph had told us, when I had raved about some beauty spot or other on the island, that there were even better views from Għargħur. I had mentioned to him at breakfast that we were off there. No way could we face him at dinner and say we couldn't find it.

'Can we walk there from here?'

The woman was non-committal. 'My father used to send me there when I was a little girl, with a basket of the biggest and the best tomatoes on my head. I could always get a good price for them up in the village.'

She frowned. 'I don't think I could do it now.' She looked us up and down, spending more time on my legs than she did on Katy's. I shouldn't have worn my shorts. 'But you are young and strong. I think you could do it.' She looked back at my legs. She was less than convincing.

She suggested the alternative gentle downward walk to a place name I had difficulty in catching. I looked at my map. It was Bahar iċ-Ċagħaq, site of the acrid burning landfills along the coastal route to Sliema, whose odours regularly invaded the passing buses. A spot to be avoided.

I would have welcomed a little more confidence from the woman before climbing up to Gharghur, but Katy had no doubts.

'What the heck! Let's go for it.'

The woman offered us a coffee or cold drink before the assault. We declined politely, so she then asked Katy if she would like to use the bathroom. 'No thanks,' Katy said. She didn't ask me.

A breathless hour later, we were gulping in as much air as possible and sitting on what looked like a standard British-issue park bench on the same crest that the woman had indicated. It was a superb vantage point giving views of the bays on each side of the island and even on the nearest coast of Gozo.

The location marked the start of the Victoria Lines, the defences stretching across Malta. They had been built in the Hey-day of Empire to protect the populous south of the island from any landings on the sandy bays to the North. They were never needed, but perhaps that just showed that they had a deterrent value.

So magnificent were the views that a little park had been created, complete with those benches, to provide well deserved relaxation for all who had made the effort to get there.

We made the most of it.

'*You* should be used to hills like this,' Katy insisted, as I continued panting long after she had recovered.

'We have hills, mountains even, but that doesn't mean we spend all our time walking up them,' I said defensively.

'Are all your family roots in the Highlands?'

'Yes, I suppose so. Both my father and mother were born and brought up in the same area and the Smiths and the Roses had toiled on that land for generations before. On the same crofts.'

'But now you're all moving away, I guess.'

'Well, maybe. Colin, who is two years older than me, is a forester, but a modern-type forester, all computers and budgets and man management and forward planning. He and Catriona look to be well settled in Inverness. They've started their family. I have a young niece who adores me.'

'That's wonderful,' Katy said.

'Well, she's too young to know any better!'

'No, I mean having a niece, not having a girl that adores you. I haven't any nieces or nephews yet. Joe and Paul are both married, well Paul has a partner, but no signs of a passing stork so far. Maybe that will be the news when I get back. And what about your sister, the one who sent the card?'

'Popsy – Dorothy on her birth certificate, but it's the same name as my mother's and a couple of cousins so we needed some way to pick her out. She's a law to herself. I can't see any man keeping up with her. She is the bright one of the family, a first in mathematics at Glasgow, but too creative to be just a numbers person. She's doing weird and wonderful things with computers for some flashy magazine publishers in London. I don't think she'll ever make it back home. But *she* thinks she will. She says that one day she'll be able to do everything from Glenbraith and won't ever need to go to London, so who knows?'

'She sounds fun,' Katy said.

'Fun, but frightening. I don't understand minds like that.'

'I often think that what we all do now would be just mind-blowing to our grandparents.' She stood and stretched out her arms. 'We're into something that they wouldn't even think of as work.'

We walked slowly along the ridge. 'My father has always been a fisherman with a croft and he just can't believe people pay Popsy and me to play with numbers and words. Of course he can see what Colin is doing and understands it, but us?'

My mind went off at a tangent.

'Do you know, Katy, I think you must have lost out on a lot. I mean going to a University on the doorstep! It's just like an office job. Part of University must be the away-from-home bit. I think people should be banned from going off to any university within 200 miles of their home.'

'But that's just not the way we do it in the States. Joe went to Boston and Paul across the river to Harvard.'

'And I suppose all of you then landed up with jobs in Boston?'

'Yes, we did. Well, Paul didn't. He's nearest to me in age, just a year older. He was last heard of in the Himalayas, trekking with Donna. Is there a country called Bhutan? But he promised to be back for Thanksgiving. He's kinda political. I think he'll land up in Congress at some point in his life.'

'Well, at least, he's had the chance to look around. There is a world beyond Boston, even beyond the US of A, you know.'

'We all got to travel quite a bit, Johnny. We saw the world. Well, the world on our side of the Atlantic.'

'Is this your first time in Europe? I just assumed you'd been …'

'We went to see our grandparents in Ireland when we were

younger. County Wexford was a world away from Boston. And they were marvellous. So warm, so touchy-feely. Grandfather Mifsud was nothing like that. When they died, we stopped going.'

'You must come and see Scotland. Your roots may be Maltese and Irish, but America's roots are distinctly Scottish. Remind me to tell you all about it one day.'

We rose to our feet and waved wildly down to the Lilliputian cottages below. Just in case the kind woman with the bathroom was looking in our direction. Somehow I felt she would have followed our progress – and particularly mine – with some apprehension.

We meandered down the other side of the ridge to the aforementioned Bahar iċ-Ċagħaq, bypassing the refuse pits and catching the bus back to Mellieħa. We both had an important appointment near Mdina that afternoon. With the family of the young man who had disappeared in Edinburgh.

*

When I had phoned that morning – this time from the comfort of my hotel bedroom knowing I was on *Capital News* expenses and it was only a local call anyway – the missing man's mother, Mrs Micallef, had been suspicious, but eager to do anything that might bring her son back safely to Malta. We were invited to meet her and her daughter-in-law at the Micallef home.

And so Katy and I found ourselves walking up the garden path to a large, attractive one-storey villa on the slopes in the lee of Mdina. The name had intrigued me – 'Two Hoots' suggested a playful attitude to life that would hardly be in evidence in present circumstances.

The garden was colourful and formal with a couple of the classical statues that stand in for England's garden gnomes on this heritage-conscious island. Malta also goes in for brass doorknockers in a big way – to the disappointment I imagine of many a British tourist seeing the large sign on a Bugibba shop 'Larger knockers inside.' The Micallefs were no exception and a pair of gleaming, beautifully moulded brass owls underlined the house's whimsical name. A rat-tat-tat from the left-hand owl brought the younger Mrs Micallef - Dante's wife - to the door.

She was taller than most Maltese women, almost as tall as Katy, and dark, with a wistful, Madonna-like face – Raphael rather than Evita – emphasised by a razor-sharp centre parting. Her maternity dress of pale blue Thai silk – I could see it was blue, Katy told me later it was Thai silk – displayed a bump that suggested the next generation of Micallefs would be arriving not many days into the New Millennium.

She introduced herself, forcing the welcoming smile expected when greeting a visitor. 'Joanna Micallef. You must be Mr Smith, you spoke to Dante's mother.' She turned to Katy, the smile becoming more trusting and less cautious. 'And Miss Mifsud.'

'Hi! Great house,' Katy said, shaking hands with her and placing her left hand comfortingly on the wife's shoulder.

I apologised for our intrusion. 'But, as I mentioned, I'm here because I believe I can help.'

'Of course, of course. Come in.'

We followed her into a spacious lounge, very simply but elegantly furnished. The Micallefs just had to like entertaining if the settees and chairs to accommodate a dozen bums or so were anything to go by.

Near a pale marble fireplace designed more for decoration than heat, Mrs Micallef senior sat in a plump armchair upholstered in rose-pink damask. I already had an image of the Maltese grandmother-to-be in my eye, amended in places by the sound of the voice on the telephone, but I was not prepared for the frailty of Dante's mother.

The high-necked, loose dress with its chaste collar of

80

cream Maltese lace (I'd been to enough market stalls not to need Katy's input on this one) failed to hide a very thin frame. Underneath a stylish cut of blue-black hair showing a dramatic streak of silver going back from her left temple, the lined face suggested a history of worry with origins beyond her current problem. But most striking of all were the intense, dark, young eyes blazing with energy. If the face suggested a struggle, the eyes declared her the winner.

She remained seated, but greeted us warmly. 'How do you do? Marija Micallef. Mr Smith, Miss Mifsud, please sit here.' She gestured to a sofa for two facing her own chair across a low, beautifully grained marble coffee table. We both sat obediently.

'What a really cool room,' Katy enthused. 'It is so calm and relaxing.'

'It was at one time.' The mother played with the lace on her dress. 'We look forward to it being so again.' Her English, as with most Maltese, was perfect, but in addition there was an elegant accent, hinting perhaps at an education in a good school in the Home Counties.

The wife sat on a chaise longue, completing the three sides around the hearth.

'Tea?' the mother offered in my direction, 'or coffee, Miss Mifsud? You sound American.'

'No, tea would be just right, thank you,' Katy smiled in her endearing mode. I thought the Bostonians would have had enough of the stuff at that Tea Party she keeps going on about.

The wife poured out our teas into bone china cups from an ornate silver teapot. A matching bowl housed a supply of sugar cubes and sugar tongs. Thin slices of lemon were at hand on a salver. It all seemed eminently English.

'You've explained on the phone what you can do to help us, now what can we do to help you, Mr Smith?' She crossed her thin hands on her lap, calm and reposed.

'Well, as you know, all that has appeared so far is a very brief news item with a far-from-helpful photograph. In the time available my colleagues had to blow up – enlarge – a section of the group photograph taken when the mission first arrived in Edinburgh.'

'We've seen it,' the wife said. 'It didn't look at all like Dante.'

'The newspaper wants to try and follow it up with a fuller article, more likely to jog people's memories. If you have a better photograph of Dante, it would help. We might also try and get some shots of the two of you – to emphasise the family element.'

'Of course, we have plenty of photographs,' the mother said. 'He is our only son and he and Joanna are not long married. It is their first wedding anniversary next week.' She gestured to a large wedding photo of the couple on the mantlepiece. 'We have been so happy and proud and that means lots of photographs.'

The wife, her eyelashes moist and shining, opened a box and turned out a dozen or so photographs on to the table. 'When mother told me what you were after, I thought you might want some photographs and I picked out some of the best.'

I flicked quickly through. They were good, great even, showing a handsome, happy young man, the sort of man who couldn't possibly be up to no good. The mystery deepened. I picked out two good likenesses.

'May I take these? I'll get them back to you when we've finished with them.'

'Please do,' the wife urged. 'Are you sure these are enough?'

I assured her that they were just what the paper was looking for. We chatted for another twenty minutes or so, about Dante and the visit to Edinburgh and the disappearance. The two women were anxious to talk, to elaborate, to persuade, as if Katy and I somehow had it in our power to bring back Dante.

The facts were so simple as to be banal. Dante had gone from school to University, graduated in business studies and joined a local agricultural firm. He had lived with his mother and father, until his marriage to Joanna, a primary school teacher whose family had long been friends of the Micallefs. Dante had known her for many years. There were no money troubles and, looking at Joanna, I just could not believe there was any hint of houghmagandie, or hanky-panky, as the Sassenach would say.

The wife gave me the name of his boss and invited me to ring him to get any work details. He had, said the wife, been promoted only six months before and this, his first business trip outside Malta, had really given him a buzz.

The telephone rang. The wife walked over to a carved rosewood bureau, picked up an old-style black telephone and spoke for a few moments.

'It's Tony.' She spoke directly to the mother. 'He'll be a little late this evening, but we're not to worry, he will be here in time for dinner.'

The mother turned to us. 'That was my husband. Joanna's parents are coming over this evening and he was ringing to reassure us. He is a very considerate man.'

'I stay here with Marija,' the wife explained, 'until Dante is back. We have a flat in Sliema, but I don't want to be on my own.'

I got up and thanked the two for their help. 'We mustn't keep you any longer.'

The mother stood for the first time, reminding me of her frail frame.

'Mr. Smith, is my son alive?' Those dark, anxious eyes were imploring. I felt deep down that deception was pointless, but I made the effort.

'Mrs Micallef, Edinburgh is not a violent city. Visitors

are usually perfectly safe and we would surely have heard if Dante had … well … met with an accident. And crimes like detention of innocent visitors are rare and kidnap unknown. It is not Italy.' Did I hide from them the flash of fear that came to mind as I remembered Norman?

I tried to reassure them. 'I cannot pretend to have an explanation, but there is hope – and your help today will give us a better chance of finding him.'

Katy interrupted. 'I think maybe we should get a photograph of the two of you? It might be just what the paper needs. Shall we go for it?'

The mother opened her arms expressively. 'Of course, whatever you feel will do the trick.' The idiom came easily. She turned, caring, towards Joanna. 'Is that all right? You are not too tired?'

'No, mother, not at all,' the wife insisted, smiling weakly. 'I am quite mobile, even if I don't look it.' An unobservant male like me could see however that going over the story of Dante in detail had aggravated her understandable weariness.

Mother and wife patted their hair and primped their dresses. Katy took her camera from its jumbo leather case, manoeuvred them in front of the wedding photo and started playing the art director.

As the flashes bounced off the white-and-gold plaster ceiling, I wandered around the room looking, in particular, at four oil paintings on the wall facing the three bay windows of the lounge, simple, calm landscapes, blocks of colour, solid rocks and shifting trees, shadows, shapes. I recognised the style straightaway. They were from the same brush as the paintings in the public areas of the Seacrest. I had admired them, coveted them, from the day I arrived and had pestered Mr Joseph for more details. He had bought the paintings for the hotel and told me that the painter, George Fenech, was a local man and had a studio in Mellieħa. I had tracked down the studio and passed an enjoyable hour with him, a fascinating dynamo of a man in his seventies. I loved his work, hated his price tag, reasonable, cheap even, but beyond my short reach, and I had left, sadly happy and empty-handed.

Katy had finished. We made to leave.

'I see you admire George Fenech's paintings as much as I do, Mrs Micallef,' I said.

'You know his work?' She seemed surprised.

'Only since I came to Malta.'

'He's a wonderful man and a very … poetic … painter.' I think she would have talked further, but I felt we should go and I made for the door.

The wife remained behind, lying back on the chaise longue. The mother followed us slowly.

'Thank you, Mr Smith, Miss Mifsud.' The mother's gratitude was tangible. 'Excuse the impertinence,' she addressed Katy as she held her hand, 'but your family must be Maltese. We have a limited number of names here and some of them are very distinctive. Where did they live on the island?'

'My grandfather left Valletta after the War. All of his brothers and, I think, his only sister were killed in the bombing.' I thought back to how I had made her sit through the previous day's audio show.

'My grandmother died a little later.'

'A sad reason for leaving. Indeed all reasons for leaving are sad, but I hope you are happy in the United States. We know so many people who are. May I push my impertinence further? Are you,' she asked, looking from one of us to the other, 'what young people call an item?'

'No!' I believe my reply came only a thousandth of a second after Katy's.

'Forgive me, you seemed so much in … harmony.'

I smiled at Katy. She poked her tongue out at me, disrespectfully. We left.

As we walked down the path, Katy wanted to know how I recognised the paintings in the Micallefs' lounge.

'You must have seen that they were the same as those in the hotel. The style is so individual. And Mr Joseph, who's a bit of an artist himself, told me all about George Fenech. He's exhibited all over the world, Edinburgh in my place and New York in your neck of the woods.'

'I guess I should take a closer look at them this evening,' she said, thoughtfully.

It was starting to rain as we donned our helmets. Katy teaspooned into me and we headed off for 'home.'

Before dinner, I had time to write my story and fax it to Phil in Edinburgh. The Micallef photographs and Katy's film were picked up by DTL and I was sure they'd be in Edinburgh in time for the Tuesday paper. Nothing to do now but wait.

*

There is a long-forgotten Gaelic word, targhairm, which once even made it into an English dictionary. It refers to an old Highland custom of standing under a waterfall, covering one's head with a bullock-hide shield and contemplating the eternal verities. Apparently the incessant drumming and vibration provides inspiration for visionary insights.

I can now vouch for it. Just before dinner, my good deeds done and the fax away, I was indulging in a long foamy shower – one of the luxuries of long-stay holidays is the constant supply of hot water and fluffy white towels. Under the buffeting of the deluge, a half-fact emerged from my subconscious, a past link between Scottish money and Malta.

Try as I could – and I even put my head under the waterfall for another five minutes – I could not clarify the connection. But like the true professional journalist, I knew someone who could. She appeared in every Scottish journalist's list of contacts and she was certainly down in my little black book. Olga Jones.

Olga was an Edinburgh institution, a chubby lady of uncertain age. She was an alleged spinster, but it was rumoured there was once a common law Mr Jones, variously described as a Welsh rugby fan who stayed over in Edinburgh to wait for the next game two years later and the viola player with an East European orchestra playing at the Festival who had defected to the West. No one had ever had the courage to seek clarification.

The delight of nearly every Scottish journalist, Olga was a dilettante and proud of it. What was a label of contempt to others was a badge of honour to her. She wrote well and was that rarity a funny female after-dinner speaker. I knew of witty males chosen to propose the Toast to the Lasses at Burns Suppers who had paled visibly when hearing that Olga would be replying.

It was however another aspect of her talents that I needed to tap. She was an expert on an array of exotic topics and one of her specialist subjects was banknotes, a legacy of her spell as a bank press officer.

I rang her from the hotel room, too impatient to wait for the cheap rate up the hill. Olga was a serial dinner guest and I thought that whatever her diary looked like, she'd be in at this time of the evening, but maybe not later. I was right.

'Johnny. They told me you'd emigrated!'

That line was now being stretched to breaking point.

'Yes, but even exiles have to earn a crust. Now, Olga, I'm sure you're getting ready for some dinner or other, getting into your most glittery number, trying to do something with that flowing mane of yours.'

'You flatter me, Johnny. But you're right. The SFE dinner. Up at the Signet Library, no less.'

'Only the best venue for the best, Olga. Now before you get back to the make-up mirror, a quick favour from you, please.'

'When do you ever ring for any other reason?'

'Do you know of any connection between Malta and Scottish banknotes?'

'Indeed I do, but what a strange question. A few years back, no, more than a few, time flies, the Royal Bank had its banknotes printed in Malta!'

'It may seem a silly question but why?'

'De La Rue produces notes for all the Scottish banks, usually printed in the north of England. At one stage they were snowed under with extra business – the new republics created as the USSR split apart all wanted their own currency. Latvia, Lithuania and Estonia were the first in the queue.'

I wasn't following her logic and told her so.

'De La Rue asked the Royal if, as a special dispensation, they could print some of its regular supply in Malta, even flying a few RBS people out to Malta to reassure them of the quality and security of the operation. There was a bit of a flurry in the newspapers at the time because news leaked out of the arrangement and even details of the ship bringing the notes over. Something of a security gaffe, but it all turned out OK.'

Yes, that must have been the report that bubbled up from my shallow subconscious. In any newsroom, there are so many conversations going around at any one time that bits of information get lodged in the cranial crevices of anyone working within earshot. If you're not actually working on the story, you don't notice them. Until something triggers off those strange processes called memory.

'Are there any plans to repeat the arrangement?' I prompted.

'Not that I know of, but then, they wouldn't tell me, would they?'

'Olga, be a darling and ask around,' I appealed.

'It won't be easy but I'll try. There should be someone sitting near me tonight who can help out on that one – there'll even be one or two of the men who sign the notes. Give me a call, let's say tomorrow, same time.'

SFE was the public relations vehicle for Scotland's financial services industry and I was as confident as Olga that she would get me what I wanted to know.

*

After dinner, we went off on a coach trip to see the Christmas lights in the villages and the big towns. And with Sam and Sadie keeping us company and on top form – and no sign of Dougie and Gus – it was impossible to return to the tangled knots of speculation which were threatening to take over our lives.

Chapter 11
Tuesday 23 November

The following day the wind and rain of the night had blown themselves out and, straight after breakfast, Katy and I walked along the sand and across to the other side of Mellieħa Bay, up to the Armier cross-roads and north along the Marfa ridge.

I was, although I say it myself, smartly but appropriately dressed, in a dark brown polo shirt, light chinos topped off with a useful broad-brimmed straw hat. Katy, predictably, wore jeans, a T-shirt depicting a map of Massachusetts, large sunglasses and a cap relating I believe to some baseball team. To display to the world her fierce independence of mind she wore the baseball cap the right way round in rebellion against the fashion of wearing it back to front. At least that's what she told me. I thought it was because it would keep the sun out of her eyes.

As we walked, high above Mellieħa Bay, the morning developed into one of the warmest of our holiday. Around us was the greenery of the short rainy season. Strange conifers and small bushes broke up a patchwork of rocks and rough pasture. The soft slender leaves of trees I could not identify failed to hide the pale nude trunks and boughs. Occasional cages reminded us of the singing bird lures used by the locals to bring migrating birds within gun range. It clicked: the people at the racetrack had been selling them!

To our right, we caught glimpses of the bay, the village of Mellieħa with its splendid trademark, the dome and twin towers of the Church of Our Lady. The silhouette of Selmun Palace broke the smooth flow to the opposite headland and behind we could see Saint Paul's Bay and the rocks where the fervent saint was shipwrecked in the early days of Christianity.

The air was still, there was no sign of the rain and the cold winds returning and the sun was at last delivering its promise of warmth and maybe even heat.

Katy had started the walk in her inferiority mode and the surroundings gave me the cue for retaliation. We left the road for a narrow track to our right to get a better view of the bay and the village.

I began to harangue her on the subject of Maltese pride.

'Look over there.'

I pointed and she screwed her eyes into the sun.

'Underneath that great church is a small sanctuary, by no means the first home for Christianity on the island but the first spot dedicated to Mary. Now, your people, Miss Mifsud, were worshipping there when Seb's were drinking blood on the banks of the Rhine.'

Katy dimpled obligingly.

'If tradition is your thing – and God knows why it should be in this day and age – understand that Seb's lot are just carpet-baggers.'

Katy found this fine Deep South analogy a trifle amusing.

'Imagine. Out in that bay in 1565, the huge Turkish fleet at last having to retreat back home to Istanbul and admit they'd lost the battle for Malta. The Christian knights on the beach all cheer – they had beaten the most powerful force in the world and sent it home, with its tail between its legs. I know how that Turkish Admiral must have felt. I once had to face a news editor to tell him I'd gone to the wrong hotel and missed an exclusive with Tony Blair.'

Katy smiled. 'And what punishment did he dream up for you?'

'I was sent to sub – that's sub-edit – the Women's Page. For three months!'

'You made that up, Johnny. I'm getting to read you,' she said pertly, wagging a finger.

'Maybe,' I conceded.

The girl was right. She was beginning to spot my creative tweaks.

'But back to that Admiral, Katy. Having to return and tell the most powerful man in the world that his army had failed to cuff 800 knights of Saint John and a few thousand Maltese! I imagine Sulieman the Magnificent would have had more ways of showing his displeasure than even three months on the *Capital News* Women's Page. After all, his armies were already battering down the walls of Budapest and Vienna and now he's told that he couldn't take some godforsaken rock that nobody really wanted. You saved Christianity then. If the Turks had made it here, the Italians could never have stopped them. There'd be nothing but mosques in Rome and Paris today.'

Katy was moved by my passion.

I hadn't finished. 'And what were Seb's gang doing at this time? There was only one Englishman left here in the Knights. The Sassenachs were too busy cutting off their links with Catholics – and the head of the Queen of Scots, my queen …'

'You know, Mary had red hair and freckles and was very sexy,' Katy interrupted.

'… and shouting four-letter words at the Spanish Armada as the gales did their job for them and sank it. Tell Seb and his toffee-nosed toffs that, when you get back.'

'He wouldn't believe me!' Katy laughed.

'He doesn't have to. You know it's true and I thought we were trying to bolster your pride not destroy his!'

'You can be quite hot-blooded. For a Scot. I thought they were supposed to be mean, moody and miserable.'

'My God, the colonials are revolting! We are warm, welcoming and …'

'Wulnerable?' Katy suggested.

I jumped up, knocked off her baseball cap and ran off. She retrieved it from the edge of the cliff and chased me back to the road. I let her catch up. Well, to be honest, she was a faster runner than I was in any case. We walked and bantered for some twenty minutes until we reached the headland with its blue-and-white statue of the Madonna and its tiny chapel for fishermen.

A few Maltese men were letting their racing pigeons out of large wicker baskets and shooing them off to their lofts and their mates in the south of the island.

I knew a bit about pigeon racing. It had been my first venture into journalism when still at school. I'd cycled all the way up to John o' Groats to see thousands of birds being released for one of the big British races. Although my photographs failed to come out, my words made it into the feature pages of the Glenbraith Clarion.

I tried to explain the principles to Katy. She got bogged down on the mathematics of clock timing. One of the fanciers, true to his name, took a shine to Katy and came over to tell us how the birds were trained. He poured us each a plastic cup of warm lemon tea from a huge Thermos. The big race, he told us, was from Rome.

I pitied the poor birds having to run the gauntlet of the Neapolitan and Sicilian sharpshooters in addition to the usual hazards of long distance flying.

Nicky, the fancier, was unloading from the baskets not just his own pigeons, but those of his friends. They took turns, he explained, and this was his Sunday on duty. He still had more than a hundred birds to be released. Two at the time. Waiting for the previous pair to disappear before opening the basket for the next pair. It was going to be a long job. We thanked him for the drink and wished him luck – and Katy even kissed him on the cheek. Had she no shame!

We wandered away and walked through the groves of small stunted trees.

'Look, real grass,' Katy said and sank down on to a bed-size patch of soft, thick, green grass. There was even a rare nebula of daisies to remind me of home and, for a split second, of the meadowy Sebastian. She lay back, flung off her sunglasses and baseball cap and closed her eyes. I looked at them. It seemed a shame to cover those bright, shamrock-green eyes, but the blue-veined lids and the soft, dark lashes almost made up for it. I think it was Keats who wrote of azure-lidded sleep. He must have known someone like Katy, known her well.

Maybe it was the thought of all those randy pigeons homing back to their mates, or perhaps it was just a question of familiarity breeds attempt, or possibly just the sight of the map of Massachusetts undulating gently as she breathed, but for the first time I went further than the few little kisses we had exchanged with our Good Nights. Firmly, I laid my hand well to the south of Martha's Vineyard and moved purposefully on to Cape Cod. Katy's eyes opened as widely and as instantly as Snow White's at her abrupt awakening, her hand gripped my wrist and pushed me firmly away.

If I had been Philip Marlowe, the dame would have said something like 'Slow down, Mac, you're approaching a built-up area.' I could have parried with 'Sorry, baby. I must have missed the speed limit signs' or suchlike.

Instead I stared into those sun-flecked eyes in the shadow of my shoulder, looking, wanting to see 'Wait!' I saw only 'Don't!'

Katy sat up, asked me to dust down the grass from her back, but didn't mention her front. We walked homewards along the ridge, chatting as if nothing had happened. Which I suppose was only right. Nothing had happened.

*

I was back in my room, trying to paper over memories

of my faux pas with the equivalent of a cold shower – a few more pages of *MacAbre* – when I had a call from Marisa at Reception to tell me there was a fax waiting for me.

I went down and collected the fax. It was from Phil and it included a photocopy of my *Capital News* story. He was delighted with the Micallef piece. He had scribbled at the bottom of the fax, 'Couldn't have done it better myself – and the pictures were great.'

I looked at the cutting. Just what I needed. First edition of the day and likely to run right through. Page 3. Big heading. Big 'John Smith' by-line. Big pics. Should be no difficulty picking up a job with a few like that in my portfolio.

They'd used a good portrait of Dante from the pictures we had been given and Katy had managed a bit of luck with that pricey camera of hers. She had caught mother and wife looking up at the wedding pic with very sad expressions, the pregnancy curve tastefully visible. Corny, but it worked.

I tried Katy's room on the house phone. She was in, 'writing a letter to Megan.' The letter writing was suspended immediately and she was down in a shot to look at the newspaper cutting. She was ecstatic about her photograph and when I pointed out that if she looked carefully she could see, even on the faxed copy, a little line running at the side of the photograph PHOTO: KATY MIFSUD, she went into emotional orbit.

I thought for one moment there might even be a chance of her giving up her academic social work and coming to Edinburgh to train as a journalist. But I think that was asking too much of Saint Whatsisname.

She wanted to order a dozen copies of *Capital News* for Megan to circulate in Massachusetts. She had obviously been keeping her up-to-date with the happenings. I wondered if they included me.

When I faxed Phil to report safe receipt and delight – and

also to check what payment I could expect – I asked him to send them off, airmail. I knew he'd complain so I pointed out he wasn't paying Katy, since I had just bought her a bottle of Glayva. I found out later that he had sent off the copies at once and boosted *Capital News* transatlantic circulation to new heights.

I imposed on the hotel's accounts office to give me a few photocopies of the fax and posted one off to the Micallefs and a couple to the Maltese dailies to show that back in Scotland we were not forgetting their missing compatriot. Oh, and I left one at the Reception for Mr Joseph. He'd want to know anything that was happening to his island or its inhabitants.

Mission accomplished. With some style.

Chapter 12
Wednesday 24 November

The morning began with an unexpected letter from Don Blaikie. Not for him the immediacy of the fax or the e-mail. As I opened the envelope, the evocative odours of his office escaped like an antique potpourri. The letter itself on imitation vellum was a studied defiance of modern technology. The handwriting was a flowing copperplate, possibly written by a fountain pen but perhaps even with a quill. And the language was no less traditional. After the opening 'Dear Boy', the letter became quite a challenge, a sort of continuous crossword puzzle. I really needed to have to hand the Oxford Concise, a book of quotations and Brewer's Dictionary of Phrase and Fable to make full sense of it. What on earth did 'inenarrable' mean? How could Malta, the 'wee island' convert me into a 'nesophile'? Or was that 'nesaphile', he seemed to have sharpened his quill at that point? And who the hell was Philoctetes?

In essence however the message was simple: how was I progressing with 'The Malta Job'?

I acted with rare haste and faxed a quick note to assure my patron that his project was bubbling along and would be delivered on time. I determined to put in some extra work over the next few days to make that information more truthful than it was at the time of transmission. But there was the planned return visit to Valletta with Katy to take priority that afternoon. Maybe I could try and get a little of the chapter on witch-burning done before we set off.

Then I remembered the more immediate task of washing some socks and pants. I couldn't carry out even that simple procedure without interruption. It was Katy on the phone.

'Can you pop down to my room? We have a couple of visitors.'

I walked down the one flight of stairs, whistling cheerfully. When I reached the corridor to Katy's room, I suddenly stopped. A couple of visitors? Not Dougie and Gus?

The more I thought about it, the more convinced I was that there was something odd in Katy's voice. I had assumed it was Sam and Sadie, bringing a bottle of wine, or Bonnie and Sid with another consignment of mead. But no, it must be a more sinister situation. Had Dougie phoned home and told someone to check up on me? No, with a name like John Smith, they'd never track me down. Perhaps I was better off with that name after all. They'd soon have found Hugo Catchpole or Dwayne Lightning! Besides, the telephone directory still gave the name of the previous occupier of my old flat.

I slowed down almost to reverse as I neared the room. At that moment, salvation came along in the shape of Gerhard, a huge German visitor who had joined us on a few occasions in the bar. He was weighed down with shopping bags which betrayed a gift-grabbing spree at the Craft Village of Ta' Qali. I greeted him warmly and kept him talking as I knocked at Katy's door. I might at least be able to wedge him between Gus and me.

When Katy answered it, there was a smile on her face and no fear in her eyes. I looked behind her to see not the two villains but the two Mrs Micallefs.

There was no longer any need for Gerhard's protective bulk and, to his confusion, I waved him away and went in. I must have looked very relieved, because Katy wanted to know what the matter was. I promised to explain later.

The two women were sitting in the room's only chairs. Katy sat on the bed and I leaned against the long counter in front of the mirror. The two ladies greeted me warmly and with overlapping contributions thanked me for sending them the press story and apologised for coming to the hotel unannounced.

The mother spoke, slowly and deliberately. 'After seeing your work, Mr Smith, I thought that there was perhaps one thing we had omitted – a reward. What do you think?'

'Why, yes, that would certainly be worth trying,' I agreed, ticking myself off for not having thought of it before.

The wife was more agitated. 'Do you think £20,000 sterling would be right?' She held out a bulky manilla envelope and opened the flap. There was the money, bundle upon bundle. By way of explanation, she said with some agitation, 'Mother took it out of the bank today. We can afford it. And it might bring Dante back.'

The mother calmed her down, laying a thin, restraining hand on her daughter-in-law's lap. 'We discussed this with my husband but Tony was not enthusiastic. I didn't know why.'

I thought for a moment. 'Two things, Mrs Micallef. I don't think we need to go to this amount. I am sure it would be good enough to offer £10,000 or even £5000. You might wish to increase that amount later. And of course, you don't have to give me the cash now!'

'It's a very good idea, you know,' Katy said, putting her arm encouragingly around the wife. She turned to me. 'What would you need to do now, Johnny, and how quickly could you do it?'

'I'll ring the paper immediately. They like this type of thing. It gives them something new to say and keeps their story running. It should be in tomorrow's paper. The family offering a reward is always a good angle.'

'Would it be possible to offer it anonymously?' the mother asked. 'I don't usually go against my husband's wishes, but in this case I feel he is wrong. That is why we came here to speak to you.'

'I'm sure that would be possible. I don't think *Capital News* will object.' I closed the envelope and gave it back to the wife. 'You won't need this until we have Dante back with us – and I think it would be better with you. I've nowhere safe to keep it.' When I first arrived at the hotel I had toyed with the idea of renting the small room safe, but had felt that the back-up floppies of *MacAbre* were not worth the small but accumulating daily rate.

The two Mrs Micallefs rose, the mother with dignity, the wife with difficulty, and thanked us again. We chummed them down to Reception. I offered to call a taxi, assuming that that was how they had arrived. Joanna was at a stage where driving would be uncomfortable. To my surprise, I found that the frail but redoubtable mother had driven to Mellieħa in Dante's large four-wheel-drive Cherokee. We waved them off, the mother reminding me not to send her a copy of the news item mentioning the reward. She would trust me to get it done.

'What was the matter with you when you came to my room?' Katy asked as we walked back into the hotel. 'You said you'd explain.'

'On my way down, I suddenly thought that when you mentioned two visitors you meant Dougie and Gus. They could have discovered that we were poking our noses in. You might have been … well, tied up … and they could have been waiting behind the door to pounce on me.'

Katy shook her head, just as my mother did so often when listening to what she called 'excuses' and I called 'explanations'.

'That's what happens when you watch too many movies, Johnny,' she warned.

'I'm sure that's a line from Sleepless in Seattle. But it doesn't matter. Nobody can watch too many films. Now I must phone this piece about the reward through to Phil and then we can get off to Valletta on the motor-bike.'

Not even the breathtaking views across Grand Harbour to the Three Cities could inspire us. All the deeds of derring-do in the fight against the Turks or the defence against the

Axis bombs failed to help us make sense out of the tangle of intrigue that was emerging – Dante disappearing in Leith and Dougie and Gus turning up in Malta. We had long ago ruled out coincidence, but had nothing to put in its place. Strangely enough, it was something as simple as a flurry of rain that gave us the breakthrough.

We had been sitting in the Upper Barracca Gardens, many feet of rock above the War Rooms where minds more fertile than ours had grappled with the problems thrown at them by Germans and Italians. The city is cramped for space, but there are two oases of greenery, this one and the lower version along at the tip of the peninsula.

We had wandered at leisure among the trees and the statues. A very animated sculpture of three street urchins, hand-in-hand, was the most eye-catching. It was called 'Les Gavroches'. Neither Katy nor I had ever come across the word and decided it was the French for 'scallywags' or 'ragamuffins'. Most of the monuments were however to famous folk, often to British naval heroes killed elsewhere in the Med and even a couple to Einstein and Marconi.

At a fine bust of Churchill in his most bulldog-like pose, an old man bent almost double, turned to us with watery, yellow eyes and said, in a West Country accent, Devon or Cornwall, 'We would never have made it through without Winnie.'

At his beckoning, we followed him to the wall high above the waters. He gestured downwards to the nearly empty harbour. 'When I was last here, there were sixty Royal Navy ships or more out there. I was on one of them ...'

He fell silent, alone with his reminiscences and perhaps his long-dead comrades. He did not to want to speak any more.

We went and sat on one the benches. I had given up the cat-chasing-tail thoughts about the Micallefs and, caught up in the atmosphere of the place and the old man's words, I remarked to Katy how impossible it was to imagine the bombs that had fallen within sight of our bench.

She reminded me quietly that some of that tonnage had wiped out her family.

'I wonder what the real people thought when they were told they'd all won the George Cross,' I said. 'Today, we'd all be cynical, but I think they may have felt something we've all lost.' As soon as the words were out, I knew they were ill chosen given Katy's family history and her Bostonian aversion to kings called George.

'They probably thought why don't they send us food instead. It's what they needed. Most of all.'

'I just can't get my head around it,' I retreated. 'I read somewhere figures of five months of continuous day-and-night bombing. And nearly 7000 tons plonked down on this area here. Just think – while all that the USA – Seb's people – could boast were a few crackerjacks thrown out of balloons during the Civil War.'

'What about Pearl Harbour?' Katy countered.

'Hawaii wasn't even an American state when the Japs invaded. And in any case, it's further away from Boston than Malta is.' I couldn't work out the logic of that last bit and neither could Katy.

'How did you meet Seb?' I chanced. 'Was he the boy next door or the knight on the white horse who came and swept you off your feet?'

Katy looked at me for a while and then smiled, a smile of reminiscence. 'I can thank old, doddery Professor Culpepper.'

Culpepper! I was sure she was making it all up. She noticed my disbelief.

'No, honest injun. He was laid up – and I think it was actually gout.' She laughed out loud. 'It sounds like a comedy script. Well, he asked me to get him a text. I can't remember for certain what. It was something to do with les philosophes, you

102

know, those intellectual lefties who were stirring it up before the French Revolution. Perhaps someone called D'Albert or D'Alembert.

'Well, I couldn't find it in Boston although I walked up and down Newbury Street, so I took the train over to Cambridge. That's where Harvard is and there they have all sorts of wonderful old bookshops.'

'I don't believe it! Seb was running a bookstall.'

'No, but I tried Grays and had no luck and was in Schoenhof's when Seb heard them telling me that they didn't have the book. He told me where he had seen a copy. He even walked with me to the lane …'

'Chummed you to the lane,' I amended.

'I would never have found it on my own. It was so quaint, a narrow alleyway off Linden Street. It didn't even have a sidewalk. And, gosh, it all happened from there. He asked if he could give me a lift back and …'

'Don't tell me!' I interrupted, 'let me guess. I've seen all the films. He had a red MG sports car.'

Katy had the good grace to blush. 'Yes, he did as it so happens. And on the way back he asked me to go with him on his sail boat the next weekend.'

I raised my eyes to heaven and presumably the abode of the idle Saint Whatsisname. This was very unfair competition. What are you lot up there going to do about it?

'I know this sounds loony,' she stammered with some embarrassment. 'I've never said this to anyone before, but when I met him, well, I felt the same shiver, the same tingle as when I first saw a tiger at Boston Zoo. He was so sleek, so powerful, so beautiful.'

You're right, I thought. It is loony.

She looked directly at me and asked, 'Would you believe

someone can fall in love just like that, Johnny?' She clicked middle finger and thumb to emphasise the point. 'Well, I certainly did.'

I couldn't believe she should be so insensitive as to ask me that question. So I just nodded dumbly.

She interpreted my expression quite wrongly. 'It wasn't a question of poor little Boston girl being bowled over by rich young Harvard man. We were a very well-off family, with our own boats, and one of my brothers had gone to Harvard. It was Seb who impressed me, not his … trappings.'

A cloud passed over the sun and darkened the gardens. Within seconds, a flurry of rain ended a conversation, which was bringing Katy as much delight in recounting as it was bringing me sadness. At least I now knew who was to blame. It was some ivy-covered, port-swilling Yankee academic called Culpepper.

We fled in the direction of the main gate of the walled city where I had left the bike. But the rain got heavier and we looked for shelter. Fate was lending a hand yet again.

A piece of advice – if you're ever in Malta around Christmas and see a sign 'Presepiju' follow the arrow – the sign means 'crib' as in Shepherds-and-Wise-Men and the Maltese have turned it into an art form. At the one extreme are the huge, public Cecil-B-de-Mille-style versions, with a cast of hundreds, with towns vying with each other like Premier League football teams to win the awards.

Two nights before, our coach trip had taken us to Qormi to see the bookies' favourites to win this year. Over one hundred miniature people and nearly two hundred animals in a set the size of a decent suburban lounge and with the most ingenious mechanics to make camels swagger, carpenters saw, donkeys haul, children toddle, wise men proffer and angels peep. And dramatic lighting and music to set it all off.

At the other end are the metre-square, personal flights of

imagination, painstakingly assembled, ingeniously conceived. When we saw the hand-written 'Presepiju' sign down an alleyway, we made for it and gingerly negotiated the wet, narrow steps down to a dimly lit basement. On display were the dozen or so winners of this year's competition, the Crufts of the Cribs. How could anyone possibly have thought of making a Nativity scene out of melon seeds? Or matchsticks? Or bottle tops? Or even dyed women's tights?

'Oh, look, pantyhose,' Katy squeaked, camera flashing. I shivered – and not just with the cold of the cellar. The Yanks usually have a sure touch with words – compare their 'jet-lag' with our 'circadian dysrhythmia', or thank them for 'drive-in', or 'check out'. But 'pantyhose'! No thanks.

Katy loved the cribs, bubbling with enthusiasm, flashing away with abandon and eager to share with me each revelation of the Maltese crib-makers' infinite wit.

Suddenly, she froze and pointed at the little family clustered at the centre of a symphony in dried fruit and veg.

'That's it! That's it! We've missed the whole goddam point.'

I looked at her and back at the crib. There didn't seem much to miss. All the usual ingredients were there – newborn babe, adoring parents, genuflecting extras.

'Saint Joseph!' Katy was impatient at my obtuseness.

I looked more closely at the figure next to the mother-and-child tableau. He consisted solely of eight broad beans and a rakish halo. Frankly, I thought she had flipped or undergone a profound spiritual experience.

'We've seen everyone except Dante Micallef's father! Is he the key to our mystery? What does he do? We know nothing about him.'

I was less than chuffed. Why hadn't I, a trained journalist, thought of that? I'm a professional, she's some sort of social worker. That's it, of course, she's used to thinking in family groups and missing fathers.

'You may have something there,' I said, coolly, but inside I knew she was right. We had so many pieces of the jigsaw, but she'd at last worked out just which one could make them all fit into place.

We made our way up the steps into a Valletta showing only a covering of puddles to remind us of the rain we had escaped. We walked down Republic Street, the city's spine, and looked for a phone box. Katy spotted one at the bottom of yet another flight of steps.

We picked our way down steps especially measured, our guidebooks assured us, to let the armoured Knights Hospitaller of Saint John crank, waddle and swivel, back and forth like Frankenstein monsters. Time and the Luftwaffe had made them less user-friendly and we proceeded with care.

I put in my phone card – encouragingly bearing an image of the Nativity – and dialled the Micallef home.

The mother answered.

'Mrs. Micallef, so sorry to trouble you … it's John Smith here. I phoned your offer of a reward through to *Capital News*. They were delighted and by now the good folk of Edinburgh should be reading all about it … no, thank you … I didn't meet Mr Micallef when we called. He was at work. My editor has asked me to check up on one small point. What does your husband do? I mean, what is his work?'

There was a pause.

'He works with Goodhill Redpale.'

'What do they do or what does he do?'

'He is head of a large printing unit.'

'What do they print?'

There was a longer pause.

'It's a security printing unit, producing stamps and ... other items.'

The metaphor might be inappropriate, but the penny dropped.

'Does that mean it prints banknotes?'

'Yes, but you can understand that he doesn't talk about that side of the business. For obvious reasons.' She was uncomfortable discussing this with me.

I reassured her. 'Mrs Micallef, you're a treasure. I think this may help us. Do you have a number I can get him on at his office? Yes, I realise it's not something you give out readily, but please believe me, it is important.'

I wrote down the six-digit number in my trusty black contact book and thanked her. She reminded me that her husband's name was Tony. Katy needed no briefing. She had pieced together the whole picture from my side of the conversation. I squeezed her with excitement. 'Well, done, Ms Mifsud. I do believe you've given us lift-off.'

I would like to claim that my planning was meticulous even in the smallest matters. Unfortunately, it wasn't. I had to clamber back up the steps in search of a shop that sold phone cards. By the time I found one that was open – Malta has a virtual commercial siesta, hiding from the heat of the sun from 1 o'clock to 4 o'clock even when it's cold and raining – and got back to the phone box, I found I'd just missed Mr Micallef. I decided to phone him at work the following day. I had the feeling that a call at home would be unwelcome. I would forget everything for the moment and concentrate on the drive back and dinner at the Seacrest with Katy. And this was the special Maltese night with garlicky rabbit on the menu.

*

Once again, we haggled across the table on the subject of rabbits. Katy seemed to think that eating rabbit was wrong. She didn't like the sign I told her I'd seen in an Edinburgh butcher's shop – 'Watership Down, you've read the book, you've seen the film, now eat the cast.' But I remembered her saying how Seb's family had served venison at dinner when she and her father were invited over for the first time. I chided her with inconsistency, being happy to eat Bambi but squeamish when it came to chewing Thumper.

Going off to phone Olga brought the argument to a close.

As expected, Olga came up trumps when I rang her from the draughty phone box.

'I don't know where you got your tip-off from, but it's spot on. There is a big contract going through Malta at the moment. Same situation as before, but it's not the Royal this time. And it's new work from Scotland that's proving difficult to digest.'

'Why is that?' I asked.

'Well, Albion Bank has suddenly decided to produce £50 notes. Don't ask me why. Should have done it years ago. They and the Royal have had nothing between £20 and £100 for a century and a half. To get it out for a special Millennium launch, Albion's given De La Rue the OK to print in Malta.'

Olga was getting very enthusiastic. 'Only yesterday I arranged to see a preview of the note. I'm doing a piece on it for The Collector and had to file copy before the official launch. It's a cracker. Albion is still showing Scottish wildlife on the reverse. This one is an engraving of two Scottish wildcats, even better than that giant stag on their £100 note, and that was the best note since the old Commercial Bank's view of people strolling along George Street.'

I couldn't recall ever seeing a £100 note from any Scottish bank but let that one go.

'And they're even putting a hologram on the front. The Royal did it in 1998 for their Alexander Graham Bell £1 special, first in the European Union, but that was just a gimmick, no one really needs a hologram on a £1 note. This time it's a forgery-deterrent for real.'

108

'Olga, you're a darling. I don't know what it all means yet but I'm sure it's important. If there's ever anything I can do for you ...'

'There is, there is. Johnny. Get around the record shops in Valletta and see if there are any CDs of Oreste Kirkop.' She felt it necessary to start spelling the name.

'The Maltese Tenor,' I interrupted.

'How on earth did you know that?' Olga sounded deflated. Few people surprise her and it gave me some satisfaction. 'He's not in many of the books.'

'I know your mania for tenors, but you've strayed on to my patch now. When obesity stopped Mario Lanza acting, they got Edmund Purdom to mime – Student Prince, 1954. When it stopped Lanza singing, they got Oreste to do it – Vagabond King, 1956.'

'You're a mine of totally useless information, John.'

From Olga, this was equivalent to a knighthood.

'Oreste died not long ago,' she continued. 'The Hollywood stuff was pretty tacky, but I've heard he did some good work on the US opera circuit. In Malta, they may have brought out some compilations.'

'If they have, I'll find them and you'll get them.' I bade Olga a Good Night and thanked her, promising to tell her the background to my questions when I was back in Edinburgh.

As we crossed the lane to the little bar, Katy told me she was impressed by my knowledge of Maltese tenors.

'Easy,' I explained, 'Olga only collects tenors, so if ever she mentions an obscure name, the best bet is he's a tenor.'

'So she's into tenors and tenners. How droll.'

'I wish you hadn't said that, Katy. Leave the corny puns to me.'

'But I couldn't understand all that about Scottish banknotes. Isn't Scotland part of the UK? Don't you use Bank of England notes?' Katy asked.

'Yes, we do, but not many of them. In Scotland, the commercial banks, the ones you see in the High Streets, issue their own notes and they are the ones you'll see being passed around. Only one in ten would be a Bank of England note.'

'That's weird,' she frowned, 'that's like Texas or Hawaii issuing their own banknotes.'

'It's not quite the same. It's more convoluted than that.' We each took a stool at the bar. 'Olga could explain it all, but here's the instant version. I once made the mistake of asking Olga that same question and I'm now a second generation pundit.'

The barman, Hubert, took our order, a pint of Hopleaf for me, a glass of Cabernet Sauvignon for Katy. She was getting to like the tipple, costing a little bit more than the usual Maltese red as the grapes were brought in from Udine in the north of Italy.

'Well, let's hear the answer. And then I can be a third generation pundit,' Katy prompted. Her willingness placed me on the spot.

'To start with you must realise that at one time all banks issued notes, promissory notes, undertaking to pay whatever was the face amount. People passed around the pieces of paper because they were easier than bulky coins.'

'So what was the problem?' Katy was exercising that argumentative curiosity of hers.

'Well, you've seen the cowboy films. The James boys breeze into town, rob the bank and the folk in Tombstone or whatever are left with useless bits of paper. The bank can't pay up.'

'But that was the Wild West!'

110

'Yes, but that's what happened everywhere. Even in England, our neighbours in the South. If the Bank of Luton, say, went bust – a robbery, a loan gone wrong, a crooked manager – anyone holding their notes went phut. So the Government – indeed most Governments – keen to protect its citizens, banned the issuing of banknotes by anyone except the central bank.'

'That makes sense. When did all this happen?'

'Oh, mid 1800s, I suppose.' I was vague on this one. 'But the Scots objected.'

'Well, they always do, don't they?' Katy was getting to understand my fellow countrymen better than they understood themselves.

'No, but they had a case. They had come up with an alternative to the usual pattern of thousands and thousands of small, vulnerable banks scattered all over the countryside. They invented branches, so that any local difficulty could be shrugged aside and covered by one of the few big banks operating through a network. When the Bank of England – did I tell you it was set up by a Scot, Katy? – tried to get the monopoly to protect the customers, the Scottish banks and public wanted to know why they should be penalised just because the English couldn't run a banking system.'

'And they got away with that?'

'Yes, Westminster followed up the legislation with a concession excluding the Scots from the ban on banknotes. And it's held for the past century and half.'

'So they all get to produce their own notes …'

'All those that were around at the time, Bank of Scotland, the Royal, Clydesdale and Albion.'

'Isn't it confusing?'

'Not at all, although I can see it must appear so to a country that has all its banknotes the same size and the same colour.'

111

Chapter 13
Thursday 25 November

Before going down to breakfast, I sniffed at my after-shave. I had been sent it a Christmas or two before by Auntie Jessie and Uncle Robert. I suspected that it had originally been a present sent to him, but Aunt Jessie, a great one for decorum, must have decided it was far too racy for the hen-pecked Bob. Whatever it said to me, it didn't say 'manly' or 'meadowy.' I left it carefully next to the litterbin. Maybe the chambermaid would like it for her boyfriend. Or even for her Uncle Roberto.

I avoided Katy after breakfast and slipped off by bus to Sliema. That would be the place for a real after-shave. On my way up an escalator, I saw the shop sign 'UnCommonScents'. It was buzzing with young men-about-town and their ladies. It took me ten minutes to find my way back, down escalators, up escalators, across escalators. I am not a Shopping Mall man. The assistants, all looking like black-haired Stepford Wives, did not rush to me. Perhaps I didn't look right. I eventually tapped one of them on the shoulder. She spun haughtily around, but the smile didn't vanish.

'I'd like some after-shave,' I ventured. I suppose it was like going to Glasgow's Mitchell Library and asking for a book.

'Do you have any particular brand in mind, sir?'

'No, I would like to try something new. Perhaps you could recommend something.'

'Of course, sir. Have you any preference for fragrances?'

I mined the seams of my normally reliable vocabulary, but could find nothing.

'Perhaps I could try something, well, manly but meadowy,' I suggested. The wide smile widened.

'It is so rare to find a gentleman with such precise views.'

I smirked modestly. She consulted the crowded shelves like a golfer looking for the right club, an angler searching for the perfect fly. She took down two expensive looking flasks and sprayed a little from each onto two small expensive looking pieces of cardboard.

'Perhaps one of these would fit the bill.'

I sniffed at each just as I have done many times before when presented with the first mouthful of a wine. This time, buoyed with confidence, I paced up and down the shop, sinking deeper into the carpet with each stride, breathing deeply over each piece of cardboard in turn. I tried a gamut of expressions from perplexed investigation to ultimate approval.

'This is …?' I enquired, doing a Roger Moore eyebrow hitch as I held out to her the one of the pieces of cardboard.

'Ganymede,' oozed the acolyte, showing me the box.

'And this …?'

'Endymion, both typically Guareschi fragrances …' she elaborated.

I shrugged, hoping my shoulders said 'Mais, oui. Cela va sans dire!'

'… but created for a New York company.'

Before my shoulders had finished saying their bit, my voice said, 'Two excellent suggestions. I'll take this one … Endymion.'

She returned the samplers to the shelf and took down the real thing. She then lovingly wrapped up the already excessively packaged liquid in a lavish metallic paper, and rounded it off with an elegant, slickly tied bow, seemingly loath to part with a treasured possession.

'It is so much easier when a customer knows exactly what he is looking for,' she observed as she sandbagged my Visa card.

I left, a happy man.

Fasten your safety belt, Mifsud.

*

That afternoon, Katy came up to my room with another batch of photographs. She'd been keeping me well supplied with copies of her holiday portfolio.

I suggested that we phoned Tony Micallef from there. 'It's only a local call and not worth a walk up to the kiosk. We deserve a little luxury after all our exertions.'

Katy agreed and settled into my one armchair. I dialled the Goodhill Redpale number. It was speedily answered with a rather curt 'Yes?'

'Mr Micallef?'

'Yes. Who is speaking?' He sounded impressive, in control.

'Mr Tony Micallef?'

'Yes.' This time with a hint of anxiety.

'John Smith here. I met your wife and daughter-in-law a few days back and ...'

'Yes, of course!' Did I detect relief in his voice?

'They both told me you were very kind and understanding. And we appreciate your help very much. Have you any news for us?'

'No, sir, and I'm sure you'll agree that no news is good news at this stage, but there is a ... development which I'd like to talk to you about.'

'Development? I don't understand.'

There were very tense vibes coming from Mr Micallef.

'Yes. I have an idea that the police in Edinburgh may have been asking the wrong question. They wanted to know why anyone in Scotland would want to harm or ... detain ... a

Maltese agricultural merchant and not a very important one at that. They may even have progressed as far as wondering, more specifically, why anyone would be interested in Dante Micallef. What they should have been asking, as you and I know, is why anyone would want to kidnap the son of Tony Micallef.'

There was a distinct intake of breath from the other end.

'I don't follow you. There has been no contact. There have been no demands.'

'I think you do follow me, Mr Micallef, especially if I tell you that for the past few weeks I've been pondering over the answers to another question. Why are two of Scotland's most notorious criminals taking a winter's break on your most friendly island?'

He continued the pretence of not knowing what I meant, but there was something of a panic creeping into his voice. I suggested that we should meet and that it might help resolve the situation. This seemed to steady him.

'It would be difficult to meet here at the office. And my home would be no better. My wife and Joanna know nothing of this matter.'

And you, I thought, know nothing of their idea of a £20,000 reward. I was rapidly becoming the Micallefs' piggy-in-the-middle.

I asked him to suggest a place, but recommended that we should meet at seven o'clock in the evening. 'I am sure I know where the other side will be then,' I explained, the mental image of Gus Graham tucking into the Seacrest's roast beef convincing me that he would not be easily prised away from the hot buffet table.

Micallef hesitated and then, audibly regaining his composure, took control. 'Let's meet at the Casa Notabile in Mdina. It is a restaurant, but I can reserve a private room. We could speak in absolute confidence. But it must be tomorrow,
116

we cannot wait.' There was an urgency in his voice, which puzzled me, but I put it down to the stress he was under.

He gave an address in Villegaignon Street, the most prominent of the many narrow winding lanes in the Silent City designed to provide privacy and protection to much earlier generations.

'I look forward to seeing you at seven o'clock. I understand from my wife that you have transport.' The noise of our motor bike had not gone unnoticed. 'Good night, Mr Smith – do I take it your … associate … Miss Mifsud will be with you?'

I assured him that my associate would indeed be there and bade him Goodbye with one of the few Maltese phrases to stick in my memory, 'Bonġu'.

Katy nodded appreciatively. 'You handled that very well.' There was too much surprise in her voice for my liking. 'Oh,' she added with an impish smile, 'I liked the bit about "associate" too.'

I shrugged. 'It's what Perry Mason would have said. And I thought it was better than "moll".'

'It was certainly better for you.' She ruffled my hair, knowing it would annoy me.

I pondered on the following day's appointment. Why did he insist we couldn't wait any longer?

'As a special favour, Katy, could you look out a decent frock if you have such a thing? I get the feeling the Casa Notabile will not be a McDonald's.'

'And how do you propose I ride the bike if I'm wearing the sort of dress that turns you on? But I will wear something smart.'

I gave up any hopes of seeing her in a flowing gingham frock and looking like something out of Oklahoma or Carousel. I wondered why she always wore trousers. Ugly legs? Hairy legs? Varicose veins? Tattoos? I dismissed them all.

Katy must have detected the carnal images going through my mind, as she jumped up suddenly from the bed.

'See you downstairs for dinner.'

Exit, pursued by a glare.

*

I took out a new yellow disposable razor and carefully set about producing my closest ever shave. For once it was successful, a bloodless coup.

The Endymion creation was reluctant to leave the flask but I coaxed out a baked-bean-size blob of the pale green cream. The expensive pale green cream. Was it too much? Too little? I could not afford to haggle and slapped it on, adding another blob for luck or safety. And another.

My shave had indeed been close and the cold astringent brought tears to my eyes. I was sure the sacrifice would not be in vain.

Katy was waiting near the door of the hotel dining room. She must have sensed something, because she was wearing a stunning trouser suit in what I think of as Gainsborough blue. I sauntered over, trying to reproduce the swagger Steve McQueen had used when he went over to Faye Dunaway in the auction room in *The Thomas Crown Affair*. It didn't seem necessary as Katy affectionately slipped her arm into mine, sniffed and wrinkled up her nose approvingly.

'There's no hiding that smell,' she said, excitedly. Was Endymion that distinctive?

'Smell,' I queried.

'Yes,' she replied, nodding to the dining room. 'Roast turkey – they've not forgotten that it's Thanksgiving!'

'Thanksgiving? Tonight?' I was deflated.

'You'd better believe it!' Katy replied, bouncily.

She hurried me through the door. You lose some, you lose some.

'They' had indeed not forgotten the Americans, despite the fact that Katy was the only one in the hotel as far as I could make out. As we walked past the hot counter, looking for a table, we couldn't miss an enormous roast turkey, surrounded by ashets of beautifully carved meat.

'And look,' Katy said, pointing beyond it, 'pumpkin pie.'

I knew that Mr Joseph had been in the States for some time and he was well up on his Thanksgiving rituals. He had even changed the piped music and we were given a rest from the Christmas tunes to have instead a selection of Sousa marches, some good Gershwin and rousing film music, from *The Way We Were* to *The Bodyguard*.

Katy was as happy as a toddler with the hotel's efforts and her bliss didn't end there. We were barely seated and only two spoonfuls into our soup, when Mr Joseph himself came over and deposited a bottle of champagne in a standing ice bucket.

'Thank you, thank you, that was a swell idea,' Katy enthused, 'I really appreciate it!'

Mr Joseph raised his hands in protest. 'Not mine, Miss Mifsud, not mine.' All was explained. Just a step behind him was Anna, our regular waitress. She put down a slim bouquet of delicate mauve orchids in front of Katy.

Katy blushed and picked out the small silver card. I noticed that, as she looked at it, she automatically reached for the barely noticeable profile of the hidden emerald ring. There were tears in her eyes when she looked up.

By way of explanation to the three of us looking on, she read aloud, 'You are not alone at Thanksgiving. Love, Seb.'

'Mr Palmer was very persistent,' Mr Joseph explained. 'I believe we were the fourteenth hotel on Malta that he had phoned.' So Megan hadn't broken Katy's confidence. Clearly a best friend who could be trusted.

The happiness in Katy's eyes was intense and tangible and I found it impossible not to share in it, despite its origins.

Seb had not left me an easy act to follow and the turkey stage of the festive meal was very much an occasion for homesickness and maudlin. Katy told me of little incidents from earlier Thanksgivings with the family and was quite upset as she spoke of her mother's surprise for them one year when she produced a clever replica of the Mayflower in marzipan and icing.

I tried to relieve the mood with a change of topic, back to the two meetings with the Micallef ladies. Katy had been very impressed by the way in which the two women had coped with the pressures of losing Dante and at the same time not having any idea of what was happening to him.

'It can't be easy. The mother looked very frail and yet she must be only in her early fifties I guess,' Katy said. 'And Joanna is at the stage when she should be taking every chance to rest, not frantically searching for a lost husband. I don't know if I could cope so well.'

'I thought Joanna looked especially lovely,' I commented. 'It's quite weird, but I think expectant mothers often look more attractive than usual.'

Katy smiled, 'And how many expectant mothers have you been familiar with, Mr Smith?'

'No, I mean … well, a couple of the gang from Napier had babies last year and the wife of one of my best friends and my sister-in-law Catriona … and … well they all looked … I can't think of a better word than "lovely".'

'And did you ever tell any of them they looked lovely? I'm sure that's the very time they would appreciate it. Many of them think they're unattractive when they put weight on.'

'You can't go telling another man's wife how attractive she

is,' I protested. 'It's not done, it's not … right. You'll never get me telling a pregnant woman she looks lovely – well, not until it's my baby, of course.'

'You know something? You men are so uptight about these things,' Katy said, shaking her head. 'You don't seem to be able to cope with a purely platonic relationship.'

I looked at her. Yes, I might manage a purely platonic relationship if only she would help. She should be gaunt, unsmiling, waspish, nagging, less irresistible. She should be moody and sulk – be a sulky came to mind as I thought back to her little bit of information about the trotters. Then I might possibly stand a chance. But to get in practice, perhaps I could just carry on thinking of her in an impurely platonic way. Just for the time being.

I hadn't realised how long I had been silent, until I noticed that she was waiting for an answer and at least a reaction.

'Yes, you're probably right,' I nodded, forgetting what the actual question had been or if, indeed, there had been one. 'But let's get over to the pumpkin pie.'

We returned to our table, my plate trying to cope with too large a slice of the pie and a scoop of ice cream, and, to my astonishment, Katy's mean, metal bowl easily holding her frugal portion of uncorrupted fresh fruit salad.

'What's wrong with the pumpkin pie? I thought it was an essential part of the religious ceremony.'

'To tell you the truth,' she whispered, 'I don't really like it. But there's no way they'd allow me to miss out on it back home. Not eating pumpkin pie would be seen as treason, as overthrowing the nation, undermining the family.'

That opened up a line of thought I had meant to pursue earlier. 'This wedding of yours, Katy. I can't believe that the daughter of a good Maltese father and an Irish mother is going to get married in a Protestant church.'

Katy looked particularly serious. It was an issue she had obviously thought long about.

'If mother was still alive, it would have to be in a Catholic Church. But she has been dead some time.'

'Some time? She must have died young.'

'Yes, I was twelve when she got sick. It was just after Thanksgiving, the one when she made the Mayflower cake. We Americans seem to have cornered the market in discovering new diseases to die of. She contracted one of them. I forget its name, somebody or other's syndrome. It was a drawn-out and painful death. Because I was young, they kept me away from most of it, but not all. That wasn't possible.'

I expressed my sympathies as best I could and ended, 'It must have been awful for you at that age.'

'It was. It had an even worse effect on Dad. Only in the past few years, with all of us kids establishing our own lives, has he become the father I knew once again. I think it was the combination of the loss and the responsibility.'

She thought for a moment and sighed, deeply. 'Grandfather Mifsud may have survived the horrible bombing here in Malta, but his faith didn't. It must have been the loss of what was virtually his entire family. I remember him as a very distant man. He didn't want to relate to any of us. I couldn't understand. Do you know, he never wanted to hold me.'

She continued pensively. 'It must have been the same with Dad in some ways. His faith couldn't cope with the death of my mother. I know it weakened mine. My own religious convictions are now negligible.'

She shrugged off her serious musing and said briskly, 'But with Seb, his parents and his sisters the convictions are so strong, so deep-rooted. Their religion is part of them. I couldn't be stubborn on this point.'

It was a cue to get up and leave the dining room.

We spent a platonic evening in the bar, rounded off by a platonic good night peck in the lift. Back in my room, I made a promise to myself that I would get in my riposte to the champagne and the orchid. Someone called Sebastian had thrown down the gauntlet and I had to respond. It needed thought, it needed planning, it needed ingenuity and it needed a helluva lot of luck. And I had no control of the deadline. Still, five days ought to be enough for someone of my ability.

Chapter 14
Friday 26 November

Despite the impending meeting with Micallef, I cast away all thoughts of its intriguing possibilities and, with no little feeling of guilt, all responsibility for the moribund *MacAbre*, to concentrate on my riposte to Seb's Thanksgiving triumph, my Operation Claymore. It was after all merely a matter of standard journalism procedures. I made telephone calls and took notes. I came up against brick walls. I shrugged and started up again.

By the afternoon, I had got nowhere and decided to try my luck with another chapter of *MacAbre*.

It was not a good idea. Reading of malevolent Scots invariably took my thoughts away from historic criminals to today's versions and to the evening date with Tony Micallef. I was really looking forward to it – and not just because it had allowed me to turn down the entreaties of Sam and Sadie, Sid and Bonnie, to join them for a line dancing session. My relationship to the dance floor was roughly in step with Rabbie Burn's links to family planning.

Katy must be right. Micallef would surely prove to be the key to the whole mystery. Once we had that, we could sort everything out and I could get down to finishing *MacAbre*.

True to our arrangement, the Bostonian, no doubt invigorated by her overdose of Stars and Stripes from the evening before, met me at the hotel reception at 6.30, wearing not her blue Thanksgiving outfit, but a smart trouser suit I hadn't seen before, in a colour I think is called taupe, over a pale green blouse. The earrings were very pretty, not her usual ones which always looked as if they had been applied using an industrial riveter. And she actually wore a brooch. She told me the design was pre-Columban.

'You mean BSG, Before Seb's Gang,' I teased. 'But the suit

is super. It makes you look so … boyish.' That line had worked for Ian Carmichael in School for Scoundrels, but didn't prompt Katy to prove her femininity immediately. She must have seen the film.

Fortunately the evening was dry, cool but not cold, and the starry skies above Mdina gave it the appearance of a Sunday School illustration, black silhouetted towers, a spangled sky and an emaciated new moon in position over the pro-cathedral of Saint Peter and Saint Paul, twin to the great Cathedral of Saint John in Valletta.

Parking and driving regulations are formulated to keep the Silent City silent, so we parked outside the impressive entrance to Mdina, crossed over the bridge and entered alongside the Tower of the Standard, now, I was comforted to see, given the eerie darkness of the streets beyond, housing the local police station.

We must have taken a wrong turn at some point because we found ourselves in Pjazza Mosquita, its three stunted oleander trees and limited lighting giving it a ghostly feel.

Katy sneezed and a disembodied voice called 'Bless you'. We looked around. The square was empty. I don't know about Katy, but I was seeing flashes of extracts from far too many films of the occult for my liking.

Katy sneezed again. Another 'Bless you' floated to us. This time, with a better sense of direction, we looked up. There, one of those prying balconies had actually opened a shutter and a nun was silhouetted in the oblong panel like some stained-glass window. She moved her head sideways and we caught the impish smile on her face. We thanked her for her blessing and asked the way to the Casa Notabile. She directed us back to the junction where we had made a wrong turn. It brought us quickly to the restaurant.

Inside the door, the vestibule was lit by a lantern of ecclesiastical proportions. We were greeted, as always in

Maltese restaurants, effusively. The name of Tony Micallef merely multiplied the effusion and the maître led us through to a small inner room that looked like a set of a BBC classic serial. Mr Micallef was there to meet us.

He was, I felt certain, the man who had met Douglas and Graham at the Marsa Races, but he had been a long way from us then and I was not sure what he would look like close up.

He was impressive, perhaps in his late fifties, slim, of medium height or possibly on the short side, wearing a double-breasted navy blazer and grey flannel trousers, his hair black with a little silver at the sides, a self-contained assurance, and, in a wrinkly sort of way, handsome. Katy, of course, fell for him straight away. I'd seen it all before – Rossano Brazzi and Jean Seberg in A Certain Smile. These Mediterranean old men have something. Give them Viagra and we youngsters won't ever get a look in.

'Mr. Smith, Miss Mifsud, it was good of you to come.' He sounded like George Sanders' Shere Khan in The Jungle Book. Just what was it with tigers? 'I'm so sorry we weren't able to meet in my home.' The Maltese are big on hospitality and his regret was genuine.

'I have arranged some light refreshments, as I take it you have skipped the renowned Seacrest dinner to be here.'

He guided us to a side-table with a mouth-watering variety of Mediterranean sea creatures and imaginative salads.

'You'll take some wine, Chardonnay all right for you?' Without waiting for an answer, he filled three crystal goblets. Some smooth social chat on the inclement weather, the attractions of Mellieħa Bay and the paintings of George Fenech brought us to three well-upholstered easy chairs, a mountainous plate on our laps and the glasses within reach on small tables.

His mood changed. 'Your call was interesting, Mr Smith. I had thought that certain … events … were known only to myself and two of your countrymen. It seems that I was wrong. Are you in possession of some knowledge of my son's position in Scotland? What is your interest in this?'

He looked with his big grey eyes, firstly at me and then, more deeply, at Katy. I had to put all of my cards on the table, plus a few that I didn't actually hold.

'Well, I am what I say I am,' I declared. 'Not a policeman, not a criminal, not even a … banker.' I saw a flicker in his eyes at this last category. 'I am just an insignificant writer, using Malta's splendid and, let's face it, very cheap hospitality to finish a pot-boiler.'

'And Miss Mifsud?' He turned his head and smiled irresistibly at her, raising an eyebrow like some exotic question mark. Well, the smile would have been resistible if she'd made any effort. She didn't.

'A friend of John's. A recent friend. Here to provide him with some moral support.' I would have preferred it if she had left out the simper and the hint that I needed support, moral or otherwise.

I continued. 'I was surprised to find Douglas and Graham, two Scottish criminals here on the island. My contacts back in Edinburgh told me enough to convince me they were not on holiday. By luck, perhaps coincidence would be a better word at this stage, the same contact asked me to follow up the story of your son's disappearance. When I spoke to Mrs Micallef and your daughter-in-law, I had nothing more than a sense of unease about the two Malta stories. I did my job and, as you saw, produced the desired story. A straightforward reporting assignment.'

I paused to pop another calamaro into my mouth. I had fallen behind the others during my monologue. We all sipped Chardonnay.

'It was only later,' I admitted, 'that I …'

I felt Katy stiffen alongside me.

'... that we,' I gestured generously in her direction, 'worked out the link between Dante's disappearance in Edinburgh and the printing of Scottish banknotes in Malta.'

Although we had not by any means fully worked out the link, Katy and I looked at Micallef for a response.

He looked grave and spread his elegant, well-manicured hands expressively.

'You have the whole picture, what do you plan to do?'

I had no plans to reveal, because I had no complete picture. 'I have the broad picture, but ...'

Katy stepped in. Her first question of the evening was to the point. 'What happened at the Marsa races, Mr Micallef?'

'You were there?' He was taken aback and unable to hide it. 'You have been doing your homework!'

He stood up, smoothing down his navy jacket, and walked over to the sideboard. 'Some more wine?' He brought the bottle over to us. I held my hand over my glass, reminding him of my motorbike duties. He turned and filled Katy's goblet, absent-mindedly almost letting it spill over the brim. His movements seemed to be on autopilot as he thought carefully about his reply.

'Last week, I had a very strange telephone call on my direct line at work,' he continued. 'I gather from Marija that you know that I work at Goodhill Redpale who print among other things banknotes. Naturally I operate in a high security environment. That direct number is known to very few people. It was a man's voice and I recognised the accent as Scottish. I have had many dealings with Scottish businessmen and indeed my wife and I have spent two holidays in Scotland.'

He apologised directly to me: 'I am sorry for my unwelcoming reaction to your call, Mr Smith. Another Scottish accent was suspicious.'

He frowned, trying to reconstruct the exact circumstances
128

of the call. 'There was something very strange. My secretary told me that she had had a call a week earlier. Because it was on my direct number, she assumed it was a genuine business call and told the caller that I was away in Germany looking at some special machinery. She also told them when I would be back. She was trying to be helpful.'

'That explains why they took so long after they arrived to get in touch,' I suggested.

'And why Gus was talking about going back home for a week,' Katy added.

'From the first words, I sensed this call was different from any I had had from my business contacts. There was menace there. The man knew a lot about my family and me, far too much. More worryingly, he mentioned Dante. He knew I was an occasional visitor to the Marsa racetrack and that I went there on my own. He suggested – no, he told me – I should be there at the next Sunday meeting. I was to be at a spot away from the main crowd before the third race. As I believe is common in these cases, he told me to contact no one.'

I interrupted him. 'Can we take it that you did as you were told?' He nodded rather guiltily.

'I would have thought,' I said, 'that your standing instructions in a high security organisation would be to contact your security people immediately you received such a call.' The attention I had paid at Lothian and Borders Police briefings was bearing fruit.

'You are quite right, young man,' he said, almost apologetically. 'But I felt – or perhaps I persuaded myself – it was right to bend the rules and play along with the caller and find out just what the situation was. That may have been the wrong response, but it was the one I went for.'

'We saw you meet at the races,' Katy prompted. 'It didn't last long. What was said?'

Micallef stiffened at the recollection. 'Two men approached

129

me. One was obviously the man in charge …'

'That was Douglas,' I interrupted.

'… the other just "muscle" I believe the term is. The leader – did you say he was called "Douglas"? – took out a mobile phone, dialled a number, spoke for a few seconds and handed it to me. Dante was at the other end. He spoke only long enough to tell me that he was well and to send his love to his mother and wife. I was telling him that Joanna was proceeding well with the pregnancy when the phone was taken away and contact broken.'

Micallef was not at ease going over the encounter. He stumbled over the words and I felt strongly that he was recounting the conversation for the very first time.

'The man then said something like – "Now that you know who's in control, you'll want to know our demands. They're quite simple: £2 million – and we're not greedy – that's sterling, not Maltese.".'

Micallef cleared his throat.

'I protested. I'm well off, but not wealthy. There is no way I could find money like that. If I could, I would. Dante is my only child – I presume you have no children …'

He looked from Katy to me and went on.

'I asked the man his name. He told me I didn't need a name to follow his orders. He then showed that he had really thought the whole thing through. He said that the £2 million was to come not from me but from the £400 million we were printing for Albion Bank.'

I just could not see how someone like Douglas could plug in to information like that and told Micallef so. 'How could he have discovered that? These men have always stuck to their patch in Scotland. I'm sure there are no Interpol files on Douglas. He has planned some complex jobs, but at heart he's just a local shotgun-and-knuckle-duster man.'

130

Katy managed to deliver a painful kick to my shin.

Micallef sighed in resignation. 'Dante is very out-going and talkative and, like all Maltese, perhaps a little too proud of our small nation.'

Katy, who was unable to take her eyes from Micallef, nodded with understanding.

'My son had heard from me of the Albion deal. It was a big feather in my cap and, I admit, I spoke about it at home. It was only natural that Dante should have mentioned it to his Scottish hosts. You know how these things are with overseas business visits. If anyone has a link or a connection to talk about, it's a conversation piece. I cannot blame the boy. It must have been away from the business meetings, perhaps in a bar or a restaurant, because this man Douglas spoke of someone overhearing the conversation. A waiter or someone sitting nearby, perhaps.'

Dougie would not be short of contacts on his own patch, eager to win favour and a few banknotes in return for a tip-off.

'No matter how he got the information, he must have acted very quickly, without any real plan in mind. He picked up Dante, forced some more information out of him and sniffed an opportunity.'

Micallef took a sip from the wine goblet. 'You must understand, Mr Smith, that a contract of this sort is very unusual. We don't usually do work for advanced countries such as Britain that have their own security printers. We did a similar job only once before.'

'To help out De La Rue with Royal Bank of Scotland notes,' I broke in, anxious to show the depth of my research.

'Yes, yes – we work very closely with De La Rue, one of the world's top designers and producers.' Micallef's words began to flow more freely once more. This was a subject he had covered many times.

'They create the notes, but we have invested heavily in specialised equipment and security processes so that we can do the printing here in Malta. We don't, for good security reasons, produce Malta's own banknotes here, but we have the capacity to work with them to produce banknotes for other countries. Especially when those countries have no quality security printing of their own.'

Katy then asked a very perceptive question. 'If Douglas is an experienced criminal, he must know there is no way you can just take out £2 million without Albion noticing. If they get less than they expect, they'll just tell the police and hold back the other £50 notes.' It was a point I think I was just about to make and we both looked at Micallef for an answer.

'You do Mr Douglas something of an injustice. He was quite clever in realising that he knew of no way to get at his £2 million, but he knew one person who might be able to work out a way.'

'And who was that?' I asked, puzzled.

'Why, Mr Micallef, of course,' Katy said, peering into those sloppy grey eyes of his.

'Quite right, young lady,' Micallef complimented her. 'The ultimatum at the racecourse was simple. I confirmed to him that we would complete the printing of the notes and send off the finished order early in December. He gave me a week to come up with a way in which he could get £2 million without Albion or my employers knowing.'

I felt a grudging respect for Dougie's lateral thinking.

'I assume he backed up his request with something more in line with his usual style,' I prompted Micallef.

'Yes, if I did not come up with a scheme – and deliver – Dante would die, painfully. Douglas spelled it out for me. My son would be found, close to death if not dead, hooked on drugs, in the bedroom of a prostitute who would be stabbed to death, apparently by him.' His lips quivered and he avoided
132

Katy's eyes. 'The prostitute would not necessarily be female.'

There was a silence as Micallef recovered his composure. I could not believe for one moment that Dougie would carry out such a melodramatic threat. But, of course, Micallef wouldn't believe that and, with Sicily on his doorstep, he must have known of cases where such threats had been carried out.

'Death with dignity I might accept, in time. But that, never. And it is not just my son. It would kill his mother and disgrace those of us left behind. You have seen my wife. Marija is a fragile woman, brave but vulnerable. She nearly died giving birth to Dante and emerged frail and unable to bear another child. That is why we have only one child, rare for a family here in Malta.'

Micallef looked drained and defeated.

'Now, twenty-eight years later, that tragedy returns to deliver us a double blow: Dante is dearer to us than any child could be – and Marija is unable to survive any harm that may come to him.'

'And,' Katy said quietly, 'there is the risk to Joanna.'

Micallef held his chin in his hands, emphasising his impeccably manicured nails, and stared at the empty plate in his lap.

More as a means of breaking the silence than as a step I had worked out fully, I suggested that we should go to the police.

'Do you think I haven't thought of that?' There was anguish in Micallef's words. 'What could I tell them? Until now I had no idea even of these men's identities. They were just two men, two unnamed foreigners I had met at the racetrack. They could disappear and Dante would die. I decided to go along with them.'

There was another long silence, this time broken by Katy. 'You say Douglas gave you a week. But that means you have to meet up and give him your plan any day now.'

'Correct, Miss Mifsud. That is why I had to have this meeting tonight. I have been ... encouraged ... by what the two of you have said. Thanks to you, I now know precisely who they are – and they don't know that. For the first time since all this began, I feel I am not helpless, I have something to build a resistance on.' Some of the old confidence came back into his face.

'I would like to suggest we meet again tomorrow. I have not yet worked out all of the details, but I would welcome your views on my offer to this man Douglas. It may be that together we can see a way through.'

Micallef turned his gaze fully on me. 'You know these men better than I do. Will I ever see Dante again?'

I shifted my eyes and mumbled, 'Murder is a big step for any criminal and it is not one Douglas has yet made, to my knowledge.' In my mind's eye, however, I suddenly saw the twisted body of sad, harmless Norman, thirty feet below his balcony.

'I am sure he will keep his side of the bargain.'

'You don't believe that, Mr Smith, and neither do I. Tomorrow, I hope we can build into my scheme some guarantees more copper-bottomed than Douglas' word as a gentleman.' The distressed father was now the efficient businessman again, summing up at the end of a board meeting.

I emphasised that we would do whatever we could and agreed to meet same time, same place, the following evening. He shook Katy and me firmly by the hand, adding a kiss on both cheeks for her. I was pleased to see he was an inch or two shorter than she was. We left and made our way through the eerie alleys of the Silent City, no words passing between us to challenge its epithet.

*

There was a fax for me when we got back to the Seacrest. Don Blaikie, stimulated by the speed of my faxed reply, had

134

come back to me via the same route. His letter was still written by hand in that impressive copperplate and occupied six pages, but I didn't get the full impact of the parchment and the smells of the New Town. He was excited by my 'progress' on *MacAbre*. I had made the mistake of hinting at my ignorance of Philoctetes. He enlightened me.

'As every schoolboy knows,' the letter ran, 'Hercules on his funeral pyre handed over his bow and arrows to Philoctetes. They were the nuclear missiles of the Trojan War, the decisive factor. Philoctetes killed Paris with one of them. I still see you at Geordie's funeral pyre at Mortonhall, taking up the stricken warrior's arrows.' It rambled on and on.

Anyone who could believe that every schoolboy knew all that or who saw Geordie as Hercules and my writing of *MacAbre* as in anyway comparable to Homer's Iliad must be a couplet or two short of a sonnet. But it did make me feel guilty. I stayed up until two, trying to advance the progress of the book and to get down on my laptop the tale of the respectable Edinburgh family returning from Church to find their daft son eating the remains of their housemaid. It was not a story I could get my teeth into.

Chapter 15
Saturday 27 November

'St Julians. Paparazzi's. The balcony. It is the best spot on the island for eating, drinking, sun-basking and people-spotting,' Don Blaikie had insisted weeks earlier in his Georgian den. 'You can't miss it. You mustn't miss it. Oh, and you'll love the menu in more ways than one, Smiffy!'

Just after breakfast, I had made a few more unrewarding calls to jolt Operation Claymore into life, when I got a call from Katy suggesting we should kill time before our war council with Micallef with yet another visit to Valletta. This time we would join the 11 o'clock tour of the famous Manoel Theatre, proudly billed as the oldest in the Commonwealth, the third oldest in the world.

As the morning was warm and sunny, we had left the bike at the hotel and taken the coach to Valletta to give us the chance of a good walk to God knows where.

We had the conducted tour of the miniature gem of a theatre, just over 600 seats, fooled around on the stage, took silly pictures, marvelled at the elaborate Rococo dome and relished the museum. Then I noticed that the current stage production was 'Barefoot in the Park', one of my favourite films.

'Let's get tickets and come along to see what it is like on stage,' I suggested. The Box Office was open, but the young man behind the hole in the wall flicked through his clipboard and had the disappointing news that performances were booked out.

'Two nights ago we had the premiere and the reviews were fantastic. All the regulars had already booked, but since then the phone has hardly stopped.'

Katy pleaded, with eyes a-flutter. 'We've heard so much about the Maltese theatre back in the States. And we're going home soon.'

The young man searched again. This time I noticed a more earnest scanning of the lists.

'There are two tickets just returned for Sunday. But they are in the Gods. There is not a lot of room up there.' He leaned out of the hole and looked down at my legs.

'The young lady will be comfortable, but Sir might find things a little, well, cramped.'

I shrugged. If I had managed the three-hour flight to Malta with my chin resting on my knees without succumbing to Deep Vein Thrombosis, I could surely survive two hours of Neil Simon's wit.

'We'll take them.' ·

Tickets tucked away, the next item on the agenda was lunch and I knew where it was to be. We rushed down the steep hill to the sea, pausing to note that Walter Scott had stayed at a hotel there, and caught the little ferry to Sliema.

A brisk walk along the Prom had brought us St Julians, with only one essential little detour, triggered by the garish windows of a record shop. Another task ticked off. On the harbour front, an illuminated 'Paparazzi's' reminded me of Don Blaikie's recommendation.

I shouldered a path for Katy through a few Christmas parties for local office workers, loud with camaraderie and Cabernet Sauvignon, and found a table overlooking Spinola, a bay as fishing-boat-bobbing as any. Don was right. It was a real sun-trap.

Just a narrow lane away was Paparazzi's larger terrace, bustling and noisy. Below us, many-coloured ducks and British tourists, heavily disguised as British tourists, haggled over space on the congested quayside. A young boat-builder was placing a new eye of Osiris on the prow of his freshly painted blue-and-yellow luzzu, with white-haired, weather-beaten locals offering him advice – too high, too low, to the right, to the left.

In the shallow waters of the slipway, a jolly, squat barrel-of-a-man coaxed his horse, brown and shiny as a new conker, carefully into the salt water until it came halfway up the spindly brown legs. He tied the long reins to the arm of the nearest quayside bench and – to the surprise of the English husband and wife sitting on it – walked nonchalantly away to the shops of St Julians. The couple made friendly gestures and noises to their foster horse – a Mr Jim, if his blue coat was to be believed.

Katy was enchanted and used up a complete film on the bustling dramas below us. I just wallowed in her delight. At last she opened the large, colourful menu and laughed.

'Now I know why this spot is made for you.'

I emerged from my trance and opened the menu, puzzled by Katy's enthusiasm. Don had been right. This was my spot. The owner of Paparazzi's was a film buff, the whole menu was Hollywood-inspired, in its wording if not its cuisine. The puddings were listed under Planet of the Cakes, for example, and all the pizzas were named after Bette Davis films. But although she was one of my idols, Katy and I both went for the pasta, resisting the pull of *Love Me Tender* steaks.

Don had warned me to ask for a small portion, but looking for a second opinion, I asked the waiter what a standard portion was like.

'Very … substantial.' He looked around for guidance and then pointed over the balcony to a pigtailed young colleague ferrying a huge plate of spaghetti to a customer on the terrace. 'That is a normal helping!'

We both got Don's point and ordered small portions. Avoiding the Popeye conchiglie – spinach seashells! – I went, perhaps with the impending battle with Dougie and Gus in mind, for spaghetti *Die Hard*, a bolognese to kill for, fiery, confrontational. The aroma coming from Katy's penne *Dr Zhivago* – salmon, vodka, cream and caviar – gave me the well-known feeling that I had made the poorer choice.

The next two hours on the balcony were the happiest, sunniest in my life. The warmth, the light, the bustle, the wine, the pasta – these were just the backdrop to the sharing, the interaction, the revelations, the laughter, the blushes, the smiles, the surprises.

It occurred to me that this must have been close to that Impressionist painting Katy had spoken about, bubbling, uninhibited chatter in the frame of a sixteenth century Spinola boathouse. But I didn't want thoughts of Sebastian intruding, so I didn't mention it.

Katy and I talked of everything. Shoes and ships and sealing wax, cabbages and kings didn't get a look in. We told each other of sun-drenched summers and rain-drenched winters, of childhood friends, of favourite poems, of what we loved about our parents and those things for which we never forgave them, of school teachers, of work, of young loves.

We dredged up memories untouched since they were real, live happenings. I tried to get Katy to swap embarrassing moments, our hitherto unspoken secrets – I had once bought pints for some local builders to get them to whistle at Popsy, the only girl in the village who didn't come in for wolfcalls. I had once written a letter to the Editor, under a false name, praising my own work. Katy wasn't really playing the game. I'm sure she could have come up with something better than a middle name of 'Virginia'. I chanced a guess. 'Was that because you were born in Virginia? Thank heavens your family didn't move to Massachusetts until later!'

Katy blushed delicately. 'No, it's because I'm a Virgo, my birthday is 30 August.'

With great restraint, I restricted my comment to 'That method might have worked for me – John Scorpio Smith. It's catchy.'

We moved on to the cinema and argued over the funniest comedy ever filmed. Katy was being provocative when she started the bidding with *Braveheart*, I retaliated with Love Story – but we eventually amicably agreed on *The Great Race* from me, *Roxanne* from Katy.

'The original Roxanne married a red-headed man, you know, Alexander the Great.'

'Ah, but, as I've said before, she was turned on by the power bit not the red hair. And you still haven't come up with a sexy male redhead,' I protested.

We were almost in accord on the best film – she'd been taken to see *Citizen Kane* by a former boy friend and had been bowled over, but she eventually plumped for *Sleepless in Seattle!* It's one of my own favourites too, but I didn't let on.

'You're not old enough to appreciate that,' I argued. Then I had second thoughts. 'Is that the one about the girl who gives up the dreary Mr Rich Guy for a man from the other side of the country just because he appealed to something deep down in her?'

'Oh, it's much more than that,' Katy protested.

I knew, but that was the story line I liked.

On the worst film ever made, she'd never seen *An Honourable Murder* and wouldn't have believed me if I had described it. And she wouldn't agree with me on *Hannah and her Sisters,* so we gave up on the film games.

We described to each other our ideal home, but as she'd never known the glory of Edinburgh, I failed to get her enthused over Ramsay Garden, that frenzied collection of flats on the very threshold of the city's castle. She insisted on what I think was a beach hut at Cape Cod close to the sound of breaking waves and a source of clam chowder, whatever that was.

The end to the bliss came almost poetically. For once we were silent, perhaps just saving the words and images of the past hours to our astonished memory banks. A small cloud came over the sun, reminding me of one that had been similarly intrusive at the Upper Barracca Gardens, and for a moment the sea was grey. Katy shivered and asked: 'Do you think Dante will die?'

There was no way back from that. It was the third time I had been asked that question, in different forms, by his mother, his father and now by Katy. I had asked myself that same question very many times more. I was still frightened by the answer deep down inside of me.

*

That evening the Council of War took place once again in the back room of Casa Notabile. When Micallef took us through to the same chairs in the same room, I was taken aback to find a fourth person already well into a goblet of Chardonnay.

He was a large, expansive man, with more than overtones of Peter Ustinov in *Death on the Nile*, but without Poirot's affectations. Bushy eyebrows, drooping to left and right like a pair of Valletta streets gave him the air of a deeply perturbed clown. If his face and frame were large, his hands were even more dramatic. It would have been easier to keep your eyes off Cyrano de Bergerac's nose than to stop staring at his hands.

He stood and greeted us in a friendly, grizzly bear manner. To say I shook hands with him is like saying that Jonah met a whale.

Micallef combined introduction and explanation.

'Miss Mifsud, Mr Smith, this is my head of security, Guido Abela. I decided that we needed his co-operation and, indeed, his advice if we are to see this thing through.'

Abela charged our glasses and gestured to the cold buffet. In an unnatural atmosphere of normality, we ate the cold

141

meats, seafood and salads, again with the stilted exchanges of information I would have expected of guests thrown together at a hotel breakfast. Abela had been to Britain on many occasions, had an Irish wife and, that very day, his eldest son had returned at the end of his first term studying business management at the London School of Economics. He had even visited Boston and he and Katy relished memories of walks along the Charles River in the fall.

Eventually, as a sign that it was time for business proper, we got up from our easy chairs to sit around a large carved wooden table in matching high backed chairs.

I wanted to clear up one point before we became too embroiled in details. 'Can we start by answering a simple question? Why don't we call in the cops? I've asked it already, but I must put it again.'

Micallef and Abela exchanged glances. 'We have,' Micallef confessed, 'gone over that possibility today. Douglas told me that his men in Scotland had clear instructions. If the police were involved, if any arrest was made, if he failed to make his regular evening call, if they were unable to contact him – all had the same message. Get rid of Dante and the evidence.'

'It sounds like a big bluff,' I argued. 'I can't see Dougie chancing a murder rap.'

'But what evidence would we have to make a kidnap charge stick?' Abela shrugged, his huge red hands, palms up like church collection plates, emphasising his point. 'We could land up with no body, no suspect in Scotland and two villains here in Malta protesting their innocence, claiming they were just chancing their arm. They could get away with it.'

'I still think they're bluffing,' I persisted.

'But we're not talking about a poker-hand with a pile of money in the pot.' Micallef was agitated. 'My son's life is the price we pay for getting it wrong. Let's assume that there is no question – at this stage – of bringing the police into the game.

142

There is too much at risk.'

There was finality in his voice and we all nodded acceptance. Micallef continued. 'This morning, as promised at the racetrack, I may have forgotten to tell you that,' he said apologetically, gesturing to Katy and me, 'Douglas phoned me at work. He wanted to know if I had worked out a plan and when I told him I had, he arranged to meet me tomorrow to hear what it was and, I hope, to agree it will work.'

Katy and I were eager to hear what Micallef had come up with, but I assumed that Abela had already been involved.

Unlike the stuttering account of the Marsa meeting, Micallef's presentation was now calm and professional, as if he outlining a business proposition to the board of Goodhill Redpath.

'It is not easy to steal £2 million in banknotes, even from a plant whose sole business is to print huge numbers of them. Indeed, perhaps, I should say, especially from such a plant. Our security is, please take our word for it, even although Guido and I are hardly impartial, impregnable. Checks and procedures and the most comprehensive of electronic surveillance would make it impossible to bring notes out, other than for their official purpose.'

I expressed my doubts. 'I seem to recall cases of one English bank losing notes carried out by female employees in their knickers. That bank must have felt equally cocky about its security.'

'I can assure you, we would not need to search our ladies,' Abela said with some force. 'They could never have got the notes in their hands, let alone in their underwear, in the first instance. We had to come up with a plan, together, that would need a little connivance between the two of us.'

'I'll try not to bore you with a quick run-through of how banknotes are produced,' Micallef continued. 'The main thing, believe it or not, is the paper – very special, very difficult

143

to copy, very limited in its sources. It comes to us with the watermark already incorporated.'

Despite the stress of the occasion, Micallef could not hide his affection for the mysteries of banknote printing.

'We do not, obviously, print individual notes, any more than your newspaper prints individual pages. We print a sheet with anything from 20 to 30 notes on it. Firstly the one side, then the other.'

I'd had a lot to do with printing so I was naturally interested, but even Katy seemed enthralled. Again it could have been the Micallef touch.

'The printing is much more complicated than would appear. Your newspaper is, I imagine, printed by one technique, web offset now, letterpress a decade or so ago. Banknotes are printed using three separate processes. The engraving is printed by gravure, ink captured in minute grooves and transferred to the paper. If you run your fingers over the surface of the new note, you can easily detect the raised ink of this process.'

I nodded. Olga had shown me that trick.

'The subtle multi-colour graduations are printed offset, complex patterns and anti-forgery devices built in. Those are the very smooth, almost slippery areas you can also feel on a new note. And finally we add the serial numbers, different on each note, and this time they are printed letterpress, with special devices to avoid skipping or duplication.'

Katy looked out of her depth, but I winked at her and mouthed that I'd explain later.

'All of that takes time. We have to stay ahead of the forgers and, with all the modern computer technologies at their disposal, we can't do that easily or speedily. In the old days, the number of men capable of the quality engraving needed to produce a forged banknote was very limited. We and the police knew them. Now everyone has access to quality colour separation facilities and litho printing machines. As these
144

make the forgers' task easier and easier, we have to think of ways to make it harder – perhaps even impossible.'

It was a cue for bringing in some more of Olga's work. 'And my contact back home tells me that includes putting a revolutionary hologram on Albion's fifties,' I added.

Abela reacted instantly. 'How on earth did you know that?' the security chief demanded, his eyes gimleting into mine with all the old penetration that must have unnerved a generation of Maltese criminals.

'You're not going to ask a journalist to disclose his sources, Mr Abela?' I had a distinct feeling that given encouragement by Micallef, he would have tried and succeeded.

'Can I assume though that this little … elaboration … is not widely known?' Micallef asked, dispersing the heat.

'You certainly can,' I assured him.

Micallef and Abela exchanged nervous glances and there was a mysterious overtone that I could not pinpoint. I noticed that Katy was looking equally puzzled. The moment passed.

'I have, with Guido, come up with a way of getting £2 million to Mr Douglas, without arousing the suspicions of Albion Bank or our employers. It was not easy. Our entire operation is based on making sure that such a thing cannot happen.'

'And how will you do that?' Katy asked. The two of us had already discussed how Micallef could possibly siphon off £2 million and, with the best of our lateral thinking, had not come up with an answer. Albion Bank would not accept £398 million – and Micallef's bosses would not allow him to print £402 million.

We waited for Micallef to explain. He looked to Abela for support and began to outline his plan.

'I shall at a point during the final run – the printing of the reverse side – identify a lapse of quality in 2,000 sheets,

145

40,000 notes, 2 million sterling. I shall be studying the area through a powerful magnifying glass. I shall order the printed sheets to be scrapped.'

'Can you do that on your say-so alone?' I was surprised. 'I would have thought someone else would expect to confirm this non-existent flaw.'

'But it is not non-existent, Mr Smith. I shall arrange for a tiny blemish, too small to be seen by the naked eye, but too significant, in view of our proud record of top quality printing, to allow through.'

Katy and I were impressed – and showed it. 'But would spoils not have to be shredded immediately?' I asked.

'Normally, yes, but in view of the nature of the fault, I shall remove all of the sheets, intact, for further examination. We shall then reprint for the contract all of those rejected sheets, using the same serial numbers.'

'So you'll have £400 million for Albion Bank and a separate £2 million for Douglas,' Katy said.

'Yes, and I'll arrange to have the extra sheets trimmed – cut into individual notes – by a different shift. There will be nothing suspicious as far as my colleagues are concerned.'

'It sounds convincing to me, but will Dougie buy it?' I asked.

'Why shouldn't he?' Abela countered, thinking perhaps that I had some insight into Dougie's labyrinthine thought processes. 'He has Dante, that should be enough to convince him that Tony's on the level.'

'Tomorrow morning,' Micallef was back in his efficient mode again, 'I shall meet Douglas and his man. I have to be at the Sliema end of the Valletta ferry for 10.30. Douglas wants to be sure of some privacy without being led into a trap. He has obviously thought this through very carefully.'

'Mr. Micallef,' I tried to be as matter-of-fact as possible

to hide my thought processes from him. 'It might be a good idea if Katy and I could be on the ferry, well away from you, of course, but able to witness the meeting. We've both seen Dougie and Gus around the hotel, so they've probably noticed us. But they wouldn't think it odd to see us on the ferry.'

Abela was not fooled and forestalled any reaction from his chief. 'I think, Tony, it would indeed be very valuable to have independent witnesses of the meeting. It might even be possible to get you and the Scots together in an innocent looking tourist photograph by Miss Mifsud. I think you told me she has some experience with a camera.'

Micallef stared long and hard at Abela and then at Katy and me, his thoughts so transparent that we knew, long before he spoke, that he had seen through our own thinking.

'You're looking ahead, Guido, like a good policeman and you, Mr Smith, like a good reporter. If anything happens to Dante, we'll want as much proof as possible to back up my account of the blackmail.'

Abela made no attempt to avoid Micallef's sad gaze and just shrugged in agreement.

'Katy and I will not jeopardise your meeting.' I was determined to persuade Micallef. 'I can assure you of that. We've become used to acting as romantic young tourists.'

Abela smiled and Katy narrowly missed my shins with another of her under-the-table contributions to the discussion.

'I suppose you are right,' Micallef said, 'but you must be on the ferry well ahead of us. You should be there, too, Guido. If we need Maltese justice at any point, no one can work the courts better than you.'

I thought such things happened only in novels, but his face actually drained of colour as he envisaged the circumstances in which Abela's experience would be needed.

*

On the bike trip back to the Seacrest, Katy and I aired our concerns for Dante's safety, perhaps for his life. On impulse, I decided to ring Olga again, more to confirm my fears than anything else. In case she was out for evening, we didn't wait to get back to the hotel but stopped off at Bugibba to find another windy phone-box in another windy alley or a 'sqaq' as the Maltese sign identified it.

'Olga? Great to find you in.'

'I'm always in, these days, Johnny. Do you recommend Malta as a place to go to pick up a wealthy, not too demanding sixty-year-old?'

'Wall-to-wall, Olga, wall-to-wall. The square here in Bugibba is so full of shocks of white hair that it's known to the locals as Snowdrop Corner.'

'You tempt me, Johnny, but let me guess. Are you phoning me at vast expense to let me know you've found my Oreste recordings or do you have some follow-up questions? I'll bet you've forgotten all ...'

I popped in before she could continue. 'You are so cynical, Olga. The recordings, of course! My ceaseless quest took me, eventually and at no little personal danger, to a minuscule old shop in the back streets of Valletta. There, in a dark, cob-webbed corner, I managed to unearth a rare 2-CD set, including not just the Hollywood tosh, but also many pirated recordings from his days on the USA opera circuit.'

Olga was taken aback. 'You're a genius.'

'It was just persistence, you know my dogged reputation,' I replied modestly, not mentioning I'd found the CDs at that first shop I'd tried on the walk to St Julians. 'Oh, and by the way they gave me a cheap little pocket calendar which I must pass on to you.'

Olga sniffed at the hook. 'Why would I want that?'

I read from the card I had been practising on with some help from our waitress Anna. 'It's from Għaqda Għad-Drittijiet Ta' L-Irġiel.'

'Who on earth are they?' Olga took the bait in one gulp.

'Oh, that's the Association for Men's Rights, here in Malta, reminding you that 7th February is International Men's Day.'

Chivalry and good taste prevent me from listing Olga's expletives.

'Olga, you mentioned follow-up questions. How could I turn down such an offer? Firstly, how much would, say £2 million, actually weigh?'

'Good God, Johnny, redundancy has hit you hard. Are you planning a heist?'

'No,' I hedged, hinting at another book in the offing. 'Well, come on, fount of all knowledge, turn yourself into a speak-your-weight machine.'

'All right, I'll try, but not in pounds or kilos. What denominations?'

'Fifties.'

'Well, that makes it easier. I went along to the Royal Bank's shindig – seven years ago or so – to mark the last incineration of banknotes in Scotland. There was, I recall, a million on the table then. In £10s and £20s.'

She thought for five phone card units. I swear I could hear the sounds of pencil meeting paper as she made her calculations.

'Let's say £2 million in £50s would take up the space of about £600,000 in those mixed notes. Less than that if they were brand new notes, of course. It's surprising how banknotes thicken as they are passed around, rather like playing cards. I'd think ...'

And she did, for another five phone card units.

'… you could get £2 million into two large suitcases. I don't imagine I could lift one of the cases, but I'm sure a strapping lad like you could.'

My word! Dougie and Gus had been doing their homework. So that's why they had asked for £2 million. And I thought they were just embarrassed at being too greedy in asking for more. They were obviously going to take the money home as holiday luggage! We should be thankful for one thing at least. If the cases were full of banknotes, Gus might have to dump his various changes of shell suit somewhere in Mellieħa Bay.

'Question number two, Olga. How would I shift the £2 million I'd acquired illegally?'

'In new notes?'

'Yes.'

'In Scottish notes?'

'Yes.'

'My, you are making things difficult. You'd have to do it in Scotland, whereas with Bank of England paper you'd have many more options. And new notes would stand out.'

This was going to take some time and I fed in another phone card.

'The easiest way would be to have access to as many casinos and bookies as possible.'

'Yes, that might be arranged,' I said, thinking of Dougie's and Gus' life style, 'that would certainly be possible.'

'Buy chips with new notes, cash in for old, you know the form. But of course there are the surveillance cameras to contend with these days.'

'But how long would that take? Forget the cameras for the moment.'

'Depends on how many casinos you frequent, how many

bookies you know, how many friends are sharing the loot. Unless you're onto a very clever wheeze, you'll be struggling to do it in less than a couple of weeks or so.'

'But then I'll land up with £2 million used notes. I presume I would still need to launder them if I plan to set up in the south of Spain. Where would I go from there, Olga?'

'Give me an evening when you're back in Edinburgh, Johnny. The game's changed now. For "speed" with the new notes, read "patience" with the used ones. Do you have plenty of time to launder the notes? Scottish ones are difficult.'

I said I would think about the time element and thanked her profusely. Yet another phone card wheezed its last. Katy and I walked slowly down the hill to the Seacrest. We didn't speak, but Katy had got the picture from my side of the telephone conversation. I knew that we were both convinced that Dante would not be handed back when the money was handed over. Douglas needed time, plenty of it, before he could launder the money and feel safe. And time meant more chance of something going wrong.

These were not the thoughts to ensure a good night's sleep. Nor was the fact that I had got nowhere with Operation Claymore and time was running out there, too.

Chapter 16
Sunday 28 November

I am not really a dreamer. To put it more clearly, I rarely wake up and remember any details of my dreams, even although the experts claim that we all fill our sleeping hours with dreams of one sort or another.

But, just as I had feared, that night had been an exception. Chased by an astonishingly speedy Gus, Katy and I had run all around Malta and had eventually come to rest in, of all places, the Hearts football ground at Tynecastle. Amongst the cheering crowd, we felt safe until suddenly a blizzard of Scottish banknotes rained down on us and, looking up, I saw Gus standing on the roof of the grandstand which morphed into the balcony of our hotel. Gus leaned over and fell, gaining momentum and size by the millisecond and just as he was about to crush the two of us, Miss Emily Carstairs wandered into his path and was flattened.

At that stage I woke up feeling more tired than when I had gone to bed. A cold shower and a hearty breakfast, at which I could narrate my dreams to Katy, put me back on my feet again and ready to face an enticing day.

Katy and I were the first aboard the ferry alongside the promenade at Sliema, the ferry we had taken in such high spirits only a week earlier but in what now seemed to be a different world. On the other side of the dual carriageway, the smart boutiques and stores of Malta's prime shopping area were busy with tourists and locals, but the prom was, as yet, only sparsely populated.

We took up a position in the boat nearest the jetty. I behaved as any doting honeymooner would, while Katy spoilt the cover by wriggling out of even the lightest embrace.

To be fair, she had made an effort. She was dressed in a fetching pair of jeans – yawn – and a T-shirt extolling the

152

virtues of an American ale. Her large sun-hat festooned with fabric flowers added a touch of gaiety and also helped keep off the light rain drizzling half-heartedly through the thin, irritating mist which had crept up on us when we weren't looking.

A few minutes after us, Abela arrived, smartly dressed as a Valletta businessman, with appropriate raincoat and, nice touch, a voluminous golf umbrella, bearing the name and logo of one of Malta's leading estate agents.

I pointed it out to Katy. 'The guy's a real pro.' To keep up our cover, I kissed her. She giggled.

Just before 10.30, Micallef came up to the gangplank, but did not step on to it He stood at the quayside, waiting, looking anxiously at his watch and at the crew of the ferry busying themselves with ropes and other nautical impedimenta.

Suddenly, Douglas and Graham appeared, one each side of Micallef, and led him from the ferry to a small boat with an all-embracing striped canopy, a dozen or so yards down the promenade to the left. All three stepped gingerly down into the boat, and, as our ferry cast off and made towards the formidable bastions of Valletta, the smaller craft's outboard motor started up noisily and the boat set off, at right angles to our course, to the hilly Dragut Point. We were left completely out of the equation.

Abela, Katy and I stood disconsolately at the rear of the ferry, exposed to the rain. We had been so determined to get a good view of events that we had let everyone else make for the sheltered area of the vessel and now there was no room there. We thankfully shared the large orange and black golf umbrella and watched Micallef, Douglas and Graham move further and further away from us.

'Do you think they suspected a trap?' Katy asked.

'No, they're just behaving like criminals all over the world – they're cutting out the risks,' Abela shrugged.

'I think you're right, but so much for our evidence.' I made

153

no attempt to hide my disappointment.

'Oh, I don't know,' Abela said, with some conviction, if that's the right word. 'Three of us saw Tony being led away and, if I can't track down their boat-man when I know what he looks like and have the name and number of his boat, I've lost my touch.'

I cheered up.

'And when you were blowing in my ear, I managed a picture of all three of them, with Douglas and Graham holding his arms,' Katy added. 'The lens hood kept off the little bit of rain and the lighting was quite good, despite the mist.'

I was pleased that she had taken the photograph, but slightly put out that she could keep a cool head when I was moving into my top wooing gear.

When we got to Valletta, we did the obvious – and came straight back to Sliema. The rain became more aggressive and not even the mighty golf umbrella could save us as we left the shelter of the boat to scurry across the wide road to the nearest bar.

The dye from the painted flowers on Katy's hat had run riot. She was angry enough to stuff the hat in the nearest litter bin, but recovered to see the joke when she discovered why Abela and I continued to laugh long after she had got rid of the hat. She returned from the ladies' loo, having seen in the mirror the rainbow coloured forehead that had amused the two of us so much. She was subdued, but at least monochrome once more.

*

Abela and I had been keeping an acute eye on the landing stages, but there had been no sign of Micallef. An hour later, he arrived by the Valletta ferry! Yes, he had been left at the very spot from which we had returned so disheartened. The other side had won hands down.

We were eager to hear what had happened on that little boat

154

and, with the bell-towers of a dozen churches reminding us that it was one o'clock, Micallef offered us all lunch in a quiet corner of the restaurant in one of Sliema's smartest hotels. As the opposition might still be around, we made it to the hotel separately. No matter what happened, Douglas and Graham must believe that Micallef had shared his problems with no one.

The food was tasty and the news was good. Dougie had actually patted Micallef on the head when he heard the plan. He had grilled the printing chief on every step and the schedule was now in place. In five days' time, the £400 million for Albion Bank would be taken to Marsamxett Harbour under strict surveillance and would be loaded for shipment to Newcastle, near De La Rue's northern printing works. In the corner of the same security van as Albion's notes would be eight packages clearly identified in the manner of the printing trade – a page proof of the contents pasted on the package.

In this case, the pack would show a public poster announcing a new series of Maltese postage stamps and showing exactly how they would look. Inside would be Dougie's £2 million. As the posters were low security, they would be taken to a warehouse alongside Msida Creek and delivered there. A storeman would be on duty to sign for them. The two Scots would pick up the notes and Micallef would be told the arrangements for the safe return of Dante.

Although he had phoned Marija before lunch to warn her he would be late, Micallef was anxious to get back home. His wife knew nothing of the negotiations, but he was fidgeting to be away. Eventually, he shook hands formally with all of us, even forgetting to kiss Katy on the cheeks, and left.

Abela, Katy and I were alone for the first time. It was an opportunity to cover matters that we had avoided when Dante's father was with us.

'They didn't take any chances at the ferry today. Do you think they were expecting problems?' I was anxious to get

Abela's expert opinion.

'No, as I said, I think they were just being careful. We should not underestimate these two. This is an amazing plan they've put into play.'

'Amazing?' Katy frowned.

'Well, just think of it. They weren't able to come up with the details, but they got an expert to do the work for them. They managed to recruit Tony to be the genius behind the scheme. An inside job with a twist.'

We both nodded appreciatively.

'And it doesn't end there. The Scots have been very clever indeed. Normally in a heist of this scale there are lots of people involved and with each addition to the team there is a chance of a leak. These guys are doing it with just two!'

'Three if you count whoever is looking after Dante,' I suggested.

'But still an incredibly compact team for such a big job. And there is one other thing. If they succeed, they have a bonus, an advantage that few criminals have in this type of crime. As far as they are concerned, no one will know the money has been stolen, because it never really existed! They will feel safe disposing of the money because no one will be looking for it.'

The three of us sat in silence for a while and then the great frame of Abela rose with a sudden impatience to be busy.

As he prepared to leave, I put one hand on his huge mitt. 'Could you stay for a moment, Guido? I have a worry, which I don't believe we've paid enough attention to.'

Abela sat back and looked straight into my eyes. 'I think I know what you want to say. It is difficult to discuss it in front of Tony.'

Katy, ever sensitive, looked appropriately solemn.

I continued. 'Last night I spoke to an old friend in Edinburgh who knows about money, legal and otherwise. She assured me that it would take weeks to change the dangerous, easily traced new notes into anonymous old ones. Now, no way will Dante be back with us before Dougie has exchanged every single note of that £2 million. Even one bundle left in his possession would pin the thing on him. He cannot release Dante for weeks to come. Anything could happen.'

I sipped from my glass of fizzy mineral water to moisten my dry lips.

'Maybe they never intended Dante to return. I know it's out of keeping with their track records, but there is one thing we haven't told you. I didn't want to alarm Mr Micallef more than is necessary.'

I gave Abela the whole story of Norman and his death. His great eyebrows drooped even further at the edges and he looked more than ever like a huge, grieving bloodhound.

'So,' I summed up, 'we have two men who have already shown how much this whole thing matters to them, enough for them to break their usual rules. And those two men, under very great stress as they try to convert the £2 million safely into accessible funds, are going to be holding Dante not just for a day or two but for a matter of weeks, maybe even months. The longer they have him the more chance there is of a panic, of an accident.'

Katy began to rival Abela's despondency. I never thought that those lips made for smiling could look so unattractive. I continued nonetheless.

'And to … kill … Dante would not involve any great crisis of conscience. Remember, they have already killed Norman.'

'You are right, Mr Smith, but what do you propose we do?' Abela asked. 'Should we return to the issue of calling in the police?'

I was adamantly against that move. 'If we call in the police, we have no guarantee that by the time he fails to get the

157

expected telephone call at ten o'clock this evening, the man holding Dante won't do something stupid, very stupid. What we have to do is convince Joe Baird or whoever that the plan has failed completely and that he should get Dante back on the streets of Edinburgh immediately.'

'You're right,' Abela nodded, 'what we all want is Douglas and Macdonald heading for Valletta jail, Dante heading home to Malta and the banknotes heading back to the incinerators at Goodhill Redpale.'

'But how do we achieve that? They hold all the cards.' The cheery Katy was uncharacteristically pessimistic.

'Not at all, not at all. By sheer luck, we happen to have a combination of, well, skills that gives us a card to trump the enemy's. I believe I know a way in which Dante will be released immediately and safely. But we all of us have a key part to play.'

I explained in detail just what I had in mind. It took some time to get over the understandable cynicism. But eventually, Abela became hooked and Katy, just astonished.

'Do you believe it will work?' I asked the question directly to the two of them.

'Yes,' Abela said after a brief pause.

'It has more chance than the plan we'd already put together.' Katy looked at me with something in her eyes that I was seeing for the first time - admiration. 'If someone I cared about very deeply was being held, I would go for your plan, Johnny.'

I spoke directly to the security chief. 'Well, we agree, but can you persuade Tony that it will work?'

Abela replied immediately, 'I can and I must. We have until Friday. Leave it to me. There are things to do besides persuading Tony. You've given me some complicated challenges, Mr Smith.'

We were about to leave when a policeman came over to
158

the table dragging a reluctant and rather scruffy looking man. 'Here is your boatman, Mr Abela.'

The former cop had clearly not lost his influence with the island's law-keepers. He thanked the policeman profusely and gestured that he could leave. I think a banknote changed ownership in the curt handshake.

Abela moved into Good Cop mode. He gestured to a hovering waiter and within seconds a foaming glass of beer was in front of the newcomer.

'Sit down Mr ...'

'Bruno, Commissario, Bruno Muni.' The boatman sat uneasily between Abela and me. He used the Italian police title, but perhaps that was a Maltese one too.

'These men on your boat earlier, they paid you well?'

'A little, just a little for my boat and my time, Commissario.'

'Yes, but that is no matter to me. I am looking for information not taxes.'

The man sighed thankfully.

'When did they approach you?'

Bruno did some calculations.

'A week ago, no more than that.'

Surely that was not possible. The plans were only just falling into place then. As far as we knew, the Scots had not able to know of when, where or even if they were meeting Paul.

Abela was thinking along exactly the same lines. 'How did they contact you, Bruno?'

'I was working on the engine of my boat alongside the quay'.

Abela interrupted. 'It looks a very fine boat, a very

powerful boat, a very expensive boat.' He emphasised the word 'expensive' as if looking for an explanation.

'The best boat in the harbour, Commissario.' Bruno persisted with the rank which showed how important he believed Abela to be. 'I bought it last year with money my great-uncle left me, God rest his soul. Marta, my wife, made me spend the money wisely.'

'Why did the two men come to you?'

'They admired the boat and asked me if it could get as far as Sicily. I said of course it could. The small man then asked 'Even to Naples?' I said it could on a good day. He gave me some money. Just a small amount and said they would be in touch. Then yesterday they came and asked me to take then around the bay. But you saw that, Commissario. I noticed you on the ferry.'

There was a pause and Abela looked the man in eyes. 'Did you mention anything to them about me.'

'No. Commissario, not at all. They did not speak to me. Except when they were leaving they reminded me to keep the boat in good shape and that they would soon need me for a much more ... rewarding job.'

'Thank you Bruno. You have been very helpful. Finish your beer and get back to that fine boat of yours.'

Bruno gulped back his beer and left.

'So now we know how your Scots intend to get the two million back to Edinburgh. There was no way they could have risked getting a couple of very heavy cases past our inquisitive colleagues at Luqa security.'

The information had no impact on our plans but it did give us a fuller sense of the total picture.

Abela nodded approvingly, 'Your countrymen are more meticulous in their planning than we had all imagined.'

We shook hands and went our separate ways.

*

Katy and I were back in Valetta that evening. The ground leading up to the great gate glistened with frost and the good folk of Malta were taking no chances with the unaccustomed surface, walking slowly with tiny steps as if on a sheet of treacherous ice. We had no such fears and trotted into the city, down the main street then left down Triq it-Teatru l-Antik to the Manoel.

It was our Night at the Theatre, Barefoot in the Park. Now to be honest, I am not a fan of returning to the theatre or the book that inspired my favourite films, but in this case the almost mediaeval Malta theatre, Katy's presence and the story of effervescent young lady and stodgy Yankee lawyer made it all seem worthwhile.

We scaled the narrow staircase to the third tier of seats, The Gods which all Mediterranean countries seem to call 'The Paradise', a tongue-in-cheek description of height rather than opulence or comfort. Now that we were closer to the ceiling it was clear that what we had thought during our tour was a magnificent cupola was in fact a superb trompe l'oeil on a perfectly flat ceiling.

Down below us the cream of Malta's society seemed to have felt that fur coats and fine hats were de rigueur. The sultry heat of Paradise was obviously not being endured down in the stalls.

A confession. When the lights went down and the curtains went up, I had steeled myself for something on the level of the Glenbraith Thespians annual drama festival. Nothing could be further from the truth. The direction was crisp, the American accents authentic to my ear and complimented by Katy, and the timing and pace up to anything I had encountered at Edinburgh's King's.

We could settle down confidently to a couple of hours of

Neil Simon at his best. And the fact that Corie, the heroine, free-spirited, exciting and imaginative, (back in the 60s the Jane Fonda part, turned down originally by Natalie Wood, thankfully) was linked with Paul, a staid stuffy traditional all-American lawyer would, I hoped, not be lost on my companion.

There was one hiccup. The 'hero' who, I hoped, would look like Sebastian was nothing of the sort. He was in fact, tall and thin with red hair, dyed I suspected. I could have done without that, St Whatisname!

Nevertheless, it was a super evening and we laughed aloud throughout. The zany neighbour, played by Charles Boyer in the film, was especially funny and was obviously a local favourite as his every appearance was greeted with wild enthusiasm.

And it was rewarding to see just how drunk the fuddy-duddy lawyer had to get before he dared walk barefoot in the park.

In the one interval, Katy observed that the ladies in the stalls had not removed their fur-coats. Clearly, heating was not a requirement of Malta's public buildings, although by the end of the evening the hot air rising to the rafters made our seats more like Inferno than Paradiso.

We left and made our way out into the crispy cold of an autumnal Valetta. Maybe it was just for warmth that Katy clung to me like a Koala to a eucalyptus tree on the half hour or so of the drive back to the hotel. I tried to get a conversation going on the play and the clash of the spontaneous Corie and the unimaginative Paul. Katy did not seem to find the topic interesting. Maybe she was getting the lesson, even if it was subliminal.

'And so to bed,' as Pepys would say. Or rather 'And so to beds.'

Chapter 17

Monday 29 November

The following day, a bright morning sun and a light warm breeze encouraged us to go for a really long walk. From the hotel we made our way along the flat road to Popeye Village and then turned inland, up the long rising hill. To our left were fields of vegetables and huts of animals – livestock is rarely seen out in the open – and to our right the untidy landscape of rocks and sparse, tough greenery that reminded me so much of south Harris back home in Scotland. From the top of the ridge we could see both sides of the island and in front of us the Pwales valley.

We walked down the winding road, past rough wooded areas where Maltese families were already hard at work relaxing, mothers putting out the picnics, fathers playing football with the children ...

I couldn't resist the lure of the black and white football. As one of the wee lads sliced the ball in my direction, I moved instinctively with the footballing grace that all Scots seem to possess as a God-given right. I leapt to head the ball, but tripped over a stupidly placed grassy hillock and fell awkwardly. I landed on top of a small dog who was following up the skewed pass and he, in fright, bit into the football that had fallen between us. It deflated slowly in full view of the children. One of them started to cry. I got up and apologised profusely to the father. The very least I could do was to slip a five-lira note into the hand of the greeting toddler. He wiped his eyes with the back of his hand, stared at the note in disbelief, stopped crying and smiled. I must have paid over the odds. Well over the odds.

I made my way back to Katy who was laughing uncontrollably. There was no sign of sympathy and no point in explaining.

She recovered enough to deliver the final blow to my dignity. 'I saw a film once about young Scottish teenagers and there was a boy in it, just like you. I forget the name of the film.'

I did not enlighten her. Many years back our school film society had shown Gregory's Girl in the hall. I unwillingly shed my plain name of 'John' and became 'Gregory' for a year and half. Fortunately it was then shortened into 'Gregsie' which disguised the embarrassing origins and after that, I fled to Edinburgh and the anonymity of Napier.

We walked on, away from the families at play. Beyond this area, there was evidence of some planned afforestation – the signs told us the young Germans of Thuringia, who know lots about trees, were lending a helping hand to the Maltese, who knew nothing.

We came to the village of Manikata, at that time of the morning about as lively as the street that Gary Cooper walked through at the end of High Noon. The brand new church caught our eye and Katy started clicking again. The church looked for all the world like the winner of first prize in a global sandcastle competition. But that's Malta, 365 churches and not one of them as you would expect it to be.

We descended to the valley proper, rich and fertile, the farms now boasting, by Maltese standards, large flat fields, expansive enough for tractor and harvester but still the same divides of walls, white and powdery, the stones pocked and riddled and rough, and of prickly pear hedges. Here, off the tourist track, the thick succulent leaves were virgin, unsullied by the loutish knives of lovers anxious to carve messages to tell the world that Darren and Kirsty were in love.

Two young bronzed farmers were loading gargantuan cauliflowers on to a lorry and we stopped to congratulate them on the bumper crop and sympathise with them on the eternal problems of sun and wind and rain and, even, a day earlier, the scourge of hailstones. Katy pointed to the small farmhouse, just behind them a little way off our road.

'Now, I can see where the Thanksgiving pie came from.' The flat roof of the building was completely covered with ripening pumpkins. Another couple of pics for Katy.

A Maltese family out for a walk joined in the conversation and, as we waved off the lorry, chatted to us about our holiday, while Katy admired the twin baby girls and took more photographs. The mother introduced herself as Mrs Rita Azzopardi and invited us to call on her at her home in Manikata. We told her we were out for a long walk to Golden Bay, but would take a rain check on her offer. Perhaps next week …

She told us to try the harder walk along the cliffs to the left and assured us it would be worth all the effort.

Her parting shot was 'Try and get to Mġarr – and if you ever reach the square, you must try the rabbit – the best on the island.'

We said Goodbye to her and her children at the crossroads and continued on our way. As we had neither pencil nor paper, we struggled to remember that home address she had given. It was so lengthy that Katy and I split it up and tried to memorise different parts of it.

The Pwales valley joins the bays of Xemxija and Għajn Tuffieħa and our road came to an end at a dilapidated hotel. To our right was Golden Bay, one of Malta's most popular beaches, overlooked by one of its most splendid hotels. But the path to the left along the cliffs offered, we had been assured by Mrs Azzopardi, the better experience. The narrow track slithered between rocks and bushes along to the outlandish geological shape of il-Karraba, the battleship.

We did as we had been told, trying not to look back until we reached our limit. But like Lot's wife, we peeked behind occasionally and found not Retribution, but inklings of the views to come.

When we came to il-Karraba, we sat and turned to look at Malta's most breathtaking natural panorama, Għajn Tuffieħa and Ġneyna Bay and, beyond the headlands to the north, the dramatic stark cliffs of Gozo. If Valletta is Malta's pièce de résistance as far as Man and Geography is concerned, this is Malta's tops for raw untouched nature. Forget the other contenders.

We sat close together, our legs over the cliff edge.

'It's my flight back home the day after tomorrow,' Katy announced.

The rocks a few hundred feet below suddenly looked more inviting than that devastating piece of intelligence.

'But you weren't going back until December.'

'But that is December.'

'You can't leave now. In the middle of things.'

'I know,' Katy nodded. 'I've decided to stay until next week. Things should be sorted out by then. That's when you go back, isn't it? I've changed my flight and I've told Megan. She understands and she'll explain to the folks.'

She must have been keeping Megan fully in the picture as far as our adventure was concerned.

'So Johnny, what are you going to do now that you've sorted out my life?' Katy asked.

I took some time to answer, taken aback at the sudden invitation to focus on something other than Katy, Dougie, Dante or anyone but myself.

'I'm going to finish *MacAbre*,' I replied decisively.

'And then?' Katy persisted.

'I'm going to look for a job.'

'And then what?'

The thrust and forcefulness of her nagging puzzled me. She didn't leave me in doubt for long.

'You're talented, amusing, intelligent, perceptive. You should be doing something more challenging than just bobbing from one job to another and sweeping up inferior writers' droppings.'

'What do you mean?'

'Well, have you thought of any serious writing? A novel. Or why not a film script?'

'Hold on,' I raised my hands defensively. 'I'm only twenty-seven.'

'I don't believe you said that! One day you'll be telling someone "I'm only forty-seven." Johnny, when you talk about Malta you give me a lump in the throat. But when you're like this, it's a pain in the ass! Don't you think that your Olga often says "I've wasted my talents, squandered my time. I should be doing better things than answering Johnny Smith's queries"?'

She didn't let go. 'Don't you think she would give anything to be twenty-seven again? I think I'm getting to know your weaknesses as well as your strengths, John Smith. If you're ever going to write a film script you should be thinking of it, no, writing it, now.'

I lobbed a stone out into the air and listened for it hitting the rocks below.

Katy was not going to give up. 'What about this goddam battle between the Turks and the Knights that you keep going on about? Has anyone ever made a film about it?'

I paused mid throw and mid thought. 'I don't think so.'

'You mean they haven't,' she insisted. 'Well, why don't you get off your butt and write a script before someone else comes on holiday and gets the inspiration.'

I gazed out over Għajn Tuffieħa, silver in the sun. She

167

had a point. I visualised the ideal starry cast for the three ageing protagonists, giants all. Omar Sharif as Sulieman the Magnificent, Sean Connery as the Grand Master, Oliver Reed would have been great as the wily Dragut had he not dropped dead in, by coincidence, a Valletta bar just a few months earlier. Or perhaps it could get one of the snazzy new animated treatments, like Prince of Egypt, which was billed in the Bugibba cinema, but we had not got around to seeing.

'Well?' Katy was not going to give up.

'It could work,' I admitted. 'There could even be a modern-day metaphor for the clash around the world between our Western Democracy and that Muslim Fundamentalism.'

'See, your mind's back in gear. It won't do that covering jumble sales – or even working on the Women's Page – for *Capital News*, will it? Megan – did I tell you she was a book editor with Flowerdew and Mead in Boston, but looking to get to New York – well, she said that all her authors are lazy and need to be bullied.'

She gave my arm a squeeze of encouragement, which made me feel, if only for a split second, capable of tackling an epic or two.

'Well, Johnny, now that I've sorted you out, promise me that when you get back home you won't forget all this.' She tickled my ribs playfully, forgetting the cliff face beneath our heels.

I promised, more to avoid plunging over – I lose all sense of control when I'm tickled – than any deep conviction that I would indeed tackle a film script.

'Now what do you say we find our way further up the rocks and over the top to Mġarr? We can get a bus from there.' We scrambled to the crest of the ridge.

'Mġarr. Famous for its oval dome …' I reeled off.

'I guess they made it that shape because it was the money

from the sale of eggs that financed it,' Katy interrupted, mocking my travelogue style. So she had been reading those books I gave her!

'… and for the best fried rabbit on Malta,' I added, knowing that that would guarantee me the last word.

The place offering the best fried rabbit on Malta was closed when we arrived at the door.

*

My luck was better back at the Seacrest. My first few Operation Claymore telephone calls were getting me nowhere and I was beginning to despair.

There was a welcome break when Guido Abela rang to tell me that Micallef had approved my plan. It was Green Light and All Systems Go.

That gave me fresh impetus with my own telephone calls. Suddenly a single contact produced a heaven-sent piece of intelligence. Two more calls and I could feel the log jam judder. My next-door neighbours and maybe even Saint Whatsisname must have heard my shout of triumph as I slammed down the phone in triumph. The Claymore had landed! Well, almost.

Chapter 18

Tuesday 30 November

After breakfast, I told Katy I had work to do. She was slightly offended, as she had shared in all of my activities up until then. I muttered something incomprehensible about new batteries for my laptop. And left for an address at Ta' Xbiex overlooking Lazzaretto Creek, on the Sliema side of Valletta. As some American once said, I had miles to go and promises to keep. Or words to that effect.

If the trip by bike to Ta' Xbiex was easy and pleasant in the morning sun, the return trip was nerve-racking. A breeze had blown up and the normal hazards of the road north were multiplied by the instability of the most unusual passenger clinging to my back. Nevertheless I made it back to the hotel and carried my burden self-consciously through reception to the lift. Fortunately, there was no sign of Katy. She would certainly not believe that my bulky package contained batteries for a laptop.

The hours to dinner passed slowly, like some wheezing snail. But eventually, I was out of the shower and applying, for the first time since its ineffective premiere, the magic potion that was Endymion. This time there would be no Thanksgiving to upstage me. Saint Whatsisname would have a doughty helper in the shape of the colleague whose night it was - Saint Andrew.

I had specifically made a date with Katy for dinner and had even asked her, to her puzzlement, to wear her Thanksgiving suit. After all, I needed someone on my arm for my entrance.

I knocked at the door of her room. 'Coming!' she called. She came quickly out, without really paying any attention to me, looking stunning, chattering cheerfully and turning away to lock the door behind her. She turned back and stared and was, for a brief, glorious second, silent.

'Oh my God, a kilt!'

To be accurate, it was in the fact the full outfit, black jacket with silver buttons, crisp white jabot, furry sporran, sgian dhu, laced black shoes and thick cream socks giving my legs an unwarranted hint of the necessary muscularity.

It had taken me ages to track down the outfit, starting with the Scottish Church in Valletta and relentlessly progressing from one contact to another. Saint Whatsisname must have intervened again for I discovered that, as recently as the last weekend, the unfortunate demise of one of the committee members of the Saint Andrew's Society had meant that a Highland outfit was going to be advertised for sale in the club's next newsletter.

I could not afford the asking price for the full kit, but I rang one Eric Brydon, a friend of the deceased, lumbered with selling the outfit. I suggested he might like to hire it to me for a day and swell the Club's funds. He took some persuading but eventually saw the sense of it.

All it needed then had been for me to pick it up from his house, strap the box to my back and get back to the Seacrest in one piece. That's me in one piece, not the outfit, as it was much more bulky and less aerodynamic than my usual pillion passenger and the ride home had included a number of hair-raising moments.

OK, so it didn't fit perfectly and it was not the tartan of my own Clanchattan – the Smiths and my mother's family, the Roses, both belonged to that famous warring confederation led by the Mackintosh of Mackintosh. It was however the even more flamboyant Old Buchanan, not numbered among the many sworn enemies of my own clan so I felt no guilt in wearing it. But I did feel that Seb would not have worn it if he had had red hair.

'Does this mean we get to see you dancing?' Katy asked, eyes shining.

'This is not something just for dancing. This is my national dress, proud, distinctive and worthy of any occasion,' I enlightened her.

She suddenly stopped.

'My God, the camera!'

She ran back to her room and within seconds was clicking away with that machine of hers.

'Now for our public appearance,' Katy joked, linking my arm. 'I never thought I'd get to be escorted by something out of *Braveheart*. Aren't you supposed to paint your face blue?'

'You don't deserve this honour, you tasteless Colonial,' I replied. 'I've a good mind to go and find someone else.'

She held on to my arm even more tightly. 'Golly, if only I'd had an entrance like this at the Prom back home. But better late than never. Lead on, Macduff.' I didn't correct the quote.

She found it impossible to walk into the dining room without something half way between an embarrassed blush and an uncontrollable giggle. But she did enjoy it. And so did Bonnie, who actually cried for some reason known only to her. Sadie contributed the opinion that we made a lovely couple and offered to take a photograph of us with Katy's camera. The rest of our friends cheered and whistled – and the Germans joined in. The Germans always join in.

In one respect I had failed. The only haggis supply on the island was being devoured at that very moment at the British High Commission. I had, however, bought tapes of stirring Scottish music and wistful Highland love-songs – and Mr Joseph had been happy to play them over the music system.

No orchids, but I had begged, borrowed or stolen from the High Commission dinner enough lucky white heather to deliver in the most chivalrous Highland manner I could muster not just to Katy but to Sadie, Bonnie and three attractive Bavarian frauleins at the next table. All of them asked the old question about sartorial underwear practices in the Highlands. I told the British the truth – and lied to the Bavarians, who tittered, un-Teutonically.

An impartial observer would say USA 1, Scotland 1. If only I could have persuaded the man with the bagpipes to make the one-and-a-half-hour round trip from Valletta to Mellieħa, it would have been 2-1 to me.

My self-satisfaction was short-lived. Just as long as the pudding course, to be precise.

'Well done, laddie. You've done us proud.' An unwelcome hand ruffled my hair, irritatingly. I had no need to turn around for the euphoria to turn to trepidation. I had no need, but I did.

I could have kicked myself. In the knee-jerk response to Seb and his Thanksgiving, in my overweening need to impress Katy, I had forgotten all about Dougie and Gus and my low profile. At meal times, the two men always sat in the smoking area of the restaurant, hidden from civilisation by potted tropical flora. They were usually out of sight and out of mind. Now they were neither.

Dougie stood next to me, puffing on a large cigar, behind him the brooding hulk of Gus, like some distorted shadow in the background.

Both men had also made some acknowledgement of the national day. Dougie was wearing a smart navy blazer, with an appropriate striped tie bearing some heraldic thistles and looked for all the world like the secretary of a fashionable Edinburgh golf club. Gus on the other hand was kitted out in a less bourgeois combination based around a garish tartan bow-tie and a voluminous green tweed jacket which may have boosted the business of the Scottish textile industry, but looked more suited to a New York St Patrick's Day parade.

'You'll take a dram with us?' Dougie said. The question mark was rhetorical.

'Why, yes, of course,' I replied, trying to drum up the
173

enthusiasm which would have been there had it not been for images of the disjointed Norman and of Dante trussed up in some Leith basement.

'And the young lady?'

'Sure, that's a nice idea.' Katy even managed to sound flattered by the invitation.

So our Saint Andrew's Night ended as I had never expected it to, sitting drinking large Glenfiddichs, the only malt in the bar, with Katy alongside me – that bit at least had been on the original agenda – but accompanied by Dougie and Gus.

What was it that our very own bard had to say about mice and men and schemes?

The conversation was unreal, but to be fair, Dougie was relaxed and amusing company. He had introduced himself and Gus, just using first names – and their real ones at that – and we had responded in kind.

He spoke in a very friendly manner to Katy, telling us of his holiday the previous year in Florida. She had been to the same resort of Clearwater and they swapped tales of Disney World. It would have been interesting to have seen Katy alongside another Snow White, I thought. I pictured the pair of them, surrounded by dwarfs. I've always had the ability to daydream no matter what's going on around me, in the style of Danny Kaye in Walter Mitty.

Dougie interrupted the dream. 'I didna ken you were Scottish, Johnny. I thought I heard you speaking German in the lift. Although Gus reckoned you were Scottish. He said no German would wear a Hearts top.'

'I was just trying to be friendly with them,' I explained.

'Friends! Wi' that lot?' The restricted contributions from Gus tended towards the monosyllabic and the dogmatic. 'They'd have been all over the bloody island years ago if we hadn't stopped them!' He gave the impression that he had personally co-ordinated the anti-aircraft defences of Valletta throughout the War.

'Someone said you were from Edinburgh,' Dougie continued, 'but that's a Highland accent.'

'Yes, Glenbraith, just inland from Aberdeen.'

'And what do you do in Edinburgh?'

'I'm a waiter.' I'd thought out a cover story, as I certainly wasn't going to jog their memories by mentioning newspapers. Beneath the table I crossed my fingers, hoping that whoever had mentioned Edinburgh had said nothing about journalism.

'Oh, Gus and I eat out regularly with the wives. Which restaurant?'

'Oh, here and there, I haven't found a full-time job yet. Generally American or Tex-Mex.'

'Not our scene at all, no offence, Katy,' Dougie said, smiling winningly at Katy and actually having the effrontery to pat her on the knee! 'We tend to go for the Italian or French. And of course down in Leith we have every kind of restaurant you could think of.'

To my surprise, he then handed me a visiting card! God, perhaps everything was above board after all. Criminals don't usually hand out visiting cards. It was as if the friendly Scots were real and Norman and Dante just players in a mad nightmare.

'If you've any difficulty getting a job, laddie, give me a bell. I know quite a few people in the trade. A number of them owe me.'

Dougie turned to chat to Katy, leaving me to make conversation with Gus. I had been right in identifying the green of his shell-suit on that first coach trip, confirmed by the colour of his present jacket. He was indeed a Hibernian fan, which explained his ability to spot my rival Hearts insignia at twenty paces.

We swapped incidents from a decade or so of local derbies and traded the usual insults, although, in deference to his age and size, I held back some of the more provocative. Gus was less inhibited. And to crown the evening, Dougie called over the attentive Wilfred from behind the bar and got him to take an all-pals-together photograph of the four of us. It took Katy five minutes to explain the workings of her camera, but I was sure the end result would be good enough to be used against me in a court of law.

Katy eventually rescued us by contriving a few stage yawns and, as we had bought a second, payback round, that was a good enough cue to leave the two men and make our way to our rooms. We both got out of the lift at Katy's floor. There was no way we could go our separate ways without unwinding the coiled springs of that unscheduled encounter.

Katy flopped onto the large settee on the landing, a hint that we were not going to do so in her room.

'Oh boy, was that or was that not unbelievable?' she said, slightly tipsily. 'And that man Dougie was so … normal … Do you know, his wife, was it Maisie, has dozens and dozens of Boston Pops recordings, the old Arthur Fiedler classical orchestra pieces? That's what they listen to at home in front of the fire. And he genuinely seemed to be missing her. If I hadn't known what I know, it would have been a pleasant enough evening.'

'Well, I don't want to have another "pleasant enough evening", thank you,' I said.

We sat there, not speaking, just relaxing. Katy held my hand.

After a while, she stood up. 'Thank you for the Scottish thing. That was a super surprise.' She smiled widely. 'And that ending?' she mocked. 'You should be a film producer. Who would have thought of Scotch on the Rocks with the hoods for the final scene!'

I winced. Rocks! Hoods! Katy was herself again.

'Goodnight, Johnny. I'll see you when I see you!'

'Does that mean a date for breakfast?'

'Don't push it, Braveheart.'

We kissed and went our separate ways.

Chapter 19
Wednesday 1 December'

If the evening was, well, memorable, the following morning got off to an equally unusual start. I was accosted on the way to breakfast by a tall, red-faced German in his late forties. He had been lying in wait. The early exchanges established that he was from Weimar, in the former East Germany. This explained his lack of English, as a couple of generations in that part of the country had been given Russian to make do with as a second language. At first he told me that his name was Mueller, but then seemed to change his mind and say it was Schneider.

I was confused. He wanted something from me, that much at least was clear. He kept holding his palm upwards and rubbing his thumbs across his fingertips, the universal mime for payment, but I could not fathom out what it was all about.

Help came in the curvaceous shapes of the Bavarians from the previous evening. Their English was as crisp as their blouses and within seconds they had made everything clear. Herr Muller was his name, Schneider was his profession – he was a tailor. And he wanted to buy my Highland dress!

Via the Munich Three, I explained that the kilt and all the trimmings were probably for sale and quoted him the figure in the newsletter plus a little to cover my agent's fee!

He scribbled down some calculations on the menu card and seemed happy with the deutschemark equivalent, reaching eagerly for his wallet. Maybe I should have asked for more. I told him to go into breakfast and I would come back with an answer.

Before I could rush off, one of the young girls translated an urgent question. 'Does your price include the little knife in the sock?'

I assured her that it did and wrote down its name phonetically for the beaming Herr Muller: 'sgian du'. He repeated it after me, again and again.

A quick sprint back to my room, a phone call to Eric Brydon, who was all too happy to be able to tick off another of the many tasks piled on him by the death of his friend and in minutes I was back with the muesli-munching Herr Muller. In a trice the deal was done.

After breakfast, he paid me in Maltese lire and I handed over the bulky cardboard box, leaving to the enterprising tailor the task of dealing with excess baggage and getting the sgian dhu past the metal detectors.

I put the Maltese banknotes in an envelope and addressed it to Mr Brydon. Abbie at Reception helpfully offered to pop it up to the Mellieħa Post Office on her way home at lunchtime and register the mailing.

And all that meant that, instead of a tiresome and hazardous drive to Ta' Xbiex with a large box strapped to my back, I could contemplate a morning with Katy. She had been puzzled to watch my strange negotiations from the other side of the breakfast room. I told her all about it.

'You mean you actually charged him more than you will be paid? It's people like you who give the Scots that reputation!'

I protested. 'I had to cover my costs. The drive to and from Brydon's. The registered envelope and stamp. Besides, the outfit will be worth a fortune in Germany. The ...'

'Qui s'excuse, s'accuse,' she said, laughing, in an unusual display of Massachusetts erudition. She took my arm and we walked to the front of the hotel to study the weather.

We stood leaning against the pillars, trying to decide how to spend the morning.

'We could walk up the crossroads and then go off to the headland on the left,' Katy pointed across the bay to the Red Tower on what, since our pigeon-fancier episode, I thought of

179

as the 'other' side of the Marfa Ridge.

'Or we could take the bike down to the south west. We've not really done that part.' I suggested.

'Or we could go over to the Craft Village. I've still got a couple of presents to buy.'

Our indecision evaporated with the arrival of Sam and Sadie, Sid and Bonnie, who had no doubts as to what their morning held.

'Come on, join us,' Bonnie insisted, sweeping us into the group as if we were wayward schoolchildren. 'You've been neglecting us these last few days. We're just off to Selmun Palace for a little walk.'

A five-minute bus trip took us high up beyond Mellieħa and we were soon making our way down a very steep and narrow path, enjoying the greenery that the winter rains had brought to the usually sun-shrivelled earth of the island. The fields were alive with masses of yellow wild flowers. 'Cape sorrel,' Bonnie declared, 'Oxalis something,' Sadie insisted, 'and all those little white flowers are related to alyssum.' The only contribution I was able to make was to identify the dandelions.

We straggled along the tiny deserted Mistra Bay and across the flat rocks to get the closest possible view of the pair of rocks that had holed Saint Paul's ship and forced him to take refuge on the island.

It was a pleasant hour or so. As the difficult path forced us into groups, I landed up at the rear with Bonnie, making sure she kept up with our more athletic friends. Katy, just in front of us with Sam, was in her most carefree mood and prettier than ever. I found myself looking at her with all the fondness of that first meeting between the pillars in Mosta, but now perhaps with a touch of sadness. I glanced away to see that Bonnie was regarding me with an expression which showed none of her usual bouncy optimism. We said nothing.

A scramble back up to the heights and we were soon at

Selmun Palace for a coffee and sandwich, before making our way back to the Seacrest.

We still had a fine afternoon to fill and Katy and I took the Kawasaki on a whistle-stop tour of those parts of island we had still to explore, from the most remote bays to the highest crags, from the Chadwick Lakes (ponds, really) to Dingli and beyond. But, from time to time, long silences showed that not even all that frantic activity could push thoughts of Dante from our minds. Or maybe, beyond Dante, that other traumatic D-word - Departure.

*

That evening after dinner, we received a surprise visitor. I was sitting in the lounge of the Seacrest, chatting to Katy when suddenly her animated expression – she was recounting a tale of office horseplay – changed to one of apprehension as she spotted something or someone behind me. I turned abruptly and my first impression was that Gus was at my shoulder again. It was in fact thae equally bulky Guido Abela.

He quickly calmed Katy's apprehension. 'Don't worry, Miss Mifsud, I'm just here to keep you in the picture. Nothing to worry your pretty head about.'

He also read my concerns. 'Our greedy friends are not here, Mr Smith. They are enjoying the noisier attractions of Marco's Bar up the hill. I've had a man keeping a close eye on them. Believe me, they don't go for a ...' He broke off and looked uncomfortably at Katy. 'They don't go for a walk without me knowing about it.'

Katy, who had completed the sentence for herself, smiled. 'No need to adjust your words for me, Mr Abela.'

Embarrassed, the security chief took a seat at our table, declined a glass from our bottle of white wine, but ordered instead a large bottle of fizzy Irish mineral water from springs not far from Katy's other ancestral roots. He reported that all his side of the arrangements was in place and gave us a detailed schedule of Friday's plans, including an address and a map showing the warehouse in Msida where we were to meet.

'The van delivery is expected at eleven. The Scotsmen have said they will be there just before that. My men will be expecting you. You should be there by ten to be safe, but keep an eye out for their little white car. They would be most surprised to see you two in that part of Malta.'

He produced a very efficient looking checklist and went through my own requirements in great detail.

He quickly finished his mineral water and, with a hurried 'Bonswa', was gone.

His enthusiasm had been infectious and his meticulous planning had made both of us feel more confident of success than ever. There were still worrying permutations. But, against all the odds, I slept well that night.

Chapter 20

Thursday 2 December

The day before D-Day, Dante-Day, Katy and I were at the front of the Seacrest ready to cross over to the beach for some sunbathing when I noticed Dougie and Gus set off in the Renault.

'I've got a great idea, Katy. The coast is clear. Why don't we sneak into their room and see if we can pick up any clues?'

'You'll never get into their room and in any case what do you mean by clues. We have all the information we need.'

She was right but I felt it was a chance not to be missed. 'Well, there could be something to tell us where Dante is being kept. That must be worth something.'

She didn't seem convinced. 'Well, I'm off to sunbathe on the balcony and write to Megan. Why don't you get down to some of that *MacAbre* thing.'

She flounced off, leaving me at the front door.

I was sure it could show her just how wrong she was. Back on the top floor where Dougie and Gus stayed, the room-maids were hard at work and, glory be, one was just finishing in the very room where according to my calculations the two villains had left vital clues. I smiled at the girl, rattled my keys and went into the room, closing the door behind me.

Five minutes later, I was rapidly coming to the conclusion that Katy was absolutely right. The room seemed to contain nothing but the impedimenta of the genuine tourist. No bags marked Swag, no incriminating letters, no Polaroids of a gagged Maltese hostage in a Leith cellar. I had reached the last drawer, containing what looked like nothing more than an array of flamboyant boxer shorts capable of providing shelter for a group of Cub Scouts, when I was hit by two simultaneous blows – the sight of a gun at the bottom of the drawer and the

183

sound of a key turning in the lock.

I closed the drawer and in panic fled to the balcony. A huge towel was drying on one of the white plastic chairs and I squeezed behind it.

'Well, that's the car washed and sparkling for the ladies.' Dougie seemed pleased with himself.

'Where is this place where you're going to play cards, Dougie?'

'Bridge, Dougie, bridge, no one calls it cards. Over in the big Thomson hotel at the other side of the bay.'

'Can I come and watch?'

'It's bridge not poker, Gus. Spectators not invited. I'm off to pick up Mrs Carstairs and her friend. We'll be back in a couple of hours. Why don't you have a kip? Look, you've left the bloody windaes open again, Gus.'

Dougie sounded annoyed as he closed the sliding doors over and then pulled across the curtains. The sound of the voices was deadened by the double-glazing. I listened for a few moments and just made out the door slamming closed. I assumed that it was Dougie leaving. Had Gus taken his advice and lain down for a nap? There was no way of knowing and in any case the balcony doors could not be opened from the outside.

I was really caught as Katy had predicted. Katy! I squeezed out from behind the towel and peered over to Katy's room on the side at right angles to the balcony where I was trapped. Sure enough she was there, sipping mineral water and scribbling away.

There was no way I could shout or make any sound that would attract her attention. I waved, but her back was to me.

I looked around the tiny balcony for inspiration and found it in the unlikely guise of two pairs of white socks. I rolled up one sock and shied it as hard as I could in the direction of

184

Katy. It caught on an intervening balcony and dropped silently to the floor below. The second attempt was no better. I tried a lob with the third sock and it worked. The 'snowball' fell just in front of Katy. I could see her involuntary jump from where I crouched.

She turned and looked astonished to see me there. I pointed into the room and mimed a sleeping Gus, describing a large globe with my hands and then resting my head on them.

Katy nodded and assumed that frown that always signified thought with her. I don't know what I expected her to do, but what she did was leave the balcony in a hurry.

I waited for seemed like an eternity for her to return to the balcony and let me know what she was doing. She never did come back into sight, but eventually I heard the blaring sound of the hotel fire alarm. I thought of those fellow holidaymakers we had once threatened with sunburn on the balcony. Now I was to be carbonised and all for a stupid desire to impress Katy, well to prove her wrong.

I was peering over the balcony assessing my chances of dropping on to the balcony below and so on until I reached the floor level, when the doors slid back. 'Come on, quickly. We must join the others and give some semblance of believing there's a real fire.' I kissed Katy hard and followed her out to the corridor and down into the staircase.

We were the last to arrive in the assembly point outside the hotel. As we approached our fellow holidaymakers, the resourceful Katy held my arm tightly, adjusted the top of her bikini with the other hand and fluttered her eyelashes convincingly.

'No need to ask what you two were up to when the alarm went!' Bonnie shared her scandalous observations with the crowd.

'No,' I protested, 'we were just …'

My protestations were cut off by Guido announcing that it

185

had been a false alarm and that we could all return to the hotel.

Last out, but first back. I whispered to Katy. 'That alarm was a miracle.'

'You underestimate me, Mr Smith. The alarm was no miracle, what was a miracle was that Gus left so speedily and didn't bother to close the door.'

I could not believe it. What a girl. She had saved me and all I could do in return was to tell her about the gun.

The least I could do was make the rest of the day memorable. 'Let's go on a jaunt – and I'll buy you a Thank You drink.'

'Great idea.'

Katy and I crossed over to Gozo by ferry to see Malta's greener and less tourist-bound neighbour. The island is small and compact, but we still needed the Kawasaki to get to all the interesting bits. From the harbour we made directly for Victoria, the main town set in the very centre of the island. There we marvelled at its stepped citadel and the cathedral within the great walls, a very dramatic example of the Maltese ingenuity. The congregation, strapped for cash, had not been able to afford a dome, but a wily artist, perhaps the same one who had fooled us at the Manoel Theatre, had painted another staggering trompe l'oeil which converted a flat roof on the outside into what looked like a very convincing dome to the worshippers inside.

It had missed the whole point. These breathtaking village churches are intended to tell the outside world of the inhabitants' wealth and generosity and not just fool the worshippers.

Xewkija, on the way from the ferry, showed the right approach. Its gigantic rotunda, whisper it not on Malta, is slightly larger even than Mosta's (only on the inside not on the outside, shout the Mosta folk) and it can be seen from all over Gozo and from much of Malta.

We rode to the pre-historic sites of Xagħra and Ġgantija

and to the quaint hill villages. We saw the natural wonders of Ramla Bay, of the inland-sea, of the Azure Window and of the Fungus Rock, whose red vegetation was held to cure the most life-threatening wounds of the Knights Hospitaller. And we missed the last ferry.

There was nothing to it but to stay the night on Gozo. Katy reacted with a tetchiness that took me by surprise. Did she believe it was a put-up job? I protested and brandished my timetable in vain. There should have been a ferry. It wasn't my fault that the sea was rough. Not only would she not share a room. She would not even stay in the same hotel.

Well, at first.

But we found a small, cheerful looking hotel, the Hippocampo, high above the ferry. At the reception desk there was not the usual brass bell, but a gleaming sea-horse knocker. We knocked. An apple-cheeked, motherly lady appeared.

'Do you have a room?' we chimed in unison.

I stepped back and gestured gallantly towards Katy.

'A room, please. Just for tonight.'

The lady, Doris Camillieri, proprietor, if her name badge was to be believed, looked from Katy to me.

'Another room, please. Just for tonight.'

'Two rooms?' she queried, eyebrows raised.

'Yes,' we chorused.

She sighed and handed Katy a key. 'Room Three.'

She looked at me and reached for the key to Room Four, thought better of it and gave me another from a different row. 'Room Twelve.'

She pointed along a corridor for Katy and up a flight of stairs for me.

'Let's meet back here in half an hour,' I suggested hesitantly.

Katy thought for some time and then nodded. She made no attempt to hide the fact that she viewed the prospect with little relish.

We met as arranged and Katy had thawed considerably.

'Sorry about the snappy bit,' she said, slipping her arm into mine as we set off in search of somewhere to eat.

We didn't have to endure a blustery wind and some painful hailstones for long as we found a cosy restaurant, the Crow's Nest, just fifty yards from the hotel. From its elevated warmth, we looked down to the cold waves crashing on to the breakwater.

'What if we can't get back to Malta for the showdown?' Katy worried.

The waiter looked to be a local man with some decades of experience of the weather.

'Any chance of the ferry sailing tomorrow morning?' I asked.

'No problem. It will have calmed down in the next few hours. I know these storms. I was a fisherman, before the knees went.' We both looked automatically at his knees. They were still there. We sniggered behind our menus, like children in church.

'Believe me, you'll have no trouble with the ferry tomorrow morning.'

Reassured, we focused more purposefully on the menu.

Over the meal, we deliberately avoided all talk of the following day. It gave us a chance to explore those few corners of each other's lives, which had been missed out in the many chats we'd had together over the past weeks.

At one point the couple at the next table, the only other diners, finished their coffee and got up to leave. They were well into their seventies and both of them courteously asked after our enjoyment of the meal and bade us 'Bonswa'.

We watched them as they made their way to the door, their hands linked affectionately. Katy and I exchanged glances but no words. I was thinking of the Burns' 'John Anderson, my jo' and she perhaps of those words 'growing old together,' which she once mentioned when talking about Seb.

Katy looked especially relaxed in the subdued light, the candles in their pale blue Phoenician glass globes giving her eyes a luminous, turquoise colour I had never seen in them before.

She laced her fingers, stretched out her arms, cat-like, and sighed. 'If anyone had told me a year ago, that I'd be here on Malta, in the middle of this adventure, I would have told them it was just hogwash. It's been an unforgettable month.'

I had to agree. 'And to think that when Don Blaikie suggested this was the way to complete *MacAbre* without interruption, I believed him!'

'I wonder just what we'll all be doing this time next year,' she murmured. I looked at her. Her time machine had already taken her there. She was dreaming of a distant happiness and I had no illusions whatsoever. John Smith was not a part of it.

'Oh, since I established my cover as a waiter with Dougie, I'm beginning to take to the role. I expect I shall be serving champagne to some rich kids at a wedding reception.'

Katy was angry. 'I told you once before you can be a goddam pain in the ass at times. You just never give anything away about yourself, Johnny. All these quips and put-downs, facts and figures, they're all diversions. To keep folk – us – away from the real John Smith.'

'But that's how conversation goes, people like it, they all do it,' I protested.

'No, no, no, they don't. Not all the time, day after day, week after week. I think we've become very close over the past few weeks, but while I've been pouring out my heart, you've been pouring out your head.'

She looked at me very intently. 'You've meant a great deal to me. I thought this was a great idea, this return to my roots. I came because I really thought it would work. No, that's not true, because I wanted it to work. And now I believe it has done. I know it has done.'

She was finding this bit difficult. 'But I know, too, that it would never ever have turned out like this without you.'

The sea-green eyes had never looked lovelier. 'Now what about you?' she continued with surprising force. 'Where do you go from here? Who is going to do for you what you have done for me? To be to you what Seb is to me?'

I shrugged. There was not much else to do. That she of all people should ask that question. Those questions.

'I'll sort myself out,' I mumbled.

'I don't just mean your career. I've told you where I stand there. I think, I hope, you will get down to that. It's the rest of your life I'm interested in.' She leaned over and kissed me on the cheek.

'Did you refuse to open up to Tandy? Were you the same with her as you seem to be with everyone else? Was that your problem?'

'We had no problem,' I said, irritably.

I was saved by the waiter coming over to point out of the window to the palm trees on the other side of the road and to show us how much the wind had dropped.

The respite didn't last long. Katy returned to the fray, pulling no punches. 'Were you in love with Tandy?'

'I was very … attached … to her. Too attached. It made me feel … exposed, vulnerable.'

'And was it because you felt vulnerable that you couldn't

tell her what she meant to you?'

'She knew how I felt.'

'Are you sure?'

I looked directly into Katy's eyes. 'Do you know how I feel about you?'

Katy looked bewildered. 'Of course, I do. We're … well, very good friends.'

'If that's what you think, then I admit I may have been wrong with Tandy, too.' I was harsher than I had ever been with Katy. 'I thought she understood, without having to tell her. Just as I thought you would know without getting me to spell it out for you.'

I waited for her to reply. She didn't. She sat there without speaking. It was a Katy I did not know. Her eyes were sad, perplexed. There seemed little point in searching for a fresh topic of conversation, so, two hours, some fine Maltese dishes and a bottle of Special Reserve after entering the Crow's Nest, we exchanged Bonswas with the meteorological waiter and walked in silence back to the hotel. As our pundit had predicted, the wind had dropped, the storm was over.

I suggested a drink at the bar, but Katy was on edge and declared that she was anxious to get what she described as 'beauty sleep'. They were the only words she'd spoken since we left the Crow's Nest.

We agreed to set our watches' alarms for seven in the morning and give ourselves plenty of time to catch a ferry that would get us to Msida in good time for the showdown.

I had noticed an unusual array of malt whiskies in the bar. It was the cue for a double Laphroaig and a bit of crack with the barman Sandro who had lived in Scotland for three years and was responsible for the whisky shelf.

Not even that most aggressive of all Scotch malts could help me shrug off thoughts of the encounter with Douglas

191

and Graham. If things went wrong, the fault would be mine. I had persuaded Micallef to change his plans. Yes, he had gone along with the whole idea, but I could not avoid the knowledge that I was responsible for any failure.

I found my way up to Room Twelve and sat at the foot of the bed.

I held my chin in my hands and my mind turned to Katy. Would I ever touch those breasts or must my mind alone tell me they are soft, murmur they are smooth, whisper they are warm? Would my eyes ever see her shiver to my touch? Would I ever have memories or would I always have to make do with imaginings?

'Are you never coming to bed?'

The voice was followed by toes wrinkling in my back through the bedclothes.

I turned slowly in disbelief. There, peering over the bedclothes, were those Celtic eyes underneath the thick, black Moorish curls.

'Bet you're wondering how I got here?' the voice came through the bedclothes. 'I explained to Mrs Camillieri. Lovers' tiff. She was … very sympathetic … and let me borrow her key. I said we'd pay for both rooms.'

I am one of the old school, cherishing those films when the sin in cinema was imagined and not flaunted, when the Hays Code ruled and when the only hump you would see was on the back of Lon Chaney, Charles Laughton, Anthony Quinn or Laurence Olivier. I'm not into sweaty gymnastics and sound effects more suited to labour than conception, so I close the metaphoric bedroom door and, in true Hollywood style, leave images of log fires crackling in the hearth, snow capped mountains probing the skies, lightning flashes turning the black clouds to silver, chandeliers winking from the ceiling.

And believe me, none of them does full justice to what went on behind that door.

192

Chapter 21
Friday 3 December

'There is a Divinity that shapes our ends,' observed the Southern Bard. If he was right, the Divinity was on fine form when he was working on Katy. The thought came to mind as I watched her shimmer off to the shower, the morning light capturing her outline and putting to flight forever all memory of Liz Taylor's waddle-on part in Dr Faustus.

Katy was half singing, half humming the Wannadies song 'You and me'. I had never heard her sing before. I felt curiously uplifted.

We had slept later than we had intended. Whatever happened to those alarm watches? A frantic look out of the hotel window showed us, far below, the good ship Cittadella leaving Gozo for Malta. Its sister ship would already be on its way in the opposite direction.

Decisions, decisions! If we were to catch it, we had to choose. Breakfast or shower? We both agreed to a shower, but Katy turned down my perfectly sensible suggestion that showering together would save time. She seemed to think it would have the opposite effect.

We showered, separately, brushed aside Mrs Camillieri's tempting offer of breakfast, paid our bills and set off for the ferry in clothes which, if not fresh, were at least not slept in.

We caught it with time to spare and Katy even remembered to take some photographs of the harbour, as pretty as, well, a picture, in the silvery morning sun. As she leaned across the ship's rail, the motor drive on her camera buzzing, I looked over her shoulder and noticed that the Crow's Nest restaurant was in her sights and there was even a glimpse of the upper floors, the bedrooms, of Mrs Camilleri's little hotel. I wondered if she would explain the significance of that view to the loyal Megan.

We had coffee aboard, along with some wickedly sticky buns, a Maltese speciality, and made good time to Cirkewwa. With the sea still sporting a noticeable swell, it took the skipper some time to manoeuvre the large ferryboat into the quayside there.

There was also a frustrating delay in getting off the boat. Some police divers were near the jetty, manhandling a black inflatable into the water alongside the ferry. "Inspecting the hull, a regular check," claimed the apologetic Tannoy.

But despite the hold-up, we were still well on schedule to make the Msida rendezvous. On the road south, we passed by the front door of our hotel but there was no time to stop and get a change of clothing. With a stiff wind at our backs, we were at the harbour area well in advance of the planned showdown with Dougie and Gus.

Guido's carefully drawn map took us straight to the small, neglected warehouse. With no bell or knocker in evidence, I rattled the large corroded letterbox. A narrow sliding window opened and a pair of dark eyes checked us out. The door swung up and we were hurried in. The door fell back and was re-locked. Three hefty Maltese men in their thirties were expecting us and, thankfully, Abela's description must have tallied with what they saw before them, even given our dishevelled appearance. A small, bent man, wearing a large surgical boot, left his desk in a small makeshift wooden cubicle and limped across to check out the latest intruders on his privacy, complaining in Maltese. His loose, ill-fitting grey overalls marked him out as the storeman.

'We've just heard from the boss,' the only talkative member of the trio told us, waving a mobile phone in explanation. 'Everything has gone to plan and the shipment has been taken aboard. The papers are being filled in and he expects the van to be here in thirty minutes or so.'

He sat down at a rickety table and motioned to us to do the same. He pushed over two bottles of cold Kinnie. Despite the coolness of the morning, our mouths were arid with anticipation and we welcomed even the medicinal tang of Malta's answer to Coke, IrnBru and Dandelion and Burdock.

Twenty minutes or so later, one of the men posted at the door called us over to his spy-hole. He looked out, turned and called softly.

'A car's just pulled up. Are these the two guys we're looking for?'

I peered out and saw the white hatchback with the black windows in the shadow of a dry-docked boat. I nodded.

'Like good bad-men, they came early, eh?'

I nodded again, although the precise meaning of the remark was lost on me.

It was another ten minutes before the van arrived, the Scots making no sign of leaving the cover of their car. Micallef's car was following the van. He stepped out briskly, came over to the door and knocked. The storeman opened it, slowly and with considerable mutterings, relating no doubt to his hard lot. We had by then moved well out of sight behind a stack of pallets, a narrow gap between them giving us a clear view of the open area.

Micallef called out to the van driver and his assistant, who staggered in with eight packages carrying posters stuck on the outside to indicate the contents. They put these down on a pallet and the storeman, still complaining, signed the delivery notes and gave one of the copies back to the two men. Micallef jovially handed them a couple of Maltese banknotes, slapped them on the back with a cheerful joke and sent them on their way. He came in and closed the door behind him. As far as the watching villains were concerned, the warehouse contained only Dante Micallef's father, an old storeman who posed no problems – and £2 million pounds.

I was surprised to find Abela suddenly at my side. There must have been a second door at the rear of the building that

I had not noticed. He motioned to the three men, who took up their positions nearer the pallet but still well out of sight. He sent Katy and me to the very back of the store insisting that we should play no part in the proceedings.

There was a knock at the door. Micallef went to the spy-hole and looked out. He opened the door and let in Dougie and Gus. They were carrying two very large suitcases, with an ease that suggested they were empty. Through the gap in the bales I could see the two look furtively around the small warehouse. Abela had chosen it well. It seemed to have no potential for hidden surprises.

'Here it is,' Micallef said, kicking the pallet as if in annoyance. 'Do you want to count the notes?'

'No, but I would like to see them.' By the sound of his voice Dougie was salivating.

Micallef shrugged. 'Which bundle?'

Dougie pointed to the one nearest him. 'I trust you, Mr Micallef. This one will do.'

Micallef picked it up and laid it on the table from which, I was pleased to see, our Kinnie bottles had been thoughtfully removed. He took out a small pocketknife and cut through the stout white string. He carefully unfolded the packaging and revealed rows and rows of brand new £50 notes.

The storeman stopped playing with his nose and stared in total bewilderment. He had not been privy to this part of the plan.

Dougie picked up a bundle and broke the paper band holding it. He studied the top note carefully, removed it, turned it over and looked at the reverse. He held it up to the single skylight to check the watermark as keenly as any Rose Street barman.

'Marvellous, bloody marvellous,' he said hoarsely.

'I've delivered my side, shouldn't you be arranging to

release Dante or at least to let me talk to him?' Micallef looked directly at Douglas.

'Come, come, Mr Micallef, you don't take me for a fool. It will take me a couple of days to get rid of all these. When I have done so, of course you'll get your son back.'

'Can I speak to him, then?'

Douglas sighed, took out his mobile phone and dialled a string of numbers. It took some time before anyone answered. There were no niceties. 'Put on the Maltese.' After perhaps twenty or thirty seconds, he gave the phone to Micallef.

'Dante, my boy. You'll be with us soon. I've given these men all they've asked. Are you well? Keep up your courage …'

Douglas took the phone back. 'Get off the line and put my man back on.' Pause. 'Everything's going to plan. I'll call you tonight. Usual time. You know what to do if I don't.' He switched off the phone and turned to Micallef to let these words sink in.

The storeman gazed, uncomprehending, from one to the other.

Micallef spoke, coldly. 'It is only right you should see the money that you have taken so much trouble to obtain and which you will never be able to touch.'

Dougie and Gus heard the figurative panic alarms at the same time and turned around instinctively.

Abela and his men were upon them. Dougie put up only a token struggle. In his prime he would have proved more of a handful. Gus put up much more of a fight. He savagely punched to the ground the first man to reach him and, with an agility surprising in a man of his weight and shape, made for Micallef and grabbed him. The Scot produced from somewhere the gun I had seen hidden in the sock drawer and pointed it threateningly at Micallef's head.

The odds were suddenly reversed. Gus had his arm firmly around Micallef's throat and he jammed the pistol upwards under his jaw.

I was sure that Abela, frozen in his stride barely two yards from Gus, had a gun. I had felt the hardness of the metal when he had hustled us away, but there was no way that he could ever get at it quickly enough to beat Gus in a shoot-out.

'Let him go, you Eyetie bastards,' Gus shouted at the two men holding Dougie. The men looked to Abela for their orders and he flapped his hand at them in a resigned acceptance of the inevitable. They let go of Dougie's arms and he smoothed back his hair, straightened the collar of his jacket and moved over to Gus.

'That was a very big mistake, Mr Micallef,' he said, back once more where he liked to be – in control. 'Now perhaps your flunkeys could put those packets into the suitcases there.'

This time the men looked to Micallef for a reaction. Despite the agonising hold that Gus had on his head, he nodded. They took the notes, bundle by bundle, and put them into the suitcases.

At first it looked as if the notes couldn't possibly fit into the space available. But they did. Two million pounds in two innocent-looking holiday cases.

Dougie gestured to the terrified storeman to come to him. Whimpering, the man obeyed. Dougie grabbed him by the collar of his overalls and dragged him over to his cubicle. The Scot quickly looked around the cramped space and in particular at the door.

'The key. For this shed.'

The poor storeman fumbled in his pockets and handed over a ring of keys, holding out one of them and pointing to it, no words coming from his lips.

Dougie snatched them from him and turned back to Micallef

and Gus, leaving the poor wee man, no threat to the two thugs, supporting himself against the door of his little office, forlorn and confused. His realm had been invaded.

Dougie, cocky once more, waved the keys at his adversaries.

'Well, I know it's not a prison cell, but, with all of you squeezed into it, it will keep you fellas out of mischief for a while.' With mocking politeness, he gestured to them to make their way to the cubicle.

Abela was looking straight in our direction and nodding. He had moved very close to Gus. There was something pleading in the expression on that huge, open face. What was he trying to say?

'I think he wants us to do something now,' Katy whispered. 'Perhaps to create a diversion.'

I decided to chance it. 'Follow me,' I mouthed.

We stood up and moved to one of the aisles to the side of all the activity. I took Katy's hand and walked brazenly towards the action. I was trying a nonchalant lope, which was difficult when my knees were knocking. I then attempted a cheerful greeting through my sticking lips.

'Hello there,' I called and waved as if I had bumped into them in a Valletta market rather than an Msida godown.

'Hi, guys,' Katy joined in, also waving cheerfully and, I must say, more convincingly than I had managed.

Dougie and Gus spun around and looked disoriented, totally bewildered. Instinctively, Gus took his gun away from Micallef and waved it in our direction.

It was enough. Abela's huge, red fist caught him on the side of the head. The gun went off with an ear-splitting explosion in the confined space of the warehouse. The bullet lodged dramatically in the built-up heel of the storeman's boot and he screamed in fright. I was sure that that boot would become a talking point in many a Malta bar and passed on as a family heirloom, as cherished as any saintly relic.

Gus had fallen like some puppet whose strings had been suddenly cut. The security chief turned him over with his foot and picked up the gun from under his large, limp body.

'Your son is dead meat, Micallef,' Douglas shouted hoarsely, holding up his mobile phone. 'You heard what I said. If I don't phone that number tonight, your family tree gets cut down.' He was not aware of, or had forgotten about, the fertile Joanna. 'My man will know what to do. I'm the only one who can cancel his orders and I don't do that without my freedom and my £2 million.'

Abela snatched the phone from him. 'You'll be phoning no one, Mr Douglas, and it looks as if Mr Graham has lost interest in your little venture. It's our show from now on.'

Douglas looked astonished. This was the first time he had any inkling that the Maltese knew his name. His brow furrowed as he tried to think what exactly the implications of that simple little fact were. He glared at Katy and me, knowing we were in some way responsible for his plight, but unsure of how it had all happened.

Gus stirred painfully. Two of Abela's men dragged him to his feet and handcuffed him with what I assumed were police surplus issue. His eyes had still not focused.

Douglas repeated his threat – it was, after all, the only club in his golf-bag. 'You've just signed your son's death warrant. My men will kill him – without question.'

Micallef's response was not what Dougie expected. 'But what if you were dead? Both of you? And your men knew you were dead? What would they do when the news comes through that Dougie and Gus had been killed?'

The use of their familiar names confused Douglas still further.

Micallef pressed home his new psychological dominance.

'They might kill Dante for £2 million. But would they kill him and risk their lives for a lost cause or a lost leader? Or if they thought that the money was now well and truly out of reach? Think about it.'

Douglas faltered for the first time in his dealings with Micallef. 'Killing us will do you no good, Micallef. Don't be a bloody fool,' he pleaded, with little of the braggadocio that had for so long been his trademark. 'You're no criminal, and certainly no killer. And they wouldn't believe you if you told them you'd killed me. And how could you let them know anyhow?'

Seeing he was getting nowhere with Micallef, he directed his arguments to Abela. 'You don't think I'm fool enough to leave any incriminating numbers on my phone.'

'The boss knows what he's doing,' Abela replied. Douglas turned back to Micallef, shaking his fist in frustration.

Micallef shrugged with a nonchalance that unnerved the Scots, turned on his heel, opened the doors and left the warehouse. The handcuffed Dougie needed little more than a directing hand, but Gus came rapidly back to life and it needed Abela's entire squad to retain the huge bucking frame. I appeared to be the target for his anger and expletives.

No matter which way his body contorted, his eyes were fixed on me and somehow a stabbing index figure left no doubt that Abela's blow had not wiped out his memory of my role in his change of fortune from millionaire to prisoner. His screamed threats were foul and repetitive.

Eventually they managed to squeeze Gus into the white hatchback, which, I noticed, bore the appropriate number-plate letters 'NAB'.

As we made our way back to the motorbike, I was still trembling uncontrollably. Katy looked very concerned.

'What was he saying?'

'They were just threats.'

'But what were the words he kept repeating? Not the foul ones. They're universal.'

'He was saying "You're effin' haggis, Jimmy!". It's a bit like, "You're dead meat" or something.'

I was calm enough to start up the bike and join in the drive to whatever Abela had up his sleeve.

Micallef drove off in his metallic blue Opel Astra, followed by a battered Ford mini-van driven by one of Abela's men, with Dougie and Gus presumably somewhere in the back. Abela came next at the wheel of the criminals' white Toyota hatchback with the darkened windows. Katy and I completed the eccentric procession on our trusty Kawasaki.

We drove to the north of the island as if once more making for the ferry to Gozo. The wind that Saint Whatsisname had conjured up for me so productively on Gozo was blowing again, although I was to see its relevance to our plans only later.

As we cavalcaded down the hill, bypassing the village of Mellieħa, we came close to our hotel, but at the last moment we turned left down a narrow but made-up road. It was straight enough for me to turn and mouth to Katy. 'We're making for Popeye Village. There's nowhere else to go at the end of this road.'

The little Anchor Bay had been commandeered by a film company for a production of *Popeye* with Robin Williams. Not one of his best. The crazy, higgledy-piggledy village was constructed as a film set, but left behind to give Malta a tourist attraction at the top end of the island. It was a puzzling destination, far too public for any skulduggery, I would have thought. But Micallef and Abela had kept this part of their plan from me.

Our convoy drove past the tourists' cars and coaches and came to a halt, hidden from the visitors by a shallow hill of

202

earth and stone.

Micallef got slowly out of his car and came over to our bike. 'Mr Smith, Miss Mifsud, I'd like you to see this.'

We walked away from the other vehicles.

'Do you notice the cliffs? Very dramatic, very steep, very dangerous. And yet, unlike the much steeper Dingli cliffs to the south, with a guaranteed supply of witnesses.' He looked down to Popeye Village, strung out on the lower cliffs. We could make out a few dozen tourists wandering amongst the narrow streets of the former film set. 'An ideal spot. Guido has used his unequalled knowledge of our island in suggesting it.'

He looked up the hill to the white hatchback. Abela was standing beside it and one of his men, short and stocky, the one who had given us the Kinnies, was kneeling down and pushing what seemed to be bamboo sticks into the space in front of the driver's seat. He then tied long strands of grass loosely to the door handle.

Micallef signalled up the road to Abela who spoke to the man at the car. We heard the car's engine start up and the revs rise noisily. The man fumbled inside the car. He fiddled with clutch and handbrake and stepped smartly away.

The engine of the white Renault Mégane with its distinctive black windows shrieked into life. I instinctively looked around the bleak Maltese slopes to see if the noise had attracted any attention. Of course, it hadn't. There was no one there to hear it. Well, no one who mattered.

The car accelerated down to steep track. I willed it to ignore the sharp right-hand bend at the bottom of the hill. It did, of course it did, bumping over the worn and insignificant kerb and then lurching sideways as it hit the more challenging line of stones marking the cliff-edge.

And then I heard the screams coming from inside the Renault, the screams that should never have been. Katy's finger-nails bit deeply into the back of my hand.

Something had gone wrong, dreadfully, horribly wrong. As the car corkscrewed into the blustery air above the bay, we both turned to Tony for some explanation.

He was smiling. 'We weren't supposed to kill them, only pretend to kill them!' I shouted at him.

From our high point on the opposite side of bay, we could see the faces of the tourists in the village as they pivoted in horror to see the white car with its black windows corkscrew past them into the boisterous waves. The doors of the car seemed to open as it sank and sent up a mushroom of brown foam.

Micallef smiled and gestured to the minivan nearby. There pressed against the windscreen were the flattened faces of Dougie and Gus, the big man's face distorted even more by a huge gag. I never thought I could be so pleased to see the pair. It took me a long time to forgive Micallef and Abela their dramatic 'death scene'. Micallef walked over to them. Still reacting to the shock of it all, Katy and I followed, hand in hand.

'I hope you like my friend Mr Guido Abela's production. You were of course perfectly correct. If I had been a brutal man, you would both have been in that car. But I am not and you are still alive. But thanks to Mr Abela, the rest of the world will not know that.'

'You bastard,' Dougie said, 'you'll pay for this. It's just a show. It makes no difference to your brat. He gets it just the same.'

Micallef carried on as if he had not heard the threat. 'Guido made sure that one of the 'tourists' in the village had a camera at the ready and another a camcorder. I can imagine that other, more genuine tourists will also capture the event for posterity or at least for your associates in Edinburgh. I presume they can read – and if not that they watch television.'

He smiled at the two men. 'Thank you for the affectation

204

of the black windows, Mr Douglas. It made sure that no photograph or video would show that the car was empty. Oh, and the screams? Mr Abela's final touch. I don't know what his neighbours thought when he was recording them on that old cassette machine of his last night.'

Katy held on to me. For both of us, the chilling impact of those screams would take some time to disappear.

'Goodbye, gentlemen,' Micallef said. 'I have to work with another friend now, making sure the Edinburgh journalists get all they want. My colleagues will look after you, if necessary until my son is back home with us on Malta. Then they will hand you over to Corradino Correctional Facility. You'll be at home there. Although it is our only jail, you'll find the inmates include more foreigners than locals.'

'I'm certain we've enough evidence, with that of my son which you never expected to be used against you, to make sure your long stay in Malta is just that.'

I had no difficulty excusing Micallef for making the most of his triumph.

'A little bird tells me,' he continued, 'that you had planned to retire from the life of crime to the charms of the Mediterranean. You will – but not in the comfort you had envisaged.'

Micallef had style, my God, he had style. He waved off the van to what newspapers would describe as an unknown destination.

He put an arm each around Katy and me and the three of us walked over to the edge of the cliff. Circles of mud and air were still fighting their way through the boisterous waves to mark the last resting-place of the white hatchback. Excited tourists, men, women and children, were pointing at the turmoil and looking for bodies.

In between the fishermen's cottages, the schoolhouse, the saw mill and the Seafarers Hotel, the smithy and the cemetery, they buzzed like bees, loud with excitement, jostling for position. Katy snapped away excitedly.

We waited for something to happen. It didn't. Then suddenly, around the headland came a high-powered black inflatable.

Two divers plunged into the water in the centre of the still spreading ripples. Every eye was on the fresh ripples that they had created.

'Police, the last thing we wanted.' I looked anxiously to Micallef, but there was not the panic I had expected. He shrugged in what seemed to be resignation.

The divers broke the surface and swam to their boat a few feet away.

On cue, a swirling current brought the white car up to the surface, its two open doors flapping in the waves and giving it the appearance of a stricken sea gull. Katy snapped away even more excitedly.

Micallef hugged me, Continental style, and kissed Katy uninhibitedly.

'We still have much to do, but "what starts well, finishes well". Let's get to work. We don't want Dante's warders to panic when they can't contact the boss man.'

'Don't worry,' I assured him, 'Edinburgh is an hour behind us and this story will be in the late editions – the ones that matter as people are coming home from work. And on this evening's television.'

'Start now,' Micallef urged, 'and I think it would be poetic justice if the calls were to go on their bill.' He handed Douglas' mobile phone to me. 'Abela's men know the score and the "amateur" video and still photos will already be on their way to the newspapers and television offices in Valletta.'

*

The sirens and flashing lights told us that the police were

on their way. I thought it would make good background noise and phoned Phil at the Edinburgh news desk. Much as I wanted to let him in on the story, I had to play it straight. He was hopping around with each sentence, coughing helplessly and interspersing the occasional sneeze. I finished the story, confident that it could go in virtually verbatim. Any news editor would welcome every single word.

'It's yours, Phil – and I'm giving you a few hours start over everyone else,' I emphasised. 'I'll be in touch with the television boys, but you're the only newspaper I'm ringing. And if you're quick, you'll even get a picture of the car spiralling over the cliff.'

Phil couldn't resist looking even this gift horse in the mouth. 'If you're pulling my effin' leg, I'll make sure I remove both of yours.'

'This is no joke. *The Malta Independent* will have the photo,' I explained, 'Get it wired and you've got the story of the year.'

'Now, Phil, you won't believe this now, but there's an even better follow-up. Something to blow your mind.'

'Don't leave it like that, Johnny. Just a hint.'

I hung up. Without my usual excuse of a phone card running out! I made a few more calls to contacts on the television and radio stations in Scotland. Dougie would have a big phone bill to end the year with.

*

Three hours later, Katy and I were back at the Seacrest, changed and showered, and scanning a fax from *Capital News*. We couldn't have expected any better treatment if I had written every word and edited it myself.

Making the most of the early tip-off, the story unfolded beneath a garish EXCLUSIVE banner with a headline to be stuck in Jim Pepper's scrapbook ...

TOURISTS POPEYED AT DEATH DIVE
OF EDINBURGH HARD MEN

Two well-known Edinburgh criminals, James Dunbar Douglas (56) and Angus George Graham (54) are believed to have died in Malta this morning. The holidaymakers were travelling in a hired car when it careered off the road and plunged some 90 feet into Anchor Bay, opposite the well-known tourist attraction, Popeye Village.

The police are still trying to recover the vehicle, although initial reports from divers at the scene suggest that there are no bodies inside. Seas were running particularly high at the time of the accident and the doors had been forced open.

Visitors at Popeye Village, the film set for the 1980 Disney musical, gazed in horror as the car pirouetted into the bay before their very eyes. Many of them who were filming and photographing the picturesque village turned their cameras on the death vehicle as it hit the waves and sank.

Eyewitnesses report cries from the vehicle but no signs of life in the foaming wake of the white hatchback Toyota.

A police spokesman in Malta told *Capital News*, 'I have never known so many witnesses to a fatal accident on the island. It means that we can state respectfully but confidently that Mr Douglas and Mr Graham, who had rented the car for the whole of their stay, have lost their lives.'

'In addition to the car hire records, we have recovered a number of personal items from the car to confirm the identification. We have given full details to the police in Edinburgh and they, I believe, have already informed the families.'

The two men had been in Malta for several weeks and were planning to return in the next few days.

The coverage didn't end with the bald story on page one. Phil had gone to town with a profile of Dougie and Gus, recounting a couple of their escapes from the claws of Justice and a full run-down on their many criminal charges and few criminal convictions.

The widespread memory loss, which had in the past afflicted so many of the villains' enemies, rivals and victims, disappeared miraculously as news of their demise spread. A few of them had already spilt copious quantities of beans to Phil for his opening salvo.

Phil also mentioned the wall-to-wall TV coverage that the story had attracted in Scotland and down south.

I explained to Katy that libel law did not apply to dead people and, in a case like this, journalists could dust off the old files, ring frightened men with long-held grudges and terrified women with good memories and really pull out all the stops.

'But they're not dead,' Katy observed correctly. 'If Scotland is anything like the US, I guess there'll be plenty of work to keep redundant lawyers busy when everyone finds out they're both very much alive.'

I put her right on the Scottish law scene. 'Edinburgh lawyers are eternally irrelevant, but never, never redundant.'

Because I was getting all my faxes at the hotel, Micallef and Abela had joined us there in a deserted corner of the lounge bar. Everyone else was down at the Aceline cabaret. I'd been in touch with the Lothians and Borders Police press office, emphasising Micallef's concern for news of his son and giving them his mobile phone number.

'The newspaper took up the bit about the doors of the car being open so it seemed reasonable that the bodies had been swept away' I pointed out. 'We were really lucky there. When the police divers turned up I was sure they would find a car with doors closed and no bodies inside. That would have alerted anyone with half a brain!'

Micallef smiled. 'Don't attribute everything to Dame Luck, Mr Smith. Unlike most of us on this religious island, Guido believes such a creature doesn't exist.'

Abela gave a seismic shrug. 'The police happened to be in that area. My good cousin Dom runs the diving operation. He owes me a few good turns.'

Katy shook her head in admiration. 'We should have known by now that nothing happens by accident here!'

We lapsed into silence, the tension and exertions of the past days at last bringing in their revenges. When it came, the harsh ringing of the telephone seemed like a fire alarm. Micallef automatically picked up the phone and was about to press the 'receive' button, when Katy leapt from her seat and snatched the phone from him.

'That's Douglas' phone, not yours,' she shouted.

We were riveted and immobile. Katy let it ring for some twenty or maybe thirty seconds and then answered it.

'This is Mellieħa Police Station, deceased property store. Calls to this number should have been referred to Police Headquarters, who are handling all queries on the recent fatal accident. I'm sorry for the mistake, may I transfer you?'

The reply was brief and Katy switched off the phone, turned to us and shrugged.

Micallef was trembling. He took Katy's hands in his and, his voice breaking with each word, said, 'I could have ruined everything. Another second and I would have said "Micallef". God knows what would have happened.'

No matter what the Almighty's view would have been, I knew what would have happened. Even the thickest villain would have smelt a rat if he had heard Micallef's voice at the end of a phone, which should have been either in Dougie's pocket or at the bottom of Anchor Bay – or both.

Micallef turned to Katy. 'Young lady, I may find that I owe you everything.' He pulled himself together, breathed deeply and, in an artificially normal voice, added, 'Your Maltese accent was first-class by the way.' Katy was equally upset by the drama and just nodded blankly.

'Was it them? The men holding Dante?' I pestered her. I knew I was not being very understanding, but the answer really mattered.

'I don't know. I guess it could have been. The only thing he said was "Wrong number".'

'But you must have got some sense of an accent.'

'It could have been a genuine wrong number,' Micallef interrupted.

'I gave up believing in coincidences since I arrived in Malta,' I said, dismissively. 'Was it a Scottish accent?' I persisted.

'I don't know,' Katy snapped. 'I'm trying to remember every little detail. I couldn't tell.'

Her frown and her dimples deepened.

'Never mind,' Micallef consoled her.

Katy's eyebrows relaxed, but went straight back into docking position as she struggled with her memory.

'Well, perhaps we'll never know,' I sympathised, squeezing her, platonically of course.

'At least we didn't give ourselves away or rather I didn't give us away,' Micallef sighed, shivering anew at the thought of the doubts he could have sown in even the most Neanderthal of villains.

The silence reasserted itself.

'Oh, there was one thing that was kinda strange,' Katy said hesitantly. 'The man called me "hen", just as you did once, Johnny.'

To the astonishment of the other two, I threw up my fists in a victory salute and shouted 'yes' loudly enough to wake up the gentle giant Gerhard, snoring lightly in a nearby armchair.

'If he called you "hen", he was our man,' I explained. 'The academics would say that the word "hen" is a limited female vocative, used for women or girls, known or unknown, in the Central Belt of Scotland. What it really means is that it was almost certainly Dante's jailer on the other end of the phone. He must have been checking out the phone on the off chance that Dougie had escaped the wreck. Anyone else would have asked a question and not just rung off so abruptly.'

The atmosphere became distinctly edgy. It looked as if the plan had worked but would the jailer hand over Dante as we expected or would he react differently? The ever-practical Abela suggested that we go for a walk along the bay. The four of us walked in single file and in silence for the most part, but the stimulus of crashing waves, the keen breeze and the ever moving lights delineating the bay and reflected in the waters kept my thoughts and presumably those of the others distracted from the subject of Dante.

Nearly an hour later, having seen few people on our walk other than some serious walkers making their way home to the Scandinavian holiday village at the point of the bay, we were walking up the steps of the Seacrest to the anticipated warmth of the lounge when a phone rang. This time, it was indeed Micallef's and it came from the press office of the Edinburgh police to tell us that Dante was safe and sound. He had staggered into the Gayfield Square police station, confused but ecstatic.

The joyful Micallef stammered the good news to us and promptly phoned home to tell Marija and Joanna. To them, with no knowledge of the plot, the news would come as a bolt from the blue. They had been spared the tension of the past few hours, as they had not been told of the crucial importance of that day, of Dante Day.

Again, the ever thoughtful Abela led us away to let Micallef speak to his wife and daughter-in-law in private – and to locate a bottle of champagne.

Micallef soon joined us with tales of the ladies' delight and to take a glass to toast the speedy return of the son who was lost but was now found. Abela drank only a token sip of the bubbly, reminding us that it was his duty to 'get the boss safely home.'

I looked across at Katy. Could this really be still the same day that had begun an eternity ago in Room Twelve of the Hippocampo?

Katy must have had similar thoughts. 'Do you know, if I had gone back home on the right day, it would be, say, one o'clock in Boston now and I'd be along at Dick's Diner waiting for Megan or Seb to join me for lunch from their office. It would have been the highlight of my day. And just think what we've all been through since we got up.'

It was an early night all around.

Chapter 22
Saturday 4 December

A day later, less prominence was given to the story of Mr Dante Micallef's return to life than had been given to the news of Douglas' and Graham's departure from it. *Capital News* reported that 'the Missing Mission Malteser', as the tabloid had dubbed him, had turned up at a police station in Leith. Neither he nor the Lothians and Borders Police were able to comment on what had happened since his mysterious disappearance from the Britannia exactly a month earlier.

Phil Dunne was not fooled by his own story and had the journalist's hunch of something bigger in the offing. He managed to catch me at the hotel, as I was getting ready for dinner.

'What the hell is going on, Johnny? And please don't tell me it's a coincidence. I'd never carried a story about effin' Malta in my life and now I have two, well two and a half. This afternoon, I was following up a press release from Albion Bank when they told me that their new £50s have been printed there!'

'Patience, Phil. In two days, you'll see it's just one story and you'll be crowing about the best scoop you've ever landed. And you'll get a day's start on everyone else – and eyewitness background you could kill for. Do you remember the Lazarus tale? You know how big that made it. Well, I'll have two warmed up corpses for you.'

'I'll hold you to that, Johnny. At least your story so far has rocked those cocky bastards down in their five-star hotel at the palace.' He was referring to his arch rivals at *The Scotsman* and the *Evening News*, now moved out of the city centre to sumptuous premises between the Palace of Holyroodhouse and the site of the new Parliament buildings.

It was not in Phil's nature to be complimentary and his final words spelt out just what would happen if I didn't deliver. His threats included things no journalist should ever say to another.

I had barely time to put the phone back on its hook before it rang again and I was speaking to a very happy Mrs Marija Micallef. The mother began calmly enough, thanking me for my 'unique contribution' to the resolution of the case. But gradually her formal, prepared words were replaced by a very joyous torrent of delight at the thought of Dante's forthcoming return. He was arriving at Luqa that evening. Would I like to be there at the airport, along with Katy, to welcome him back home?

'We'd be honoured to be there, Mrs Micallef, but this is really a moment for you, Tony and Joanna to cherish. Perhaps we'll come and see you all when things have settled down.'

'Yes, you must do that! You can't go back without us all meeting up. Tony will arrange it. And don't forget Miss Mifsud.'

Don't forget Katy! I assured her that I wouldn't.

*

Before Dante had landed, Malta's police had charged Douglas and Graham with a string of crimes against its citizens and institutions. Local press on the island were limited in their comments, as the case was now sub-judice. British papers didn't have a clue as to what was really happening. I kept my promise to Phil and he, safe from any legal limitations as he was in no way circulating in Malta, produced the full story. Well, not quite the full story. I kept some, most, of the juicier details for my own use.

Chapter 23
Sunday 5 December

The prime protagonists on the side of right met for a final farewell, this time in Micallef's own house, with 'Two Hoots' at last justifying its jaunty overtones. It was a particular relief for Katy and me to get away from the Seacrest. As if Norman's plunge had not been excitement enough, the sudden deaths and speedy resurrections of Dougie and Gus and the consequent invasion by reporters and camera crews had put the hotel in turmoil. My Scottish accent and those two Saint Andrew's Day drams had marked me off as at best an expert on the case and at worst a member of the gang. In a few eyes, Katy was lumped in as my 'moll' – the word was hers, thrown back at me from an earlier, unguarded remark. Our friends of course took the charitable view, but we could understand their deluge of questions.

Escape from all the interrogations or insinuations made the evening at the Micallefs' doubly enjoyable.

Dante was naturally the centre of attention and we heard for the first time the details of his kidnap and imprisonment. Dougie and Gus had certainly mounted a slick operation. As the party had left the Royal Yacht in Leith, a small dumper truck had insinuated itself between Dante and his colleagues. In a matter of seconds, Dante had been gagged trussed in parcel tape and squeezed into a Council wheelie bin. He actually remembered hearing his colleagues call out for him as the innocent looking piece of street furniture was trundled past them.

Mindful of what his mother and wife had gone through, he was reluctant to go into details of his ordeal in the following weeks, but turned instead to heaping his deep indebtedness on to Katy and me. At last, his mother and wife commandeered him. The two ladies spent the rest of the party locked in a perpetual embrace with the long-lost lamb.

216

We met for the first time Joanna's parents and Mrs Abela, another Joanna. In contrast to her husband she was thin, short and pale, a combination which made her impact on her husband all the more dramatic. It took him some time to shake off a deferential, perhaps even cowed, manner in her presence. One day I'll come up with a word to describe that almost universal change in character which occurs in the presence of a spouse.

We used to play this game at Napier of applying Scottish place names to gaps in the English language. That little wrinkle between nose and upper lip was a 'crieff', the wobbly light at the top of a TV screen to let you know that ads are on the way was a 'donibristle', and someone with whom you had a relationship verging on marriage was a 'yoker'. One of us – not me – had come up with 'cowdenbeath' to describe that effect of a woman on her partner's style. A pretty good start, but there must be an even better word lurking out there somewhere.

It is an effect which alcohol can go a long way to neutralising and soon the red wine which we were all consuming in copious amounts, or in Abela's case the Irish whiskey, took effect and he and Tony Micallef recalled loudly to each other every incident in the whole operation. Katy buzzed with the excitement of the whole affair and I immodestly accepted whatever praise was going for my part.

'There's just one thing, Guido,' I said, trying to place an arm around his vast shoulder. 'This morning's *Independent* reeled off all the various charges against Dougie and Gus, but there was no mention of poor Norman. I think we owe it to him to get the bastards for his murder.'

Abela and Micallef exchanged embarrassed glances, each waiting for the other to answer.

Eventually, Abela spoke, the words coming several seconds after his big red hands had started talking.

'The problem is, John, that Douglas and Graham had

217

nothing whatsoever to do with Norman's death.'

'But you're not asking me to believe all this was just a coincidence.'

'Apparently, yes. Some time after the inquest, a young and very nervous chambermaid from your side of the hotel plucked up the courage to go to the police. She was swabbing down a balcony – ironically enough, Johnny, it was yours – and clearly saw him topple over, with no one near him.'

'Nicky! Why didn't she tell me?'

'She had no reason to think you were involved. And she's a very shy girl. It seems that Norman was trying to see what Mrs Emily Carstairs was reading, with the aid of some exceptionally powerful field glasses.'

'Which,' I persisted, 'were later seen in the hands of Dougie Douglas.'

'That is the one of the two crimes to which they have confessed,' Abela explained. 'Mr Graham's heritage of larceny meant that he couldn't resist stealing poor Norman's binoculars when he saw them caught in the top branches of the palm tree below his balcony.'

There was a long silence, the only one in the whole, noisy, happy afternoon. Katy ended it. 'Johnny, I do believe you're lost for words.'

There was merriment all around.

'The second crime to which he confessed,' Tony Micallef added, 'was stealing a fishing rod from an angler on the prom in front of the hotel in order to retrieve the binoculars.'

'My colleagues at the Pulizija felt,' Abela explained, 'that it would not be in the interests of Norman's reputation or indeed that of Mrs Carstairs – she was reading a press cutting referring to her shoplifting offence in Brighton sent to her by a friend – to make these facts public. My colleagues were very thorough. They were not, John, some sleeping foreign Bobbies

218

who missed a murder.'

I shook my head in disbelief. 'But that was the whole reason for my ringing Phil Dunne in the first place. I would never have bothered had it not been for Norman and, well, the pair of them in the room next door and the binoculars …'

'Then that poor man's death did some good.' It was the mother, breaking away from Dante to make a rare contribution to the afternoon's conversation.

*

As we were leaving, the Micallefs having exhausted every nuance of gratitude and having plied us with hospitable invitations to come and stay with them, we went around the room to say good-bye to Marija, we were by now all on first name terms, and Joanna. Both of them remained seated, the mother exhausted by the strain of the past few days, the mother-to-be large and, if not immobile, uncomfortable.

Katy and I kissed them, and promised to come back to Malta and see them one day.

'I suppose the contents of the manilla envelope should be divided between the two of you,' Marija said. I waved my hands, trying to indicate to her not to mention our arrangement.

'Oh, don't worry. Tony knows all about our little business,' she said.

Tony smiled and wagged a scolding finger at me. 'I think you deserve something despite your conniving.'

'Well, I didn't tell the ladies about our little meetings, did I?' I countered.

'But you must accept something,' the mother urged.

'Not at all,' I said firmly. 'It is my personal crusade to rid my nation of its reputation for an unhealthy concern with money! And Katy has far too much of it, anyhow. That's why she is so spoilt.' We all laughed.

As I said goodbye to Joanna, I hesitatingly squeezed her hand and whispered. 'You're looking very lovely.' She blushed and smiled. My whisper was not enough to evade Katy. She nodded at me and chalked up an imaginary point in the air. I am sure I reddened. Or at least the bits between the freckles did.

Tony saw Katy and me to the door. Out of sight of the others, he handed us each an envelope, which looked as if it should contain a Christmas card. 'You may have a look before you go,' he said.

Like little children, we opened the envelope and took out a card bearing a special banknote.

Micallef explained 'Your colleagues in Scotland, Johnny, have already received a similar pack to this one to cover the Albion Bank launch of its new £50 note. Similar but not the same.'

I looked at both sides of the note. It was indeed as beautiful as Olga had said. The engraving of the two spitting wildcats was more animated than any I had ever seen on Scottish notes. Our banks have always taken a pride in such things, jealously keen to remain constantly ahead of the Old Lady of Threadneedle Street in the design and originality of their notes. They'd beaten her to multi-coloured notes by 150 years, to notes printed on both sides by a mere century and she still had to attempt a hologram.

Hologram? Where was the hologram? Olga had said the new note would have one. Micallef and Abela had confirmed as much. I turned the note from side to side.

'The hologram, Tony? Where is it?'

Tony smiled. 'It seems that we omitted to print the hologram on the £2 million notes for Douglas. That would have made it the simplest thing in the world to track them all down. Our original idea of a tiny flaw would not have done that. We kept it from you and I apologise. But it was a need-to-know decision. Remember, we did all this before your famous Plan B came to light.'

He was enjoying his little game.

'All of the illegal notes have now been accounted for and destroyed. But two or three were lost in the scuffle. They must have been those that Douglas checked. We never found them. If they were ever to turn up, collectors would pay a fortune for them.' He shrugged, smiled broadly at us and winked.

'That's the most wonderful souvenir anyone could think of,' Katy said, hugging Micallef in gratitude.

I too hugged him, Continental style, and we promised to keep in touch.

Katy and I closed our precious packs, precious to us that is, although I thought that if I'm ever redundant again, I might check out what Micallef had said about collectors ...

As Katy and I settled down rather noisily into the taxi that Tony was treating us to, we agreed it was a worthy ending to an astonishing experience.

Chapter 24
Monday 6 December

At five o'clock on the following afternoon, Katy's last on the Island of her Fathers, I sat on my balcony. The day had until then been totally forgettable. I had run out of the surplus adrenaline pumped into my system by the expectations and events of the past days, but at last I was emerging from the inertia. The sun was still bright as it dropped onto the silhouette of the Popeye Village church, the clouds light, not enough to hide the warmth, but enough to promise a spectacular sunset as they lined up like puffy pink chorus girls for the finale.

I heard a cheery call and looked up to see Katy retrieving a towel from the metal line at the side of her balcony. 'I almost forgot to pack it,' she said in a loud stage whisper that just about carried across the still air.

I leaned back and closed my eyes, miming the pleasure of basking in the sun as she stood in the shade. I picked up an imaginary wine bottle, poured it into an imaginary glass and beckoned to her to come over. She nodded enthusiastically and disappeared from her balcony.

Within two minutes, she was knocking at my door. She had thoughtfully brought with her a half-bottle of white wine, miraculously conjured up from somewhere. Which was just as well, as I had forgotten that I had run out of the stuff. She had come to know me very well indeed over the past weeks. I did have two glasses, well, polystyrene cups, and a corkscrew.

I poured two prodigal measures. 'Well, what would you be doing if you were at home now?'

There was no hesitation. 'Shopping!' and she actually seemed to be thrilled at the thought! 'But I still have that to look forward too when I get back. And if I'd finished my shopping, I'd be skating on the Frog Pond with … the guys.'

We took our 'glasses' out on to the balcony. For fifteen minutes or so, we sat in silence on the green plastic chairs, sipping our wine slowly and feeling, for the last time together, the evening Maltese sun on our faces.

My thoughts focused mainly on just what Katy was thinking. Was she transported back home to Seb? Or was she flicking over the days in Malta and, perhaps, thinking of me? Or even of Gozo? When I glanced over at her, there was no clue. Her eyes were closed and she was smiling contentedly. It would not have surprised me if she had purred.

The sunset performed as spectacularly as the fluffy clouds had predicted. Despite my prayers to the still needed Saint Whatsisname, by 5 o'clock the sun had dropped below the horizon, into the same bay that had caught the Renault Mégane and its canned screams. Almost immediately the air cooled.

Katy got up with what I read as reluctance and sighed. 'That was a good idea. It was just … right, exactly right. But I've got to go now. Packing still to do.'

She paused rather self-consciously and then hurriedly added, 'Oh, and you might like this card, my address back home and my phone number and all that.'

I took the card and my reply was no less awkward. 'I don't know where I'll be living when I get back to Edinburgh, but I'll be in touch. To let you know what's happening.'

She kissed me lightly on the lips, walked quickly through the room, not pausing to look at the bed and threw a hurried 'See you down at dinner' over her shoulder.

*

After dinner at the Seacrest, a rather silent affair, we were making our way almost by habit to join the usual crowd at the bar, when Katy held me back at the door.

'What do you say we go some place special tonight? That place Gino told us about maybe.' The soloist with one of the hotel's most popular evening groups had recommended we hear the singer at the Sunburst Hotel in Qawra.

'That's a good idea.'

'And let's take a taxi. My treat.'

We went over to the bar and told the others that we were off to Qawra. It was not their last night, they were staying on until Christmas, but they seemed to understand.

We were lucky enough to get a small table just to the side of the stage and were entertained to all the very best of Sinatra, and now that 'Ol' Blue Eyes' was away, the Maltese entertainer turned out to be the nearest thing to the original we were ever likely to hear. Katy loved the whole Sinatra repertoire and this made it a wonderfully bittersweet, nostalgic last night. We danced slowly and for the most part silently.

There was a surprising coup de grâce to come. One of the most appreciative of the small audience went up to the band and it looked as if he was asking if it would be OK for him to sing. The singer seemed to know him and handed over the mike. We dancers just swayed in time waiting for the new song. The dumpy middle aged Maltese with comically upturned eyebrows did not look a promising replacement for the very slick band vocalist. And when I recognised the opening bars of my favourite Chris De Burgh number I felt we were in for an embarrassing few minutes of amateur karaoke.

I was wrong, very wrong. The voice which came out was vintage de Burgh and Chris would have been proud of the *Lady in Red* that followed. My Lady was in Green, but it seemed to sum up everything I was feeling.

Never seen you looking so lovely as you do tonight …

Yes, I went along with that.

… or the highlights in your hair to catch your eyes …

Yes, there on my cheeks were the hints of red among the intense black.

224

… I'll never forget the way you look tonight.

I was sure that these were the moments between us that would always stay fresh.

Back at the Seacrest, there was a long, lingering kiss in the corridor, but Katy bade me a final, firm Good Night and closed the door behind her. I walked along the corridor, up the stairs to the top floor and straight past my own room. I found it at the second attempt.

Chapter 25
Tuesday 7 December

Despite the early hour, the concourse at Luqa Airport was a congested, chaotic and, for me, sadly unreal spot. It was Tuesday, traditionally the day for predominantly UK flights. The charter planes were ferrying out the slightly brown Brits and bringing in the pale, coughing casualties of our winter. My plane to Glasgow was to leave several hours after Katy's early scheduled Air Malta flight to London to catch a British Airways flight to Boston.

Amid tearful farewells from Sam and Sadie, Sid and Bonnie, we had put Katy's luggage aboard the airport bus and followed it on the bike. Somehow it didn't seem right to say our goodbyes at the Seacrest.

Katy was dressed for the long haul, a loose light suit in subdued browns and oranges with bold Native American symbols. She kept chatting seamlessly like some sports commentator, about all those little experiences and confidences we had shared and I had nothing to say.

'There will never be another month like this one,' she babbled, 'So much happened. They won't believe the half of it back home.'

She shook her curls. 'It'll take so long to tell I'll have to arrange a special evening to get all my friends together and give them the whole story. Maybe I should get dad to help me with a website. They'll never have seen holiday photographs like these!'

As she had ordered from the hotel shop two prints of everything she had ever taken on Malta and given me a full set, I knew just what she meant.

'Nothing exciting has ever happened to any of them.' She paused and frowned. 'Do you think I'll ever have a month like this again, ever? It's not the sort of thing that happens to us in Boston.' She looked wistful for a second or two. Had she at last thought of something that Seb and Boston couldn't deliver?

Katy regained her zest and began another excited re-run of the Popeye Village spectacular. Midflow, she suddenly stopped.

'Dominic Bunn,' she announced triumphantly.

'Who on earth was he?' I asked, confused and not for the first time by her thought processes.

'He was a very handsome redhead and all of us at school fell for him and he was the wittiest, most macho boy in our year. There, I said I would come up with one!'

'And what happened to him?' I just had to know.

Katy pouted, deliciously.

'He became a priest.'

Good old Dominic Bunn.

A loud, Scottish voice interrupted. 'Johnny! Somebody said you were here for a month or so. I've been looking for you all over the island. What are you doing here? Are you going back today?'

I turned and recognised Cammy Gow, a reporter I had met at many an Edinburgh press conference and an enthusiastic fellow-member of the Scottish Film Club. His question puzzled me, as my first thought, after some uncharitable blasphemies, was that he was following up the Micallef story.

It was soon clear he knew nothing about it. 'Great holiday, crap weather, plenty of booze. I suppose you're one of the lucky ones on the Glasgow flight. I've got to fly to bloody Manchester and drive home up the M6 and the M74. Who's the bird?' He had noticed Katy.

'A friend, but she's just leaving. I must …'

'Did you get to the Malta Film studios, Johnny? A great day out. I was sure you would have been there. I got to see the sets they built for Gladiator. The replica of the Coliseum was magic. And we all went off for a bevvy at the bar where Olly Reid packed in. You must have …'

'No, I missed it, Cammy. I've been quite … tied up … Now I really …'

'I understand, Johnny, I understand,' he nudged me in the ribs and leered up at Katy. 'Oh, by the way, I came across a great story …'

God, he was here about the Micallefs.

'Do you know they've got a statue of a snooker player in one of those unpronounceable villages in the south of the island? Some guy Muscat or suchlike. Won the world amateur titles in the 30s. Snooker and billiards. I've taken some great pics and thought I'd start a campaign to get Stephen Hendry done in bronze and …'

I earnestly begged the long-dormant Saint Whatsisname to make Cammy disappear, nothing excessive, just a puff of smoke or a gap in the marble floors of Luqa Airport.

The Saint responded speedily but undramatically.

Cammy broke off from his monologue and looked at his watch. 'Good God, is that the time? Must dash or I'll miss the duty frees. See you.'

He left as speedily as he had arrived and I was alone with Katy again.

Her flight was called for the last time and I opened my hand and showed her the little suede box, shiny with my sweat.

'Something,' I managed at last, my mouth dry with love, 'to remind you of your Maltese roots … and even, perhaps, of me.'

She opened the box, took out the best gold chain and

Maltese cross my Visa card could stand and, as I had come to expect, opened her eyes and mouth wide in delight.

'Gosh, I must wear it at once,' she said, turning her back to me. With gauche, trembling fingers, I fastened the awkward clasp and I could not fail to see, alongside my slim offering, the chunky gold chain that held Sebastian's stupid bloody emerald ring between her soft, white breasts. She whirled around. 'It's so ... perfect.'

I looked into those green, Irish eyes. She glanced down at the box and said, in surprise. 'There's no note, no words.' There was disappointment in her eyes.

'I didn't know what to say.' I thought of the dozen or so crumpled balls of notepaper in the bin back at the hotel, proof that I had at least tried.

She laughed in disbelief. 'John Smith lost for words. I shall wear it at my ... whenever I need reassurance.' She reached up with both hands behind my head and pulled me hard towards her, kissing me on the lips. Before I could respond, she broke away.

'Thank you, Johnny. And not just for this.' She touched the little gold Maltese cross. 'You have given me a lot. I would never have ...' She struggled for a word, but left it unsaid, shaking her curls in frustration '... without you.'

I swallowed hard, my arid mouth resisting, and asked the first of two difficult questions.

'Was Gozo then just a Thank You? Nothing more?'

She was silent for a moment.

'There may have been a touch of gratitude, but there was more, much more. But please don't ask me to explain. I just have to feel. It's you who have to know.'

The next question was even harder. I held her away from me and asked her directly 'Are you going to marry Seb?'

I could see in her eyes hundreds of thoughts, thousands of words, swarming. An urgent flight call, this time mentioning Miss Mifsud by name, sent them all scurrying away. Only three words remained.

'Yes. I will.' The words sounded fatefully like something from the wedding ceremony.

'Do you think he'll walk barefoot in the park?'

A smile. 'Maybe.' A frown. 'Maybe not.'

I kissed her; she broke away, turned, dropped the little suede box in a bin and walked away. Yes, it was Pocahontas going off into the sunset. Had she not saved the life of someone called John Smith and then married another man? My princess never looked back.

*

I rode back to Mellieħa Bay to return my motorbike and even perhaps to catch the tail end of breakfast. Abbie, on duty at the Seacrest's reception, reached for my key and was already holding it out for me as I walked slowly up to the desk.

'Your key, Mr Smith.' There was something odd in her smile. Another day I might have tried to interpret it. Instead, I merely noted it. I walked to the lift and was pleased that I did not have to share it with anyone.

I walked, zombie-like, down the corridor, opened the door and slumped despondently onto my bed, giving my packed cases an undeserved kick. I lay on the bed and stared at the ceiling.

A splash of colour intruded on to the rim of my vision. I sat up and stared at the wall opposite. A lyrical, luminous landscape hung there. It showed a lane, half in shadow, curving out of sight between bushes and beneath a domineering, gaunt rock. On the horizon, the creamy houses of Mellieħa beckoned. It was a lane we had walked down. Once. Together. The packing for the painting had been thoughtfully folded and was lying on the dressing table nearby.

The wall of my room had been blank when I left with Katy. She must have connived with that smiling little Abbie at Reception.

The Wedgwood-blue sky and ochre land, the burnt sienna rock shapes and the soft, shamrock-green undergrowth – all whispered 'George Fenech'.

If the signature in the bottom left-hand corner was unnecessary, the imprint of Katy's lips slap in the middle of the lane, in her trademark scarlet lipstick, was tasteless, corny she might have said. I felt I should remove it. One day. Maybe.

Part Three

Chapter 26
The Return

The return to Edinburgh set in motion a variety of frantic activity – and made it impossible for me to snatch more than a couple of days back home in Glenbraith. I chose to be at home with the family over Christmas, which helped head off my mother's grief at my absence for the Millennium Hogmanay.

I had been met at Glasgow Airport by Lothian and Borders Inspector Tucker and driven home to Edinburgh. The debriefing needed more than the hour-long car journey and I reported to Fettes HQ to fill in the details. The most comforting aspect of the interviews was Tucker's confident assurance that any threats made in Malta were not to be taken seriously.

'We've picked up Joe Baird who was Dante's jailer and, believe me, Dougie and Gus are no longer the force they once were. There aren't hoards of underlings at their beck and call. No one's going to settle any scores with you for those old men.'

*

My unusual role in the Micallef affair smoothed my way into a job with *Capital News*, I would have been surprised if it hadn't. On the other hand, there were wider issues to air.

The National Union of Journalists felt that certain basic principles of the profession had been undermined by the use of bogus stories to catch criminals, action likely to undermine the public's faith in the media. Public's faith in the media? I tried not to smile. A long-drawn out investigation of the matter and my role in it fizzled out with the NUJ giving me a stern admonition not to do it again. I willingly and sincerely promised to try and avoid such situations in future. And how I meant it!

It paled alongside the legal profession's gnawing over the repercussions of the libel committed by *Capital News*. As I had pointed out to Katy, it is not possible to libel dead persons, but, as Dougie and Gus turned out to be far from dead, the lawyers were having a field day. Those elements that concern the rest of us – time, expense and justice – have never troubled the Law to any great extent and a case in which lawyers could abandon thoughts of all three was going to run and run.

*

The Micallefs had given me not just a generous memento of Malta, an eighteenth-century framed engraving of Mdina, but also a short but important shopping list – and, from the manilla envelope, the wherewithal to pay for it. Champagne was destined for Olga, some Highland Park for Phil and, for Don, the man who set everything in motion, some bottles not of Madeira but Marsala. Tony, not one to miss a business opportunity, told me that his sister was married to the producer of Sicily's finest fortified wine. He wrote down the details and I convinced him it would be available in Edinburgh. That meant a far-from-burdensome visit to Valvona & Crolla, where the aromas alone are worth paying for. They indeed had the Marsala on the groaning Christmas shelves and I got all the other drink there as well.

*

Olga was overwhelmed by the crate which I hauled up to her second floor flat in Fettes Row, but even more delighted with the Oreste CDs. While the rest of us think in terms of the Three Tenors, Olga thinks in more elevated figures. Oreste took her tally of recorded tenors to one hundred and three, she proudly told me, 'alphabetically from Albani, no, from the new man Alagna, to Zenatello.'

But the talk was mainly of the banknote job and I could see Olga's bottomless brain-store absorb every single detail of the inside story. I showed her – and to date no one else – one of the three notes which had survived without the hologram.

'I am speechless, Johnny,' she stammered. 'Trust me. I

234

shall never tell a soul.'

I believed her.

She sealed the bond by showing me her own copy of the wildcat note. Being Olga, it was special. In addition to the usual printed signature, there in the watermark space was a personal signature of the Chief Executive of Albion Bank and, after swearing me to secrecy, she pointed out that the serial number was her date of birth.

*

I could tell by the gleam in Don Blaikie's eyes that he was pleased to see me. He was even more pleased to see that I was carrying a hefty plastic bag.

'Well, Smiffy, my own Philoctetes, I knew you could do it. Although if the scriveners are to be believed, you had your fair share of alarms and excursions.' He motioned to me to sit down and gestured towards a tray of cakes. The glass Victorian receptacle stood alongside it, the level of the tawny Madeira looking exactly as it had done all those weeks earlier.

'*MacAbre*, signed, sealed and delivered,' he chuckled, hearing the sound of cash tills ringing into the distant future. 'I have a great idea for a follow-up and this one can be all yours. An exposé of all the great cons and frauds – especially the local government fiddles. And we'll call it *MacHinations*. Do you get it? Mac-Hinations. If we do some of the more recent ones, I'm sure someone will sue us for libel, just what we need to …'

I put the brake on his fantasies. 'Hold on, Don. I've only managed about a third of *MacAbre*. I became quite involved with things on Malta. But here are some bottles of Marsala that a good friend in Malta insisted I get for you. He owes his son's life to you. It all began the moment I got there really …'

He didn't let me finish the sentence, let alone the story, but threw one of Miss Murgatroyd's currant buns at me, failing, but not by much, to shatter one of the worst busts of Rabbie

235

Burns I have ever seen.

'Don't come back until you've got *MacAbre* ready for press,' he shouted, returning the Madeira to its dusty ledge. I fled.

*

Christmas, like many before it, vanished in a blur of overeating and overdrinking as the gathering of the clans at Glenbraith brought in drouthy neebors, relatives from distant parts and old school pals now working throughout Britain and the known world. This year there was the added hazard of having to recount the Malta adventure. The local newspaper and the even more effective grapevine had meant that no one within fifty miles of my old home was unaware of 'Johnny's adventure'. I was indeed world-famous in Glenbraith.

The days had been wet and windy but by the time I was ready to leave for Edinburgh, laden down with Mum's home baking and some of Dad's best smoked salmon, a classic Scottish winter's day heralded the bluest of skies and a clear precise landscape. With it came the inevitable icy nip, all very bracing for the two-hundred-mile drive south.

I urged Mum and Dad indoors out of the cold as we waved our farewells. To my surprise Popsy followed me as I trundled my bike to the gate.

As I was putting on my helmet, she looked at me with that solemn expression I knew so well.

'Katy was quite a girl.'

I nodded.

'Were you fond of her?'

It was a strange word to use but I nodded again.

'Too fond?'

My head remained motionless this time.

Popsy lifted up my visor and kissed my nose, the only part she could comfortably reach.

She looked at me intently and I slammed down the visor.

Her expression was not one of pity or even sympathy. It was one of understanding. She knew what I had felt, what I was feeling.

It was disconcerting. I had told the tale so many times that I was sure I had erased every clue that might give away any hint of emotional links with Katy. I certainly had not expected Popsy to detect them. She was the last person I would have thought would notice, let alone understand.

I started the engine and took off, waving backwards to Popsy and my parents at the window until I rounded the small ben fifty yards or so down the road.

Three hours later, I was back in Edinburgh, the only place to be for any 31 December, let alone a 1999 one.

*

I had been away in Malta at the time of the ceremonial awarding of the entry passes to the City Centre, coloured wristbands with security holograms. These were essential to get past the cordon around the Princes Street and the happenings.

Fortunately, the gang had a free one available and I was able to share the lengthy countdown to 2000 with several hundred thousand others. Again there was a blur – this time of noisy rock bands and of even more raucous mass humanity and, inevitably, of copious drinking. In one of those miraculous encounters I found myself face to face with an old Napier pal who told me that he had seen Tandy in the crowd about half an hour earlier and that she had been trying to get in touch with me. She could be excused not knowing which of our circle had allowed me to crash out on his floor, but I could barely believe that she was somewhere within the crowd.

I had become separated from the gang, so I searched for

Tandy for a while among the revellers but eventually gave up. And so when the Millennium Bells sounded I was alone amongst a quarter of a million people, not searching for the one girl I knew was there but thinking of the one girl I knew was not. Her Millennium Moment was still five hours away. Yes, 1999 had been a funny old year.

*

The New 1000 years began auspiciously and not just with the bright crisp Edinburgh morning, or what was left of it, which greeted me on New Year's Day.

After a few weeks of sleeping on other folk's floors, I eventually found a new flat. Not in Ramsay Garden – maybe one day my best-sellers will get me the spare quarter of a million to afford that – but in a road not too far from my old home in Bellevue Crescent and from the well-kent shops and howfs of Broughton Street.

It was in the bedroom of the flat, on 6 January, at about ten in the morning, that I received a phone call from Malta. I had sent the Micallefs my new address and contact numbers and had had occasional updates via the Internet. But this was something far too personal and elemental to be committed to electronics. An exuberant Dante wanted to share with me the news he had already broken to tribes of relatives. Joanna had had their baby.

He continued solemnly. 'I have an apology to make, though, Johnny. We had planned to call the baby after you as a reminder of everything you did. I hope you don't mind if we scrub that idea.'

He paused. I assumed it was apologetically – or perhaps even guiltily. I could hear Joanna laughing in the background.

'We thought she would rather be called Katy. We're going to ring Boston as soon as it is breakfast time there.'

I was cock-a-hoop and promised Dante I would go out immediately and wet the baby's head. I did just that. And I

238

felt a little shiver as, true to my word and well before noon, I sat in the empty Barony bar half way up Broughton Street and raised a glass of Laphroaig with the words, 'To Katy'. Only the barman was there to hear me. And it was far too long a story to tell him.

The occasion was spoilt by a housewife from Trinity requesting her favourite song from the Radio Scotland DJ. It had to be '*Lady in Red*' of course!

"Never seen you looking so lovely as you do tonight ..."

The weeks turned back to a dance floor in Malta.

"... or the highlights in your hair to catch your eyes ..."

I could see them as sharp and real as ever.

"... I'll never forget the way you look tonight."

I downed the malt with indecent haste and left.

*

And talking of Katy, the older one that is, spurred by the assertive Bostonian's nagging in Malta, I did indeed buckle down to tackle a film script on the Great Siege of 1565. I pored over the books I had brought back with me, I took the train through to the Mitchell Library to top up my facts, I watched tapes of some of the great epics – Ben Hur, El Cid and even Khartoum. And I sweated for hours over my laptop – well, I call it my laptop, Don would never get around to using it. I knew that poor Ollie Read was no longer on the books of the casting agents, but I still kept his image in front of me whenever the villainous Dragut came on the scene. The script grew and one day to my surprise it was ready.

I then faced the far more challenging task of getting someone interested in it. I invested in the latest *Writers' and Artists' Yearbook*, bought a wad of envelopes and a box of 200 stamps and set about finding an agent.

*

239

Oh, and I eventually finished *MacAbre*. Not one to bear a grudge, Don greeted me cordially and despite the fact it was April offered me some Christmas cake. He must have used up his supply of Madeira, because the new drink was the delicious Marsala I had brought him. I noticed with some satisfaction that it was served not from that Victorian receptacle of dubious provenance but from its own distinctive flask. I was also pleased to see that he had not been too proud to receive the gift and had already consumed most of the bottle. And perhaps it wasn't even the first one.

Everything went genially as he skimmed approvingly through the manuscript, from time to time chuckling, gesturing with an upturned thumb, nodding. Then something in the copy reminded him of the matter of *MacHinations*. I made my excuses and left.

*

It was in early May that I received an interesting selection of mail on my mat. I needed the boost. The night before I had watched *The Horse Whisperer* on Sky and had felt some affinity with the rejected Robert Redford. He might have stood a chance of getting Kristin Scott Thomas in a straightforward fight with Sam Neill, the rich, big-city lawyer husband. He might even have managed the head-to-head battle against the lure of the girl's city home. But both? No chance, as I had once discovered. I sympathised with Bob, but the film hadn't cheered me up.

The mail consisted of letters from three literary agents on my mailing list, a small package bearing the antiquarian double Bs of the Blaikie Books insignia, a letter from Tandy and an envelope with a USA stamp and a Boston franking.

I read the letters from the agents first, familiar with the standard wording, as they declined politely the offer to read my film-script of *Bring me the Grand Master!*, returned the synopsis and pleaded pressure of work from established writers.

240

One at a time, I fed them with a sigh into a large box file labelled 'Rejections'. I was surprised to see just how quickly it was filling up. Then individual phrases in the third letter cavorted before my eyes – 'interesting and unusual', 'untouched episode', 'full script', 'no promises'. At last, a letter to action and put into my hitherto empty 'Follow-up' file. Not a light at the end of the tunnel – but the suspicion of a tunnel.

The package from Blaikie Books brought me, hot and blushing from the presses, the first copy of *MacAbre*. I admit to feeling a tingle of achievement as I saw the garish front cover with its emblazoned title and credits to 'Geordie Ballantine' and, in smaller type, 'John Smith'. I flicked quickly through to get the feel of a real book, the tickle of authorship.

It looked eminently tasteless and a worthy successor to *MacMurder*. I was sure that Geordie, now at the Great Newsdesk in the Sky, would be pleased. And not even Don would be disappointed. I wondered who he would find to write *MacHinations*. I felt that somehow he would not send him off to Malta.

Tandy was writing to tell me that she was coming up to Edinburgh for an interview for a press job at the new Scottish Parliament. I put the letter aside. I could think about the implications of that at a later stage.

Like some wee laddie holding back the icing and marzipan from his Christmas cake, I had kept the American letter until last.

I turned the envelope over and over. Eventually, I opened it. Inside I found not what I was expecting, not what I was hoping for, not what I was wanting.

The large formal white invitation card merely told me that Mr Paul Mifsud was requesting the pleasure of my company at the wedding of his daughter, Kathleen Virginia Marija, to one Sebastian Lowell Palmer.

At least it wasn't Sebastian Lowell Palmer XIV.

Mr Mifsud's IT background showed through as he gave me a variety of choices to RSVP. Via the Internet, I declined the invitation immediately, with what I accurately described as 'regret'.

I spent some time looking at the envelope. The address might have been in Katy's handwriting. I didn't ever remember seeing anything written by her. But of course there were the meticulous notes on the back of her holiday photographs, giving details not just of the subject matter but also of the camera settings and film used. One of the photographs was hanging in my hall – the one showing Dougie, Gus, Katy and me on that memorable St Andrew's Night. The others were in my desk. I took one of them out – of the evocative seafront restaurant and hotel on Gozo as it happened – turned it over and compared the writing there with that of the envelope. Yes, Katy had written it. I don't know why but it was important to me to know that.

Where had she got my address? Despite my sunset promise, I had not been able to bring myself to write to her. And the Internet would not have helped her track down John Smith, the most common name in the English-speaking world – and that includes Scotland. There are nearly 500 of them in the Edinburgh telephone directory alone – I remembered that from a bet I'd once won in a Rose Street pub from somebody called Robertson.

Oh, yes, it must have been Dante. He would have told her when he rang about the wee Katy. But only if she had asked, I thought. He would surely have assumed I had already given it to her.

I sat there thinking sad thoughts for a minute or so and then some nagging, indefinable little tic started prompting me. I picked up the invitation card and read it again, right through this time.

The wedding was to take place at noon, on 17 September 2000, at the Church of Santa Marija in Mosta on the George Cross Island of Malta and the reception would follow at the gardens of the Phoenicia Hotel at Floriana, within sight of the bastion walls of Valletta!

The determined little bugger, what a girl!

Mosta! The Dome! A wedding! It brought back memories that had dulled but not disappeared over the past few months, sharp, vivid, sad and sweet once more.

I wondered if I could learn to play the tubular bells in four months.

I looked up at the Fenech painting above my desk. Strangely, his colours looked slightly mistier than usual. More evocative than even his firm, dramatic brushstrokes was the flash of a colour he had never used, that Disney-red blotch in the sunlit part of the lane. The fairy-tale lips were still there.

Rosebud.

Some other books from Ringwood Publishing

All titles are available from the Ringwood website (including first edition signed copies) and from usual outlets.
Also available in Kindle, Kobo and Nook.
www.ringwoodpublishing.com

Ringwood Publishing, 7 Kirklee Quadrant, Glasgow, G12 0TS
mail@ringwoodpublishing.com
0141 357-6872

Silent Thunder

Archie MacPherson

Silent Thunder is set in Glasgow and Fife and follows the progress of two young Glaswegians as they stand up for what they believe in.

They find themselves thrust headlong into a fast moving and highly dangerous adventure involving a Scots radio broadcaster, Latvian gangsters, a computer genius and secret service agencies.

Archie MacPherson is well known and loved throughout Scotland as a premier sports commentator.

"An excellent tale told with pace and wit"

Hugh Macdonald -The Herald

ISBN: 978-1-901514-11-7   £9.99

Torn Edges

Brian McHugh

Torn Edges is a mystery story linking modern day Glasgow with 1920's Ireland and takes a family back to the tumultuous days of the Irish Civil War.

They soon learn that many more Irishman were killed, murdered or assassinated during the very short Civil War than in the War of Independence and that gruesome atrocities were committed by both sides.

The evidence begins to suggest that their own relatives might have been involved

ISBN: 978-1-901514-05-6   £9.99

The Gori's Daughter

Shazia Hobbs

The Gori's Daughter is the story of Aisha, a young mixed race woman, daughter of a Kashmiri father and a Glasgow mother. Her life is a struggle against rejection and hostility in Glasgow's white and Asian communities.

The book documents her fight to give her own daughter a culture and tradition that she can accept with pride. The tale is often harrowing but is ultimately a victory for decency over bigotry and discrimination.

"The Gori's Daughter is quite possibly the most compelling novel based on a true story that you will ever read" - **Dr Wanette Tuinstra - Golden Room**

ISBN: 978-1-901514-12-4   £9.99

Calling Cards

Gordon Johnston

Calling Cards is a psychological crime thriller set in Glasgow about stress, trauma, addiction, recovery, denial and corruption.

Following an anonymous email Journalist Frank Gallen and DI Adam Ralston unravel a web of corruption within the City Council with links to campaign against a new housing development in Kelvingrove Park and the frenzied attacks of a serial killer. They then engage in a desperate chase to identify a serial killer from the clues he is sending them.

ISBN: 978-1-901514-09-4   £9.99

A Subtle Sadness

Sandy Jamieson

A Subtle Sadness follows the life of Frank Hunter and is an exploration of Scottish Identity and the impact on it of politics, football, religion, sex and alcohol.

It covers a century of Scottish social, cultural and political highlights culminating in Glasgow's emergence in 1990 as European City of Culture.
It is not a political polemic but it puts the current social, cultural and political debates in a recent historical context.

ISBN: 978-1-901514-04-9   £9.99

Good Deed

Steve Christie

Good Deed introduces a new Scottish detective hero, DI Ronnie Buchanan.

It was described by one reviewer as *"Christopher Brookmyre on speed, with more thrills and less farce"*.

The events take Buchanan on a frantic journey around Scotland as his increasingly deadly pursuit of a mysterious criminal master mind known only as Vince comes to a climax back in Aberdeen.

ISBN: 978-1-901514-06-3   £9.99

Dark Loch

Charles P. Sharkey

Dark Loch is an epic tale of the effects of the First World War on the lives of the residents of a small Scottish rural community. The main characters are the tenant crofters who work the land leased to them by the Laird. The crofters live a harsh existence in harmony with the land and the changing seasons, unaware of the devastating war that is soon to engulf the continent of Europe.

The book vividly and dramatically explores the impact of that war on all the main characters and how their lives are drastically altered forever.

ISBN: 978-1-901514-14-8   £9.99

Black Rigg

Mary Easson

Black Rigg is set in a Scottish mining village in the year 1910 in a period of social and economic change. Working men and women began to challenge the status quo but landowners, the church and the justice system resisted. Issues such as class, power, injustice, poverty and community are raised by the narrative in powerful and dramatic style.

ISBN: 978-1-901514-15-5   £9.99

Paradise Road

Stephen O'Donnell

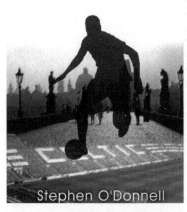

Paradise Road is the story of Kevin McGarry, who through a combination of injury and disillusionment is forced to abandon any thoughts of playing football professionally. Instead he settles for following his favourite team, Glasgow Celtic, whilst trying to eke out a living as a joiner. It considers the role of young working-class men in our post-industrial society; the road Kevin travels towards self discovery leads him to Prague, where he develops a more detached view of the Scotland that formed him and the Europe that beckons him.

"A spectacular debut novel packed with social insight but all captured in real world dialogue that flows superbly" - **Bella Caledonia**-

ISBN: 978-1-901514-07-0   £9.99